REMEMBER POMPEII

The Wanshiqi Trilogy
Book 1

KIKA EMERS

Beckett Publishing Group, LLC

Contents

*To Emerson Langley, this is the last book we wrote with you in my lap.
I think it's our best one. I miss you every day, my warrior lapdog.*

INTRODUCTION

Good and evil are so basic. So intrinsic. So essential to humanity.
It's why we reincarnate into humans. To get a glimpse of the best
of ourselves.

And the worst.

But my family's different. We're the relics the rest of the world
forgot.

And we're still here.

The fall of Pompeii? Yeah, that was me. The end of Bodie,
CA—guilty again. What happened to Atlantis? That was all Gramps.
Grams swears the demise of the Aztecs was an accident. But I think
Mom meant to destroy them. We have a long list of lost cities,
forgotten civilizations, and decimated races that can be attributed
to my family.

CHAPTER ONE

I BEND OVER TO hunt for my black T-shirt among the pile of clothes that Hunter and I discarded hours ago, but it's not there. Hunter whistles at me. When I turn around, he's still naked on his king-sized bed with the navy sheet draped over his lap and my T-shirt in his hand.

"Come on. I'm already late. Are you trying to get me grounded?" I reach for the T-shirt, but he holds it beyond my reach. If I lean in to grab it, I'll end up back in his arms and his bed. Instead, I drop onto the end of the bed and slide into my black leather boots.

"Good girl has to make it home for dinner again." His fingers tiptoe up my arm.

If they make it to my collarbone, I'm not leaving here tonight. I escape his touch by bending to zip my boots. "I've never been a good girl." Good girls learn to lock away the darkest parts of their souls.

He moves closer, and his fingers curl around my elbow. With the slightest tug of his hand, I fall back across his bed. I turn to face him, draping myself over abs that Michelangelo could have sculpted. My fingers graze his sun-soaked chest. Want flares in his Adriatic Sea eyes. I brush a dark curl off his forehead. It springs right back into place.

His lips are inches away. Everything I should want is inches away. So why do I hesitate?

An image of pissed-off Gramps appears in my mind. I leap off the bed because I can't bear to see the disappointment in Gramps's eyes or hear the frustration in his voice. "I can't miss dinner again."

Hunter gives me his why-are-you-being-ridiculous look. "Because you're a normal kid."

"I'll never be normal." By the age of three, I'd cursed seven people. I snatch my T-shirt from him, slide it over my head, move across the room.

"Kali, come back." His words tug at my heart like a Thai massage—stretching until it burns. "You want to stay with me."

"Sometimes I hate how well you know me." Almost as much as I hate being sixteen again.

The bed frame creaks. The sheets swoosh over his skin. He's naked behind me. Every inch of his chiseled human form against mine. "It's been thousands of years. But I bet you still have a few secrets."

"And you have yours." He tightens his hold on me.

I can feel the emotions shifting across my face. If he sees them, he'll convince me to stay. I lean forward, allowing the curtain of my black hair to hide my expression. "I wish I didn't."

He nuzzles my ear. "Then don't. You can tell me anything."

I wish I could, but he's wrong.

I pull away from him.

He lets me get to his bedroom door before he says, "Don't forget these in case I'm away."

I spin around and a box of special contact lenses lands in my outstretched palm. I want to thank him for understanding, for helping, for being Hunter. I should say the words, but they pile up in the back of my throat like desperate commuters on the Five. Not a single word makes its way to him.

Emotions are the worst part of being in a human body. If you're inside a bat, you get sonar hearing. But inside a human body, you get emotions. Powerful, sweeping, volatile emotions. The dark emotions—anger, frustration, hatred—empower you. The light ones—love, compassion, hope—weaken you. I'll never forget that lesson from Pompeii.

Every day, I battle my emotions.

Today, I *push push push* the love I have for Hunter down and tug my frustration around my shoulders until I have the strength to walk out.

He mutters, "Teenagers."

"Immortals." The door slips shut behind me.

Problem is I'm neither, and I'm both. So is he.

Hunter's qi, his immortal soul, is 3813 years old. Just 190 years older than mine. A tiny blip in the eternity of our existence. In human years, it's the difference between sixteen and seventeen.

I cross the cavern of his living room. A sheet of glass shields me from the thousand-foot cliff drop to the beach. The entire apartment is minimalism for three million. That glass wall is soundproof and shatterproof and sexproof.

To most, his home is the pinnacle of human extravagance. To Hunter, it's a shack.

On my way to Gramps's, I ride the brake, creeping by a car crash. The tangled roads and lure of the beaches are a distraction to any driver, but it's probably a text-at-the-wheel that brings the rotating ambulance lights. A girl is trapped in the driver's seat. A police officer leans into her car and presses his hand to her forehead while they wait for the firefighters to rescue her.

In the pit of my belly, I feel something stirring. Something soothing and sweet: compassion. My palms go swampy on the steering wheel. The light emotions lull you into a place where they can be used to compel and coerce. They strip away your free will.

I can't feel compassion. I won't feel compassion. Never again. I stamp it out like the ember of an almost-dead fire.

Then I snuggle into a memory—a reminder that I am not weak nor compassionate.

My first-grade teacher slammed her books on the desk with enough force to make her coffee mug vibrate. "It's never okay to wish your classmate dead. Don't you smirk at me, missy!"

I couldn't help myself. It was ridiculous. The one time I didn't actually curse someone, and I was going to be punished. He was one of those kids who made things up, and everyone believed him. This time, he had no idea how close he was to the truth.

"Your parents are going to have to deal with this." Absolute authority bloated her eyes.

Mom and Dad would never believe me. "Please, you can't call them." They were in the midst of a violent divorce. Anything could set them off. Her call would set them off, triggering another round of warfare in the human world.

My mother sways hearts. My father rules logic. Manipulating humans is how they work out their issues. They don't care about the lives lost. The constant conflict in the Middle East is something you can attribute to them.

My teacher's laughter trumpeted in my ears. "It's too late now, missy."

Her hand was on the doorknob. If she made it to the office, she'd call them. Sweat burst across my back.

"Don't do it." I had to stop her. I swallowed my anger and offered what I hated doing. "I'll apologize." To a human. We don't lower ourselves before them.

She shook her head. "You need to be taught a lesson." There was such satisfaction in her voice.

"Please, don't make me hurt you."

"Hurt me?" She dismissed my warning and a victorious smile slithered across her face. She opened the door and made her death a necessity.

I gave in to my anger. Shadows rose up inside me. The darkness swirled. Heat surged through me. Power. So much power poured into my qi. It felt like my skin couldn't contain it. Ancient words filled my mouth and slipped from my lips. A death curse.

She dropped to the floor in shock, her eyes bugged out by death.

Her brain blew up. The doctor's diagnosis was an aneurysm.

I knew better. I did it.

Guilt never came. Gramps searched for remorse in me. All he found was vindication. I warned her before striking, a courtesy we never extend to humans.

CHAPTER TWO

My car twists up the skinny roads of Del Mar, California, climbing the terraced cliffs into seclusion. Every seven properties or so, I catch a glimpse of the ocean down below. I pull into our circular driveway, park behind Grams's white Volvo, and check my reflection in the rearview mirror.

I finger-comb my black hair, twist it into a bun, and see a hint of my mother in the mirror. Not the mother I knew before Pompeii, but the twisted version that took her place in every lifetime after Pompeii. My brow tightens and her frown lines sneak across my face. I let my hair fall back around my face, reassuring myself that I am me. Not her.

Never her.

I walk down the stone-paved path to Grams and Gramps's Spanish-style house. The clay tiles on the roof remind me of our ranch in Mexico. But that was 200 years ago. It's so them to hold on to their favorite things across the centuries.

Like me.

While my parents blow up cities in retribution, Grams and Gramps try to teach me to be better than my parents, to control myself, to not indulge my darkest emotions.

I've never been a good student. Maybe that's why my entire class disappeared on our fourth-grade field trip. I could tell you where they went. But then I'd be called on to defend my actions.

If I close my eyes, I can still hear their constant name-calling. The taunts of bullies—secure in their power over me.

Then someone said something bad about Mom.

No matter what, she's my mom. And no one, especially not a human, was going to talk badly about her.

The rest was a Random Act of God, or so the newspapers said. Close enough. A tragic mudslide to the humans. Dad was proud; Mom scolded me.

They almost realized what I was capable of before they started arguing again.

I push open our front door—it's gargantuan and made of hand-carved oak. Then I step into the vestibule. Yes, a vestibule because Grams borrowed the interior design of our house from her old friend, Frederick Vanderbilt. It's a long, convoluted story about how I ended up living inside a Mexican Hyde Park. Even I'm impressed by Grams's ability to replicate the interior of a Vanderbilt country home.

Eight steps across the vestibule, through the glass-encased, wrought-iron doors, and I'm in the elliptical-shaped hall, a.k.a. the main room, with its Italian green marble pilasters along the walls. A second-story skylight streams light through an octagonal opening in the ceiling. Everything is done in shades of spring green, muted gold, and frothy cream. The tapestry over the mantel is our family crest circa 1560.

There are two hallways leading off the round main room at 3 o'clock and 9 o'clock. The 3 o'clock hallway ends in the living room. The 9 o'clock hallway opens up to the dining room. Those are the biggest rooms on the main floor, running along the axis of importance. Gramps's and Grams's private studies are right off the main room at 7 o'clock and 11 o'clock, respectively. The only time Grams diverged from the original blueprints was when she replaced the 12 o'clock portico with a conservatory overlooking the ocean. Gramps calls it her sunshine room.

The most annoying Vanderbilt design decision? The kitchen is down in the basement.

I check the grandfather clock in the corner. It reads 7:40 p.m. I'm ten minutes late. I dart down the 9 o'clock hallway, drop my stuff on the side table, hightail it into the dining room.

Eggplant parmigiana and chicken marsala sit on the table in serving dishes. There are four place settings. My chest tightens at the thought of sharing a meal with Mom. I still manage to get a morsel of air down my throat and send a silent request to the universe: Please, let her get stuck at work again.

Gramps is already seated at the head of the table. He looks at his watch. "Almost on time." His bushy gray eyebrows rise with his disappointment toward his tufts of white hair.

My mouth dries up, like a suddenly extinct lake.

"She's young." Grams's auburn hair is braided and wrapped around her head like a Russian crown, but she hasn't worn one of those for several lifetimes. A blood-bathed ruby embedded in three layers of diamonds swallows half of her right pointer finger. When she pours the Chianti, her ring twinkles in despair.

Gramps's chocolate-brown eyes harden. "Hunter?"

Swallowing doesn't ease the dryness in my mouth. "I was helping him prep for a test." Hades. After all these centuries, they know Hunter never needs help studying.

Grams winks. "Perhaps you can meet up on weekends."

I slip into my chair. I'm lucky Hunter gets to spend time with me here in the human realm. "He can't make his own schedule. You remember what it's like."

Gramps reaches for the eggplant. "I remember." The slightest inflection in his voice conveys the lifetimes of living without what should have been his.

It's not his words, but his tone that makes me wince. "Sorry." I've said it in every lifetime, but it's not enough.

Grams pats my hand. "This human thing is quite an experiment."

I catch a whiff of her lilac scent, remembering when we picked boughs of them in Vienna. My face can't help slipping into a smile.

"One we expect to come to an end soon." Mom's voice is insistent and demanding, even from the hallway.

She sweeps my backpack off the side table and replaces it with her leather briefcase. Her bloodhound-brown hair is slicked back in a ballerina bun. Not one hair dares to break formation as she stalks toward me. Her heels *damn-damn-damn* the herringbone hardwood floor, echoing off the chestnut-paneled walls and antique coffered ceiling. Her thumb presses beneath my chin, tilting my face toward her. Her amber eyes singe mine. I try not to flinch, despite pain like a hot curling iron glancing off my pupils.

Something relaxes in her face. "Rainbow eyes."

That's what Dad calls them. Because they are blue, green, amber, brown, gray—all at once. Dad gave me the light blue, which Mom despises. The gray is from Grandfather, Dad's father, but we don't talk about him. I can't really remember what Dad's mom, Grandmother, looked like in human form because she hated taking it. Still, I'm pretty sure the darker blue is from her. Grams gave me the green. Gramps contributed the brown and Mom the amber. I'm the perfect mix of all of them.

But Mom and Dad only see each other in me. I'm a reminder of everything they'd like to forget.

When Mom releases my chin to peel off her black jacket, I let out a breath I didn't know I was holding.

By 11 p.m., I've retreated upstairs to my room. I sit at my desk with my trigonometry book open in front of me and half a page of homework done. I blare Florence and the Machine. The dog days are not over.

My thoughts slip to my family. Grams and Gramps are on the couch downstairs in the living room, watching the news and guessing which one of my parents is responsible for the current economic climate.

Mom's off brokering some after-hours deal. Probably something to throw a kink in Dad's newest venture. Even after the divorce, she can't help sabotaging him, though she swears he started it.

And then there's Dad. I haven't gotten an email from him in days. I haven't heard his voice in weeks. I haven't seen him in months. Because I haven't done anything bad enough to warrant his attention.

For 200 lifetimes, I've craved my father's attention.

Before I can start crafting a way to catch his attention, my cell rings. Mandy. My BFF since middle school. The only girl who isn't afraid of me.

"What's up?" I ask, knowing it's some stupid high-school drama. I've seen and heard it all over the centuries, but I will listen to every word for Mandy. It's the cost of human friendship.

"Are you busy?" Her voice hitches on *busy* like she's been crying for an hour and just gained enough coherence to call me.

She's going to need special handling. I push aside my centuries of daddy issues and flop onto my queen-sized, four-poster bed. I trace my fingers along the medallion pattern of my orchid duvet cover, settling in for a long talk. "What happened?"

Tears well up in her voice. "It's not a big deal."

"So tell me." I soften my voice to coax the truth out of her.

"It's just a prank."

"Uh-huh." Mandy's a gymnast turned cheerbaby. Big mistake. She's easy prey with her wouldn't-flick-a-mosquito-about-to-bite-me smile.

"She didn't mean to upset me." Her voice wobbles, uncertainty sneaking through.

Mandy Mother Theresa's everyone, believing the world is filled with well-intentioned people. Mandy's wrong. But I can't get her to see things my way. Guess it takes a dozen lifetimes.

"I can't help unless you tell me what happened." While I wait for Mandy to say something, my gaze skims over the burnt-out-velvet-floral-patterned wallpaper. Got to love the Victorian era. My ceiling's all lilac gray with wainscoting. No one does a good ceiling anymore. Maybe I'll paint it red. Haven't done that since 1880. But that would require a whole room redo. And I don't have time for that.

She sniffs. "Everything was fine at breakfast."

She's going to take me on a Discovery Channel expedition of her day. "What did Serena do?" The cheer monarch, Serena, hates competition. She's been out for Mandy's blood all year.

"It could have been another member of the cheer squad."

I want to smash my cell phone against the wall and scream that it's Serena. But for Mandy, I entertain the notion it was someone else. "What did some unknown perpetrator do?"

"My locker." Her voice fades away and all I catch is, "redecorated."

"With?"

"Mean words. Gross pictures."

I strain to hear her. "Like?"

"Pig, slut, whore, fat ass…" She sounds as if she half-believes what they wrote and is ashamed.

"They pick on you because they're jealous. You can flip circles around them. You're gorgeous. And you're nice to everyone. They can't possibly compete with you." So they try to destroy her. I've seen it so many times. I've felt it.

All these centuries later, the memories press against the padlocked doors in my mind, trying to get out. But some things have to stay locked away. I refuse to remember Pompeii.

Mandy chokes back a sob, making a terrible snuffling noise in her throat.

I turn my attention to what is happening right now. "And the pictures?" I need to know the exact amount of cruelty inflicted because it will be returned.

"Cows. Morbidly obese women. Strung-out hookers." The pain bleeds into Mandy's voice.

Serena's MO. Too bad she wasn't on my fourth-grade field trip. "Sweetie, I wish you'd stayed with gymnastics." These girls are everything I despise in the human realm. I go to my closet and pull out a comforter for Mandy. "Come over."

I hear her neck rubbing against the phone: a quiet yes.

"I'll stay on the phone 'til you get here."

Her relief rushes across the receiver. "Thanks."

CHAPTER THREE

THE NEXT DAY, THE entire dining hall is abuzz with rumors about Serena. The cheerbabies can't tell their side of the story yet because they're sequestered with a counselor. It doesn't matter, every lunch table makes up their own version of what happened.

Without Mandy or Hunter, I've got the round table all to myself. It's achingly empty until Hunter slides into the wooden chair next to mine, throws his arm around my shoulder, and grabs a fry off my plate. "Did you hear about Serena?"

"That she's a bitch? Common knowledge." I dip my fry in the ketchup pool and take a bite.

He leans close, so close that his black curls tickle my cheek. "She plummeted from the top of a human pyramid."

"Huh." My first instinct is to cover up what I've done, even with Hunter.

"Ambulance took her to the hospital. Headmaster Holland is freaking out over the high lawsuit potential." His breath tickles my neck. "Wrist broken, leg fractured in four places, hip bone shattered."

"That'll keep her out of school for a few weeks." I can't help adding, "She might have hurt her spine, too." Herniated the L5-S1 disc, but that will flare up later.

He bows his head in a mock salute to my power. "The cheer monarch has been overthrown. Well done."

"Thanks." I can't help smiling at his praise.

"Your family will be furious if they find out you used your powers." I catch the concern in his tone.

"They're too busy with their own battles to notice an accident at my high school and realize I was behind it."

Hunter gives me his doubtful face.

It makes my voice go all defensive. "I know I shouldn't throw around curses, but you didn't see what Serena did to Mandy." I had to eat a pint of coconut ice cream and two bags of Chili Cheese Fritos last night. Mandy's an emotional eater, and you have to keep up or she feels worse. "I spent hours gluing her shredded self-esteem back together."

"You need to be careful."

"Serena should be more careful," I hiss-whisper. "She doesn't care how much she harms people. It's damage control." It's not like she's dead, though there will be nerve damage. I'm not a careless curser, purely a reciprocator.

He nuzzles the side of my neck. "You are such a softie when it comes to Mandy."

"No, I…no." I refuse to see myself the way Hunter does. I can never be sweet again. "I only jump-started karma." Mandy isn't the kind of person who retaliates. Sometimes, I admire her self-control. Mostly, I intercede for her.

His thumb strokes the nub at the back of my neck, sending tingles into my arms.

My eyes slip shut. If only we were back at his apartment. The things I would do to him. A loud clatter at the next table reminds me we're still in the dining hall. I mumble, "It was a weak curse."

"How much did your eyes change?"

He can't see the change because the special contacts he has made for me attach to my eyes and are impossible to detect. They've fooled my parents for centuries. I sit up and slide my contact to the side to show him the remaining color in my iris. "A small amount of amber disappeared this morning." An injury curse is nowhere near as draining as a death curse. "It won't register on my family's radar as something I would do."

He chuckles. "Nothing in your history suggests subtle."

"Until now." My parents don't realize how much better I am at controlling my powers.

"It might be subtle enough to stay off their radar. But just in case, take your contacts out at school and let your eyes be a little less amber tonight."

"Then they'll catch me." My mind races at the thought of what they'd do if they knew. I can see it unfolding in my head. Screams from Mom. Disgust from Dad. Disappointment from Grams and Gramps. Then they'd band together and stop me.

Fear wraps its bony fingers around my throat and squeezes until I can barely breathe.

Hunter pushes the hair off my face, reminding me he is here. "You have to let them catch you sometimes. It's the only way to prevent them from catching you all the time."

An hour later, in study hall, I get the text, "Need 2 tlk now," two seconds before Mandy's dark-blonde hair and doll-like face pop up on the other side of the glass-paneled door.

I stroll past rows of bored students covertly texting, reach the front of the room, and ask for a bathroom pass.

Mr. Behan hands it to me without looking up from his newspaper.

I take two steps into the hallway before Mandy yanks me into the girls' room. "Did you hear?!" Her words echo off the tiny tiles lining the wall and floor.

I shush her and kick each of the stall doors open to check that we're alone. "About what?"

She squeals, "I'm head cheerleader."

"That's awesome." And expected. I threw an eczema curse at the second-in-command. Blackmailed the other senior with sexts she now regrets sending to her ex.

"I mean, what happened to Serena, it's terrible." Mandy's tone digs a ditch of compassion.

I nod, pretending to agree.

She studies the floor tiles. "Am I evil to be excited?" Her voice tiptoes across to me.

"Nope." Only Mandy would still want to be good after everything Serena did to her.

"Serena will be okay." Mandy's expression shifts from uncertain to hopeful. "I'll make sure to send her flowers from the squad. It'll just be a few weeks."

It'll be the rest of this semester and all summer, too. But she doesn't need to know that now. "See? You're awesomeness cubed."

Mandy wraps me in one of her inescapable Rainbow-Brite hugs.

"Now you can put a stop to the nasty pranks."

"Yeah." She pulls back and gives me her did-you-do-something stare. But she doesn't ask.

Mandy never asks. That's why she's my best friend.

CHAPTER FOUR

A FTER SCHOOL, THE ATHLETIC go to practice and the rest of us end up in the parking lot. Alone inside my black VW Beetle, I watch my classmates break into their cliques and get into their cars and drive away. Mandy's at practice with her squad and Hunter's got a meeting back in the wanshiqi realm.

Without Mandy or Hunter, my afternoon is uncomfortably open. I could go watch the kids at the skate park skin themselves, but I can't help wondering if my family heard about Serena and suspect that I cursed her. My stomach turns on itself. Maybe I should drive down to San Diego and go hide out at Ocean Beach amongst the tidal pools and the hippies for a while.

I turn the car on, and the engine churns to life. My stereo blares Florence and the Machine. Before I can shift into drive, my cell rings. It's Grams. Oh, Hades. My family knows I won't ignore her call.

I answer. "Hey."

"Dear, we need you to come home. Family meeting." Grams's voice is gentle in its firmness.

We haven't had a family meeting in six months. Shit, shit, shit. They know what I did. "It's bad, isn't it?"

"Come home."

My pulse races with conviction. "Katrina bad?"

"Thereabouts." She hangs up.

I remember what Hunter said about letting them catch me sometimes. It's the only way they won't catch me all the time. All I need to do is stay calm, except my human body is anything but calm.

My hands shake. My heart beats faster and faster until it's pulsating in my skin.

My vision tunnels until all I can see is my odometer, and even that's starting to disappear.

I won't let the panic win. I can't.

I have to focus on something, anything. My breathing. I focus on pulling the air in for three Persephones and holding it for five Persephones and letting it out for seven Persephones. I do this until my vision clears. My heartbeat is still trapped between the layers of my skin, but at least my hands settle to a subtle trembling.

My family can't see me like this. I have to get control. I close my eyes and keep breathing my Persephones. I go deep, deep, deep inside my own mind, disentangling myself from my body. I go to that place where nothing can reach me. The place I had to create in Pompeii. I stay there until it all disappears.

When I open my eyes, fifteen minutes have passed. The parking lot is almost empty. I put the car in drive and head home.

The dark, Italian Renaissance style of the dining room magnifies my impending doomedness. My family is positioned around three sides of the rectangular table. Dad and Mom at opposite ends. Grams and Gramps across from me, providing a united front.

Dad's light-blue eyes are an unpredictable wintry mix. His obsidian-colored hair is carefully coiffed to look like it wasn't. His manicured hands rest on the table, indicating a lecture to come.

"The gray pinstripe suit really picks up your eyes." I baby-step my way into the room.

Amusement never touches Dad's lips. "Kali, sit down."

I slide into the chair reserved for me, preparing to defend myself against their four-pronged attack.

A century of disapproval fills my mother's voice. "Posture."

I unslouch a millimeter.

"What happened at school today?" Grams's voice cushions me with acceptance.

I have to deny it as long as I can. When they catch me, they need to feel it was worth it. They'll be satisfied. They won't keep digging. They won't realize how intentional my deaths are and have been for centuries.

"Hunter and I hooked up in the janitor's closet." I say it with the perfect mix of teen rebellion and pride.

Dad's eye twitches, and for a brief second, he's just a father hating the idea of some boy's hands on his daughter.

"What else?" Gramps's voice rumbles in his throat.

"I aced my physics test." I reach into my bag to extract the A-.

Mom slams her palm on the table. "Don't play with us, missy." A hair slips loose from her bun, breaking formation. She forces it back in place.

She'd love to toss her emotions at me. Stir me up like she does the rest of the world. But she's forbidden from using her powers on me during my punishment. I can't use mine on her either. Not without each other's consent, and we never consent. It's been an unpleasant ceasefire.

"Why don't you tell me?" I widen my eyes to project innocence.

"What happened to Serena Harwinton?" Dad uses his lawyerly tone.

"Cheerleader accident." I shrug, sit back in my chair, and pray that my voice stays stable.

"And now Mandy's head cheerleader." Fury flickers in Mom's eyes. She's never been partial to my BFF. Not sure if it's the human thing or the cheerleader thing that bothers her most.

"You threw a curse out, didn't you?" Gramps asks.

I'm going to say no. I have to say no. I open my mouth to say no.

Grams's gaze locks on mine. "If you did it to protect Mandy, I understand, but you promised you'd be more careful."

I need to look away, to escape the love in her eyes, but I can't. "It wasn't me." My voice squirrels up the wall paneling.

Hurt creases her forehead. "You wouldn't lie to your Grams, would you?"

She's the only one it hurts to lie to. I bite my lip, but the truth still slips out. "I was careful. Injury curses are beyond lightweight."

Mom's breath snakes through her teeth. She leaps up and grabs my chin. "There's less brown than yesterday."

The loss of brown is hard evidence that I've been using my powers. "Less amber," I mutter, but no one hears me. Brown only disappears on the big curses. Amber on the small ones.

Mom's grip on my chin is inescapable as she swivels my head toward Gramps to show him.

"Do you have a death wish?" Gramps's hands interlock tightly like he's holding it all together for us.

He has no idea how close he is to the truth. I make myself keep eye contact and force frustration into my voice. "Not particularly." Which is a complete lie. Using my powers harms my human body and eventually triggers the self-destruct encoded in my DNA. Every human body has a self-destruct. My powers just activate mine at a rapid rate. Once the brown is gone from my eyes, even if the amber remains, I begin my descent into death. Once the death spiral starts, nothing can prevent it. Death won't let any escape his grasp.

"It's been two hundred lifetimes. And you still can't make it to seventeen." Dad shakes his head at my Lincoln Memorial-sized failure.

All I have to do is live past my seventeenth human birthday and our punishment ends. Then my parents are free of me, and I'll no longer be tied to them. It's been over 1900 years, and I'm still not ready to let them go. Dying before seventeen has always been a secret source of pride for me, but I hang my head and pretend to be contrite. "I'm trying."

"Try harder." Mom's so angry each of her Rs comes out like a growl. She's sick of paying for my mistake. So is Dad.

It's the only thing they agree on. They want this to end so they can return to what they were for tens of thousands of years. But they don't understand. I can't let that happen until I fix what was broken in Pompeii.

Until I fix us.

"My control is better. I took maybe a week off this body's lifetime." I'm guesstimating. It's an art to calculate the cost of a curse.

"Remember Pompeii?" Dad asks.

Disgust writes a novel across Mom's face. Disappointment is a sonnet in Gramps's eyes. Grams looks down at her hands.

They won't let me live that down.

My inner mind quakes. A fissure threatens the deepest wall inside me. Not the one barricading my emotions, but the one barricading an ancient truth. The wall that protects them from what really happened in Pompeii.

I'm out of my chair, grabbing my backpack and needing to escape.

I ignore Gramps's command to, "Get back here. We are not finished."

I can't see the failure I've become to all of them.

I run out of the house, leap into my car, and put miles between us.

I leave them to discuss what a mistake I am. How I ruined eternity for them.

CHAPTER FIVE

HUNTER'S NOT HOME WHEN I get to his place. It doesn't matter. I let myself in, crawl into his bed, burrow into his sheets. I press my face into his pillow, needing to be near him. It smells of oceans and stars, of Hunter.

Dad's words echo in my head, "Remember Pompeii?"

I won't think about Pompeii. I can't feel that pain again. I clamp down on my worst memory, but another slips through. I relive the weeks after Pompeii. Being arrested and hauled before our tribunal, the fayuan.

All these centuries later, the smell of the fayuan's chambers still assaults me. Lilies and moon craters. Fire and moss. It disoriented me, keeping me weak in the fayuan's presence. They isolated me in the center of their octagonal stone room. Its distant dome reminding me of how insignificant I was. They made me perch on a jagged rock in human form. It sliced through my palms and scraped at my backside. Another pain to endure.

The fayuan sat above me in a semicircle, like spectators watching my undoing and taking pleasure in my pain. They opted to take human form for my trial to streamline the process. My guilt was inevitable. This was just a formality.

My trial had nothing to do with the thousands of human lives snuffed out in a moment in Pompeii. No. Wanshiqi don't care about human life. If that was all I had done, they would have celebrated my accomplishment. But one wanshiqi was trapped in Pompeii. For what happened to him, I had to suffer.

When they finally reached their verdict, the eleven voices of the fayuan rang out, "We find you to be selfish and immature. Unworthy of qifa."

A hush fell over the room. Qifa is the wanshiqi coming of age and is essential to becoming an adult wanshiqi. Without it, I don't have access to my full powers, and I cannot use my powers on another wanshiqi without their consent. Other wanshiqi aren't supposed to use their power on me either.

Even in my weakened state, panic swarmed my heart. Warning bells clanged in my ears. I glanced at my parents, but they refused to look at me. Grandfather and Grandmother weren't even there. Only Grams met my eye. Hers were filled with regret.

The fayuan waited only a moment before they handed down my punishment. "We banish you to an existence in the human realm. Your parents raised an unfit wanshiqi. The three of you must reincarnate as human until you prove yourself a fit wanshiqi by surviving your seventeenth human birthday. Only then will all of you be allowed to return to our realm. Then you can undergo qifa."

Grams and Gramps joined us by choice, not by requirement. They wanted to watch over me…and my parents.

The scene fades. My mind fast-forwards through my first dozen or so reincarnations. Back then, I didn't realize how quickly my powers destroyed my human body. I kept cursing and accidentally activating the self-destruct in my DNA. I died so fast.

Still, I desperately wanted to go home to our realm until I realized humans have what I've always wanted—a family. A real family. People who love and protect each other, people who stay together. I had glimpses of that before Pompeii. I will have it again.

Staying human will help my parents recover from the damage done to them in Pompeii. I know it will. This is my last chance to have a family.

I have to prolong my punishment here by making sure I never reach my seventeenth human birthday. So every lifetime, I select a death date. And I count down the days until the next lifetime begins. The one where we will be a family. It hasn't happened yet, but it will. It has to, right?

I don't know how long Hunter's been sweeping his fingertips over my forehead, caressing my face, and trying to tease me back to wakefulness. I open my eyes and he's right there, lying beside me on the bed. His agonizingly beautiful face is inches from mine.

My voice comes out all sleepy-slurry. "When did you get home?"

"A couple minutes ago." Concern ripples through his words. "They found out, huh?"

I nod, and my cheek rubs against his soft pillowcase. "You always have to be right."

"I wish I didn't." His voice drops low, letting me know how much he would like to be wrong this time.

I scoot closer until our heads touch. "Can I crash here?"

"Make me dinner?"

"Breakfast dinner."

"Done." His fingers entwine with mine, like the roots of the plants we once were. He stares into my eyes. His brow furrows, and his lips thin into his serious face. "There's barely any brown left."

We both know what that means. As long as some brown remains in my eyes, Hunter can use his powers to roll me back a curse or three. If all the brown disappears, my death begins. Nothing can stop it. Not Hunter. Not my family. No one.

"A few more curses will do you in." Something shifts in his voice.

"I'm thinking a Memorial Day finale." I sit up, pull my knees to my chest, and wrap my arms around them.

Hunter leans back against the headboard. "That's cutting it close."

My birthday is June 2nd. This death date is the closest one yet to my birthday. "It's the only way to make my family believe I am trying to reach my seventeenth birthday."

"Are you sure?" He caresses my cheek.

When he cups my face like that, it's hard to be sure of anything. "I have to die."

"Don't you want to be like me?" Hurt shadows each syllable.

"Not if it means losing my family." Or the last chance to be a family.

"It's temporary." He's already been through qifa.

It's a coming of age that's more like a metamorphosis. You become completely independent from your family. No longer feeling any bond to them. He swears I'll welcome the change and adapt to it.

When I don't say anything, he continues. "A teardrop in the misery of our lives." Hunter goes all Yeats in an attempt to sway me.

"I don't care if it's part of growing up. I don't want to grow up without my family."

"After qifa, you won't want them anymore. You'll be different." He moves closer, taking both my hands in his. His voice is tinged with hope. "You'll be like me. Our bond will be even stronger. And eventually, you'll form alliances with them if you want to."

I don't want to be okay with not being with my family. Grams and Gramps are everything to me. I don't want that to change. And no matter how imperfect my parents are, they are my parents. I have to fix them before my qifa. I'm afraid that afterward will be too late because qifa alters everything. I won't be the me I am now, and I won't care if my parents remain like they are. "I can't do it."

He squeezes my hands. "What about me, Kali? Don't you want to be with me?"

I hold on to his hands and lean in for a kiss. "I'm with you right now."

He pulls away from me. "These are tiny stolen human moments." He makes it sound like a crumb of bread to a starving man. "A fraction of what we are as wanshiqi. It's not the way we are supposed to be."

I stare down at the rumpled sheet beneath me.

"Let us be what we are meant to be—tonggan." His voice is ragged, like a sail that is too torn up to take this journey again.

"We are tonggan." We've been kindreds for thousands of years. We fit together, balancing each other out and making each other stronger and better.

"We are a shadow of what we could be. Only after your qifa can we be true tonggan."

I can't bear to see the pain in his eyes. Pain that I put there every lifetime.

"How much longer will you make me wait?" His tone reminds me he's been waiting for centuries.

I can't answer, so I pull him close. Brush my lips over his. Hunter tries to talk, but I refuse to answer with words. Just lips and fingers. He's a teenage boy. Physically, anyways. He can't refuse me.

A few hours later, my phone buzzes on Hunter's nightstand for the third time.

"You going to answer?" Hunter asks.

I reach for my cell and turn it off. "My family knows where I am."

"They won't come for you?"

He's everything they were and want to be again—a full wanshiqi. Seeing him stabs them in the eye with what I've reduced them to. "Doubtful."

Hunter adjusts the pillows and rests against them. "If they catch on to your plan..."

"They'll try to stop me." I cuddle into him.

"Hasn't happened yet." He traces his pointer finger over my lips. Every cell responds to his touch.

"They chalk it up to me being a failure."

"You were one of the brightest in your eon."

I duck my head, embarrassed by his praise. I trace infinite eights on his chest. "And one of the most volatile."

"That's your parents' fault." His throaty chuckle does things to me. "They are too self-absorbed to ever see you."

The truth is alcohol saturating a rubbed-raw flesh wound. I roll away from him, suddenly needing to be clothed. I lift the sheets to search for my underwear and bra.

Hunter doesn't move. "What about your grandparents?"

"If Grams discovered I've been dying on purpose, she'd hate me." Fear washes over me, goose bumping my flesh. My body trembles. Treacherous emotions threaten to undo me. I won't let them. I can't.

I remember how many times my parents have disappointed me. I summon the hurt, knowing it will bring anger along. The warmth of frustration.

I take a breath and anchor myself here in this moment. My eyes scan the hardwood floor. My panties are balled up beside the bed. My bra is hugging his chair. I grab them and put them on.

Hunter sits up in bed. "I'm sorry your parents are asses."

"They're just sick of being human."

"They aren't the only ones."

His words send a rush of annoyance over me. "No one asked you to keep coming back as a human. You are free to reincarnate as anything." My voice is fringed with fear.

"As long as I don't mind living without my tonggan."

"Then let me go."

"Is that what you want?" His eyes devour my qi.

I look at the desk, the window, even the wood floor. Anywhere but in his eyes. "You stir too many emotions in me, feelings I can't afford to have."

The bed shifts and he gets up. He stands with his back to me. The muscles ripple beneath his skin as he bends to pick up his jeans.

When he's agitated, his powers are harder to control. Since he's an energy shaper, some of the energy he siphons from the world has to be expelled. Tonight, his mood impacts the weather. The sudden rumble of thunder in the distance tells me he's upset.

I hate arguing when I'm not dressed. I grab the nearest T-shirt off the floor and slip it over my head. It smells of oceans and stars. Of beginnings and endings. It's his.

He paces across the room. His soles slap against the hardwood floor. Each step is an act of perfection. He's everything I should want. He's my tonggan. The one I was born to be with. We found each other so easily 2300 years ago. Kids in our world. But all I do is screw everything up for him.

His fingers tangle in his curly hair. "You don't get it, do you?"

"What? That you keep sacrificing your true self to be with me?" I yell, knowing he'd be better off without me. Inside, I'm arctic-iceberg cold, aching at the thought of my world without him.

His voice is so low, it echoes the rumbling thunder. "I circumvent the purpose of your punishment by helping you prolong it. Do you know what the fayuan would do to me if they knew?"

My throat tightens. His punishment would be far worse than mine.

I've endangered him every time I plotted to die before seventeen. I should have protected him. Maybe the fayuan were right about me. I'm a horrible wanshiqi. A terrible tonggan.

Hot tears slip down my cheeks. "I'm sorry."

Suddenly, Hunter's in front of me. The pads of his thumbs soak up my tears. "Let yourself turn seventeen."

Bullets of rain ricochet off the window. Tears he would never shed undo me. I love him. The kind of love that makes you want to make grand Romeo and Juliet gestures.

Instead, I clench my teeth and refuse to give in to my love for him. I step out of the safety of his arms. Hunter lets me go this time.

I count a couple Persephones before I trust myself to speak. "Why don't you leave me?"

His smile breaks my heart. "Tonggan are the essence of who we are. All we need is our tonggan."

And I make him spend lifetimes without me. Waiting on me—a tonggan who refuses to be his completely.

I step back into his arms and press my cheek against his chest, needing to hear the reassuring thrum of his heart. "I can't go through qifa. Not yet."

Hunter's arms tighten around me.

There is nothing left to say. No words to ease his pain. So I do what humans do. I kiss him. Touch him. Distract him from the inevitable pain I will bring him by pulling him back to bed with me.

CHAPTER SIX

IN THE MORNING, I can't help curling up on Hunter's couch to watch the waves break against the sandy shore below. The sky is a decisive blue.

While he's in the kitchen, I announce, "I'm not going to school today."

Hunter pads across the hardwood floor, hands me a cup of coffee, and jumps in the shower. Not the reaction I expected from him.

I meander to the bathroom door and shout over the running water, "I'm not going home either."

I wait for his response, but all I hear is the shower shutting off. I make my way to his room and perch on his bed.

A few minutes later, he walks in, towel-drying his hair. "It's your life." He shrugs into his turquoise T-shirt and gray jeans.

"You're not going to weigh in?" Hunter usually has a cent or three to add.

"Have a nice day." He gives me a quick kiss and leaves me with an entire day to fill.

That's odd. He never opts for school if he can avoid it.

I glance out his window at the azure sky. Days like this, I miss flying. I was such a good seagull. A damn fine year before I choked on something shiny. Almost as fun as living as a crab in Nai Harn until I became someone's dinner.

I'm not wasting today inside. I grab my sweatshirt and head outside.

Dad's mercury-colored Mercedes idles by the curb in front of Hunter's building. Hunter must have spied Dad's car from the bathroom window and knew I had a lecture coming, so he spared me his.

Dad rolls the window down. "Get in, Kalifornia."

He hasn't called me that since I was twelve. His Brooks Brothers chinos and gray-blue polo shirt promise a day without work, a day with Dad, a day we haven't had since I was in middle school. A day I've longed for.

I throw my bag on the floor and climb into the passenger seat. "Where are we going?"

"Lunch at the beach." He doesn't mention my running out last night. Or the two voicemails he left me.

Neither do I. "Dana Point?"

"St. Regis."

It's where we used to go, back when he had time for me. "Best nachos ever."

He gives me a quarter-lip raise. It's less than half a smile, but it's something. Then he pulls out of the parking lot and heads for the freeway. I'd love to believe he wants to spend time with me, but I know this is all a ruse. A ruse to get me to let my guard down and confess my secrets.

I have to take control of the conversation before he does. "Why don't we do this anymore?"

"We're doing it right now." The hint of humor in his voice will let him spin his absence into something innocuous.

"No, Dad." I bite the tip of my thumb. "Why'd you stop coming around?"

He stares at the traffic cluttering up the Five. All five lanes creep along. "It's what we all needed." His gaze glides from the road to the rearview mirror to both side mirrors and back again. Anywhere but on me.

"Is it?" Maybe him and Mom. But not me. Never me.

"Your mom and I can't get along."

"I didn't realize the divorce applied to me, too."

"It didn't." He adjusts his side mirrors.

"So what happened?" They've shared custody since I was seven. With each passing year, he disappeared a little more from my life.

"Life here happened." He tinkers with the temperature and adjusts the airflow. He's always been meticulous about the details, especially the ones he withholds from me.

"This is the first lunch we've had this year."

He pulls out his phone and opens his calendar. "We'll make it a monthly thing."

He's said that before. Inevitably, it's biannual at best. But it's better than nothing. "I get you the whole day?"

"Until seven," he promises.

Mom's desperate. Desperate enough to unleash Daddy time. She hates how much I want to be around him. She would never admit it, but she wants him around, too. And if she can't have him, neither can I.

My looming death date makes today more precious. After I die, if Mom's young enough, she can pop out another kid, and it's me back for another round of humanity. Otherwise, I'm forced to wait in dengzhong, where wanshiqi linger between incarnations. Sort of like the limbo humans talk about, but I don't go to heaven or hell afterward. I come back for another round of human existence.

Except I have to wait for everyone else in the family to age and die, human-style, and then reincarnate and grow to the appropriate age for my rebirth. Sometimes, I wait around in dengzhong for sixty years.

It's not as bad as it sounds. The waiting gives me time to remember what my family once was and imagine what it could be. And I still get to be me. The whole soul thing humans imagine? It's true. But their souls are one ten thousandth of my qi. I don't fragment or forget when I reincarnate. I also get infinite reincarnations. Their tiny souls burn through all their energy in one lifetime.

Dad's been a Scottish warrior and an African prince and an Italian merchant. Now he's a politocrat. A behind-the-scenes consultant ruling the politicians.

"What happens when you and Mom get back to our world? Tonggan can't separate."

He grips the wheel. "That really depends on you reaching seventeen."

"It's these human emotions. I can't always control them." The words are heavy on my tongue, weighted with my duplicity.

"You're only one month away from your birthday. It's the closest you've ever been to seventeen." This is why he really came around today. "If you feel the urge to curse, come to me. I'll take care of whatever is bothering you."

"You'd use your powers for me?" Dad's never offered to use his abilities to do my bidding. Ever.

"I will do anything to help you reach seventeen." A stark need sharpens his tone.

I slide my foot out of my sandal, brace my sole on the leather seat, and wrap my arms around my knee. I have to hold myself together. I have to hold this lie together. "I'm trying, Dad."

"Your mom and I aren't meant to stay human this long. We miss what we are." His voice cradles me. "We can take their form, we can live their lifetimes, but we can never be human." He adds under his breath, "We can never be as primitive or ruled by our emotions."

"Have you met Mom?" She lashes out in ways humans cannot imagine.

He gives me his slow smile. The one he uses to disarm all his enemies. "That's her specialty—ruling hearts. She's as close to a human emotionally as any of us. She still decimates an entire race with as much concern as a human displays when clipping a hangnail."

The ocean *whooshas* and *blblblus* behind me. Tides on the verge of change. Dad stands back to survey our work. This sand masterpiece could rival the walled town of Mont St. Michel. Our creation has withstood a few dozen waves. Mostly because of my moat digging. It's a leg and hand thing to get the right depth and width.

Sandcastle building remains our bonding activity. Several centuries ago, it was castle besieging. Dad walks the perimeter of our creation twice before pronouncing it, "Not bad," and removing the apron and gloves he wears for sandcastle construction.

I try to brush my hands clean, but wet sand is stuck under my fingernails. I spit wisps of hair out of my mouth. The back of my shirt sticks to my skin. I broke a sweat three hours ago, despite the crisp breeze coming off the Pacific.

"Picture time," he says.

A hotel worker scampers over to set up Dad's tripod.

We have a wall in his house documenting each and every sandcastle we built. It hasn't been added to in four years.

We stand on opposite sides of the sand city we've built, neither one of us willing to block our masterpiece.

The camera clicks. Six shots.

Dad checks them. "Four out of six isn't bad." He slips the guy a fifty and glances at his watch.

I pack up our tools. We've got every piece of kitchenware Mom loved when I was a kid. He says they were the only things we could use. It's another one of their ongoing skirmishes. I'm about to carry everything to the car, but the hotel worker swoops in and lifts them out of my hands. Dad steers me back toward the St. Regis. To what may be the last father-daughter lunch of this lifetime.

It's a dream view on a dream day with a dream Dad. From the patio of the St. Regis, the tan sand and turquoise waves are spread out beneath us. The sun warms my skin, and the palm trees rustle in the breeze. No matter how close I sit to my father, I still can't reach him. He has always been the Great Wall of China—awe-inspiring and insurmountable. Maybe that's why Mom gave up.

The waiter deposits a platter of nachos on our patio table. Dad pulls the best nacho from the top of the pile. It's heaped with melted cheese and olives and tomatoes. The perfect dollop of sour cream. The motherload of nachos.

When the waiter leaves, I ask, "Why'd you get divorced?"

"It was for the best."

He's never given me a reason. One that I believe, anyway. "Hundreds of lifetimes and suddenly you can't live together?" My father spent 200 years in Ancient Egypt as a sphinx. Staring at him now, I can picture it.

"We like to change with the times." Sometimes it sounds like he's trying explanations out on me. I'm never sure what's the truth with him.

Last time I was born, it was 1957. Divorce was still pretty rare back then. "Just trying something new?" My voice rises a few octaves driven by my disbelief.

"Kali." He always says my name like a monumental tragedy. "We've been stuck in human form for almost two millennia. Your mom wanted more freedom in this lifetime."

"Why even get married?"

"The commitment was required for you to return."

The nacho slips from my fingers. "What?"

"Just until you're born." He wipes his hands on his napkin and pretends that wasn't a verbal grenade he tossed at me.

"How long have you and Mom," my voice cracks, "not wanted to be together?"

"We need breathers. When I was a redwood, I had a good 300 years without her nagging."

"What about the time between reincarnations?"

"Twenty to forty years?" He chuckles.

Dad's been around 30,000 years already. That's a night off for him. He's right. I've been human too long. I forget what a wanshiqi lifetime truly means. Heat floods my cheeks. I stare down at my plate. My mind churns with thoughts. Thoughts I don't want to say out loud, but I have to. "You're sick of me, too?"

"Aren't you tired of us?"

His words slice through my heart, stinging and burning. I have to ignore the pain. It's the only way to survive it. I force lightness into my voice. "Just your obnoxious suits. I much preferred the kilt."

He throws his head back and laughs. The way he used to when I was little. And I get one last Dad Day.

CHAPTER SEVEN

D AD'S BRAKE LIGHTS flare once before his car pulls out of the driveway. His duty fulfilled, he goes back to his life. I could stay there all night staring at the dark place where his car once was. It won't bring him back. It never does.

I turn and head toward Grams's front door. I have to go apologize to Gramps for ignoring his command and running out last night. Gramps and Grams are the two people who raised me. The two people I respect most. The two people I never wanted to let down.

My stomach does a backflip over my spleen. I stop and take a breath in for three Persephones and hold it for five Persephones and breathe out for seven Persephones. After a few rounds, my scalp tingles. My feet glide over the ground. Lightheadedness gifts me with a false calm.

I reach for the knob to our front door, but the door swings open. Anna, our housekeeper, stands there. She's 250 pounds of unadulterated sunshine.

"Oh! Miss Kali, did you have fun with your dad?" She wipes down our behemoth carved oak door with a cloth.

I nod. "Are my grandparents…?"

She points to the sunshine room. "They're waiting for you."

I walk across the main room and continue straight back to the sunshine room. It is all glass, a greenhouse jutting into our yard that lets Grams and her plants soak up the sun.

From the doorway, I can see Torrey Pines Beach in the distance. The sun sinks toward the water, burning oranges and reds into the skyline. Creating a symphony of light before the coming darkness.

Gramps sits in his high-back, white wicker chair, reminding me of his past thrones. He watches Grams harvest stalks and leaves from her plants with such love in his eyes. I fear I will never have their kind of trust and love. Hunter says we'll be like that after qifa, but I'm afraid we'll be like my parents.

A sigh slips from my lips and catches their attention.

Grams's clippers pause in mid-prune. "How was your day, dear?"

I remember the sand masterpiece and my Dad Day. I try to mask my exuberance, but it inflates each word. "Dad took me to the beach."

"About time." Grams snips some leaves from her sage plant.

Gramps doesn't say a word, but his expression thunderclouds. I'm not sure if the look is for my dad or me. Maybe both of us. I love Gramps, but in moments like this I fear him. His silence and disapproval terrify me more than Mom's yelling or Dad's distance.

Grams puts her clippers down and comes to stand beside Gramps. She rests her hand on his shoulder. She gives me a quick nod to begin.

"I'm sorry for running out on your family meeting." I sit down on the floor in front of them because wanshiqi apologies, daoqian, require lowering yourself. Physically, if it's to a zhangzhe, an elder who has existed over 100,000 years, like Gramps and Grams.

I have to make a symbolic sacrifice and then an expression of agony. A hurt to repay the hurt I caused. I lay my car keys at his feet, symbolically offering my freedom. I borrow Gram's gardening knife and press it to my arm. Flesh yields only so much before it breaks. The knife slices through my skin with an all too familiar feeling: a burning sting. My blood seeps to the surface, runs down my arm, and drips onto the floor. I wait for enough to pool there and use it to write the wanshiqi symbols for apology *daoqian.*

Moments pass without a sound. There is only the heat of my wound and the blood of my apology.

Finally, Gramps pushes my keys back toward me. He accepts my apology. Grams rushes to bandage my wound. My arm throbs, but she can't use her powers to heal it. I have to feel pain for the pain I caused.

I take a breath and try to explain, "When Dad brought up Pompeii, I just couldn't take it."

"We are all here because of what happened in Pompeii." Gramps's voice rumbles in his throat, reminding me of how the ground rumbled in Pompeii.

Bile splashes against the back of my mouth and eats away at my enamel. I won't think about Vesuvius. I dig my fingers into the cut on my arm. Hundreds of nerve endings cry out. It short-circuits my memory.

I can't bear to see the disappointment in Gramps's eyes, so I drop my gaze to the mosaic tiles in the floor. The blue pieces form an intricate peony flower. I press my fingers against the tiny tiles in the floor, finding the one that is loose and rocking it back and forth. Motion to distract me from the emotions I don't want to feel. "I'm sorry you and Grams are suffering for my crime."

"We chose to come with you." Gramps steeples his fingers. It's his contemplative position.

"The fayuan may be the highest court in our realm, but they don't know everything." Grams's voice is lullaby gentle. "Your parents…aren't the best at raising a child."

Understatement of ten millennia. Grams is a healer, a returner of life. Gramps is a bringer of death, a plague giver. They know more about life and death than most wanshiqi.

Gramps leans forward in the wicker chair, closing the distance between us. "Your parents can meddle all they want in the human and wanshiqi realms. But you, if you reach your full potential, you could be greater than they ever imagined."

"What if I'm worse than they are?" Worry slips into my whisper.

"What if you're better?" The warmth in Gramps's eyes may be my undoing.

So many truths clutter my tongue. I can't share them. I swallow as many as I can. But one makes its way out of my mouth. "I don't want our family bond to become a business relationship. You still care about Mom and me. Why didn't qifa lock in your inhumanity?"

Grams and Gramps exchange one of their secret tonggan looks. Somehow they convey everything without saying a word. I've never been able to understand it.

"Qifa cements who you are at your core. It strengthens your qi," Gramps explains.

"So Mom and Dad…"

"Have very different qi than Gramps and me. They are also much younger." Grams tries to cushion the reality.

"So when I'm your age, I won't be like Mom and Dad?" I need someone to tell me that will never happen.

Grams wraps her arms around me. She holds me close and promises, "You will be who you are at your core. The tonggan bond is a reflection of each of your qi. Every wanshiqi chooses her path and becomes what she wishes to be."

I know she intends her words to be comforting, but I can't help looking at the dark side of things: the wrong choice, and Hunter and I could be like my parents.

School comes faster than I'd like. I sit in the third row of desks toward the back of the class, trying to pay attention to what my English teacher says about our poetry project. Dr. Herger looks devilishly Irish with his ruddy cheeks and curly red hair, but thoughts of my death date distract me until he announces, "Partner up with the person sitting beside you."

Hunter's not here, so I get the boy with paper-straight brown hair, the color of coconut shells. He lets it grow long enough to make it impossible to see his eyes until he sweeps it back. And then it's gray. His eyes. His soul. All I see is neutrality in decline.

He intrigues me.

I push my desk toward his. The metal legs screech across the tile floor. "Which poem do you want to use?" I stopped caring about school assignments a lifetime or two back.

He picks mine up with the slenderest fingers I've seen on a boy. Artistic fingers. Michelangelo fingers. Then he pulls a creased piece of paper from his back pocket and tosses it onto my notebook.

I unfold the page and read his words:

She lies on the couch
Swears today she'll get up
Eat something
Drink something

Do something
But tonight
She'll be on the couch
In the same clothes
Promising tomorrow is the day
The day she tries to live again.

"Wow," I say. "Powerful imagery."
He glances down at my poem.

Sometimes I sit here
Wondering is it you or me
Who set this world in motion
Careening toward infinity
Spiraling from darkness
Exploding into nothingness
Destroying all that once was
Momentum can overwhelm you in flight
Flaming lips can burn the delicateness that is you
Passion is the greatest memoir to write itself
Unfurling wings do strike me now
Remembrance unties her sash
Entreating me with her embrace once more
Into the flesh of what was
The ecstasy of her carries me away from all I believe myself to be

And I am neither you nor me

When he looks up from reading mine, a kaleidoscope of emotions whirls in his eyes. "You're trying too hard." He has one of those voices that makes my ears want to hear more.

Except his words. Wait. What did he just say to me? "Excuse me?" My English teacher loved it in 1969.

"It's good, but the lesbian overtones are a cry for attention."

Who is this kid to go all judgy on my poem?

"It keeps you from being great." His voice distills the truth in a way that is achingly honest.

"Look," I grip my pen so I don't plunge it into the back of his beautiful hand. "Tate, it's just a poem for class."

"It's Tav." His forehead crinkles up in annoyance. "Octavius Ponte, actually. I've been in your English class this entire semester."

Octavius. Suddenly the weight of Mount Vesuvius drops on my chest. I can't get a breath. Not one single breath. An image of straight, dark hair and coal-colored eyes blankets my mind. Followed by Mount Vesuvius spewing lava and ash across the entire city of Pompeii. Burying everyone I hated and destroying anything worth forgetting.

I want to leap out of my chair and smash my desk through the window. Anger ignites in my qi. The darkest feelings surge through me, making me feel like I can do anything. Take on anyone. It's a wildfire inside me, consuming everything. Fueling my rage. Words of retribution spin in my head. I bite my tongue to keep a curse from escaping.

I force myself to stay in my seat. The air betrays me. It feels as hard to breathe as it did in Pompeii. But I am not in Pompeii. I have to take sips—one tiny denying breath at a time.

He's only human, unlikely to spur me to level a civilization. A minor car accident at most. He's Tav, just Tav, only Tav.

Tav's gray eyes study me. "Don't stress so much, we can do my poem." The sound of his voice is a balm to my ancient anxiety. I see Tav, and I know he is not Octavius. We are not in Pompeii. I am safe here. I gulp down the air.

Oh, Hades. He thinks my reaction is about a stupid English assignment. I try to chuckle, but it becomes a cough. "So your poem is about going through depression?"

"We tend to see ourselves in others' poetry." He leans back and looks at me.

"Which means you've got overt lesbian tendencies?"

"Possibly." He sweeps the hair out of his eyes. A glimmer of humor appears, a nickel in the silver dollar of his irises. "We can present something about the puzzle of poetry. Give some historic examples. Then make everyone in class write down a sentence or two saying what my poem means to them."

"Then they pass them up, we read them aloud, and you tell them what it's actually about."

"Or we let them keep their idea alive." His pointer finger flicks at the bent corner of his paper.

There's something he's hiding in that poem. Something he doesn't want to say aloud. "I can do mine instead."

"No, it's just…" His eyes focus somewhere outside the window, and a sigh slips out. "It destroys the appreciation of the art when you tell someone they felt it wrong."

He has Baudelaire's soul and his flair for the dramatic. "So we let them relate to it as only they can."

He gives me a tilted-head nod.

"Great. Let's knock this out quick."

"Maybe this weekend?" He doesn't sound confident.

"I've got out-of-town plans with my best friend." I tap my pen on my lips. "I can come over tonight."

"That won't work." His voice flattens.

"Okay, how about the library after school?"

He looks at his phone. "I can be there at four."

CHAPTER EIGHT

A T 4:05, I CHECK my watch again. Tav's a little late. At 4:10, I go inside the library and walk the main floor one more time. At 4:15, I stomp down the library's cement steps. The parking lot is half-full of cars, but Tav's nowhere to be found.

He didn't show up. Didn't text. Didn't email. Didn't even pick up when I called him. It's not the first time someone has stood me up. I've had a few millennia of practice with my father. But I do not have to put up with this bullshit from a stupid human like Tav.

Sweat bursts from my scalp and trickles down my neck and my forehead. I wipe it on my sleeve. Some part of me knows I'm melting down over something ridiculous, but I can't stop it. The emotions are too strong to be denied.

Inside my car, I crank up the music, trying to drown out my thoughts. It's several Persephone breaths before I Google Tav's address so I can GPS my way to his house. By the time I get there, I've settled into simmering indignation. When I get out of the car, I'm at an adorable brown-and-cream-colored, gingerbread-style cottage. There should be lollipop flowers and gumdrop shrubs in front of it. I can't believe this is where the angsty boy from my English class lives. I follow the multicolored paving stones to the front porch.

I clamber onto the front porch and ring the doorbell a few times. I use my hand to shield the stained-glass window in the middle of the front door, but all I see is an empty hallway. There's no response, but I knock until my knuckles ache. I'm about to give up when the door finally opens.

Tav's face is a mixture of confusion and annoyance. "Kali? What are you doing here?" He glances back in the house, steps onto the porch, and pulls the door shut behind him.

No human has made me feel less important. It reverberates through my core. Reminding me of how little I matter to my parents. "We were supposed to meet at the library at four."

He shuts his eyes and sinks back against the door. "Shit, was that today?"

"We made the plan two hours ago." My vocal cords tighten like guitar strings on the verge of snapping.

He crosses his arms and drops his chin, letting his hair fall over his eyes. "Something came up."

"Oh, well, if you were busy." I throw my hands up. "I mean it's not like I have anything to do with my time."

"Clearly not. You wasted more time coming here than you did waiting for me."

It's almost five. He has a point, but I'm in no mood for logic right now. "I can't deal with slackers."

His spine straightens, and he takes a step toward me. "I always get my work done." His voice is frayed like the work has worn him down. "Don't you have anything else in your life besides this stupid poetry project?"

"You have no idea what I have in my life." The blood races in my veins, making the words sprint off my tongue. "You can text a person when stuff comes up."

His face looks like a pincushion that suddenly developed a sense of touch.

"What's going on?"

"My mom's sick." The way he says it—that's a serious sick. A sick that he is trying to save her from.

"Why didn't you say something?"

He looks down at his sneakers. His hair hides his face again. "You needed to rant."

I touch his arm. His muscles jump beneath my fingertips, pulsing with problems I don't know. "What's wrong with her?"

"Cancer." His voice is an enraged whisper.

The proper human response is the uncomfortable *I'm sorry.* Then a subject change. But I get death better than any human could. "That sucks."

"Yeah." His shoulders sag with certainty.

"What kind?"

"Breast."

"Stage?"

"Three."

The deadness in his eyes makes perfect sense now. So does his poem. He's losing his mother. It tugs at the strings that tie my heart to my parents. I have that same awful fear of losing my parents, and I will do anything, anything, anything to save them.

I've died of cancer before. Brain was the worst. But after almost two hundred deaths, I've learned something. "Life's the hard part. Death's simple. She's not dead yet."

He stares at me like I'm the anti-Christ.

Maybe I am to him. "You want to get her off the couch?"

"Yeah." I see in his eyes how much he wants it.

"I can do that." I can give him what I want most in the world. With some help from Grams.

He squints at me like he's doing pre-calc in his head. "How?"

"Have me over to work on the project tomorrow after school." I turn and head back to my car.

"Wait, what?" The confusion in his voice doesn't slow me down.

"You'll see tomorrow."

Grams waits for me in her domain—the kitchen—located in the basement of our house. White cabinets bring brightness into the room. Stainless steel appliances reflect light. Gray-veined marble counters provide the perfect workspace. A cork floor minimizes breakage. The round oak table in the corner serves as a snacking spot for us.

She stands at the island, grinding herbs to dust with her mortar and pestle. "Did you get everything on my list?"

"I think so." I set the bag of ingredients on the counter and unpack the lemons, granulated and powdered sugars, flour, butter, and eggs. The basics for lemon bars.

Her voice is soothing and insistent as she whispers words I've never known over the herbs in her mortar. The wanshiqi language is ancient. There are more words than have ever existed in any human language. Probably because our earliest speakers are still alive, which means no part of our language withers and dies.

"I've charged the herbs." A sheen clings to her forehead like she's exerted herself too much.

"Are you okay?"

She pats her forehead with a cloth. "Cancer's the hardest to ease."

Her powers don't devour her human body like mine do, but they are much more limited by it. If she were in a different form and could use her full wanshiqi power, she could heal Tav's mom and a hundred other cancer sufferers at the same time. Well, as long as they hadn't started their death spiral. Once someone is in their prelude to death, even Grams can't rescue them from Death's clutches—his grip is unbreakable. Sounds pretty clingy to me, but I wouldn't say that aloud. It's never a good idea to speak about Death, especially in jest.

"What can I do to help?" I put my apron on and sit down across from her.

"Prepare the lemon juice and zest."

I slice six lemons and squeeze them by hand. The scent of lemons fills my nose, releasing the memory of our home in Rome. Rows of lemon trees lined our backyard. I'd climb the wooden ladder and stretch my arm as far as I could into the branches to help Grams harvest them. In each tree, a few fruits lie beyond my reach.

My mother always smells of those lemons to me. Clean. Tart. Summery. Unreachable.

"It's been a while since you asked for my help." Grams's smile warms her eyes and radiates love to me. "It's always available."

"Thanks." I wring the last drop of juice from the lemon. Then I get the grater and shred the lemon skin into another bowl. "I hate having to work with this kid."

"Of course you do." She gives me her I-know-better smile.

"I'm only doing this to get him to focus."

"Kali, it's okay to be kind to humans."

"Me? Kind?" It's not something my family often accuses me of. Kindness is a weakness I can't afford.

"You aren't as bad as you like to think." She hand-kneads the dough, lacing it with healing energy. "Just because falu doesn't apply to humans, doesn't mean you shouldn't have your own code about how you treat them."

"We're supposed to practice our powers on lower life forms." Falu, the rules of our realm, dictates the treatment of wanshiqi. It doesn't concern itself with the treatment of lesser beings. "Humans don't have rules about worms."

"But they can show mercy to them." She gives me a few moments to consider it before she adds, "Falu prevents chaos in our society. You and you alone must decide what prevents chaos inside you."

"I did. Humans are fair game. As long as I issue a warning." That's more than any other wanshiqi would grant them.

"Darling, issuing a warning is fair with wanshiqi because we know what we are capable of. A human has no understanding of what that warning means." Her gaze holds me, forcing me to feel the weight of her words. "Haven't Gramps and I taught you better?"

"Probably, but you know, selective hearing and all."

"Kali…" She flicks dough at me.

I laugh. "I guess I'm a slow learner."

"It's a good thing I have all the time in the world."

Ringing Tav's door at 5:02 p.m. the next day isn't an easy task with two Tupperware boxes in my arms. I peek through the stained-glass window and see him making his way toward me.

Tav opens the door a few inches. "Didn't you get my text? She's not having a good day." His voice drops to a jagged whisper that should slice across my heart and send me home.

"That's why I'm here." I thrust my hip against the door.

He stumbles back a couple steps. "You can't be this pushy."

I step into his house. "Oh, I can. Where's your mom?"

"Watching TV." He grabs his jacket. "We'll go to the library." He tries to herd me back onto the porch, but I sidestep him and head down the hall toward the TV noises. His way hasn't worked, but mine just might.

A shrunken soul lies on the couch, shrouded in blankets. The blinds bar the day from penetrating her world. Purple bruises rim her tarnished-silver eyes. Her cheeks are thin and blanched, like the pages of a long-abandoned novel. A black ski cap traps the top of her head.

I still remember how cold my head was without hair. I stop in front of the couch. "Hi, I'm Kali."

She doesn't glance away from the TV. "The death goddess?" Her voice is barely audible.

"Not today." Dad's and Mom's perverse humor have led to a series of death-related names across my lifetimes.

"Sorry, Mom." Tav gestures toward the front door. "Library's this way."

The coffee table is cluttered with magazines and papers and tissues. I put my Tupperware on top of it all and extend my hand. "It's nice to meet you, Ms. Ponte."

She doesn't respond.

"You've got an old-school Italian name that means bridge, but I guess you don't like to meet people halfway. Maybe it should be Ms. Abisso." For the abyss around her.

Her expression curdles. Finally, a real reaction.

I sit in the chair beside her and pop the lid off a container of lemon bars. The sugared tartness wafts out. "You know everyone can eat lemon, if it's prepared properly." I take one out and munch on it.

She stares at the TV, lost in the grief of a life unlived.

Tav's forehead wrinkles like linen pants during a South Carolina summer. He edges toward me.

"In ancient Roman times, you would be flogged ten times for refusing to take a guest's hand and another six for not accepting their offering of food." I suffered for those transgressions back in Pompeii.

Tav sucks air through his teeth. It sounds like a dying flute. His fingers wrap around my arm. He tries to tug me out of the chair, but I won't budge. Not until I get through to her.

Ms. Ponte sinks deeper into the couch cushions. "Physical punishment means very little when you're dying." She says it like she will be dead in the next few moments.

"You're not going to die today. And probably not tomorrow either."

Anger flashes in her eyes. A true sign of life there.

Tav yanks me up. "You need to leave her alone."

"Because that's working so well."

Horror freezes his features. Something flickers across his face. Doubt? Frustration? I can't tell. But I hope that somewhere inside he has an inkling that I'm right.

"She eats one bar, and I'll leave," I say.

His eyes plead with me to back down, but I can't. This is simply how a battle is waged and won.

He grabs a lemon bar and bites into it. "Mom, these are pretty amazing. Please, have a bite."

"I'm not hungry," she says.

"Just one bite, please."

She puts her hand out. "All right, Octavius."

My heart trips at the use of his full name. I'll never forget the black-eyed wanshiqi who nearly destroyed me. I taste something metallic in the back of my throat. It reminds me of the blades he used to torture me. But that was Pompeii. Not here. Not now. The guy in front of me tilts his head and gives me a questioning look. He's just Tav. *Tav.* A human. A boy who loves his mother. My heart stutters to a normal beat again.

His mom takes a bite and swallows a crumb of healing. If she can heal, she will. If she can't, the rest of her time here will be more comfortable.

"Now go." His face shuts and locks like a titanium door.

I nudge the box of lemon bars toward her, making sure they are within her grasp, and leave.

CHAPTER NINE

T EN MINUTES CAN DERAIL a day. Take the ten minutes before the first bell rings at school. If Mandy finds me in the hallway or by my locker, she'll drag me into the bathroom with all the other girls to fix our hair and talk about boys. I can't listen to their chatter this morning, so I veer off the main hallway and take two quick rights into the nook that houses the soda vending machine. Eight more feet to the broom closet that I've cursed to only open for me.

"What were you thinking yesterday? Why'd you have to push my mom?" Tav's voice stops me before I reach my sanctuary.

I spin around. His eyes blaze with self-righteous indignation. A defense leaps from my lips. "She ate the lemon bars."

He comes close enough for an Eskimo kiss. "Who cares? She's got cancer, Kali. Lemon bars aren't going to make a damn bit of difference."

I can't explain why the lemon bars matter so much. I lick my lips waiting for the words to form, the ones that can make sense of this for him, but they abandon me.

He rests his palms on the soda machine. His body igloos around me. His eyes are storm clouds—dark and threatening. Emotions tumble across his face. "You can't barge into our home and upset my mother."

"You want me to leave you two alone?" My voice rises, matching his frustration.

"Yes."

"Done." I try to walk away, but he pens me in.

"We're not done until you apologize to my mom." His voice thickens around *mom*, trying to protect her.

"You want me to apologize for helping her? She was wasting away on that couch."

"And you think you made it better?" He laughs, but there's no humor in his voice. His body hums with anger. Full of life again.

I made him so mad he stopped moping for a moment. "It's better for her to be upset than despondent. There is power in anger, fuel to keep you going in the worst moments."

Rage constricts his pupils. His jaw muscle pulsates. He slams his palm into the soda machine a good foot away from my head. The sound echoes around us and bounces into the hallway, slicing through the din of students. There are a few seconds of silence, and then the Clydesdale clomping of Headmaster Holland's sensible heels warns of her impending arrival.

His eyes lock on mine. I see it now. He's afraid. Afraid of what will happen next.

His mom can't come into school to bail him out of trouble right now. He knows it. I know it, too.

I do the only thing I can think to do. I twist around, elbow him in the stomach, and punch the soda machine. My knuckles throb. The front of the machine makes a weird sinking noise and the plastic cracks.

Headmaster Holland rounds the corner. Her wavy hair fans out like a vengeance-seeking angel, the kind Michelangelo wasn't allowed to capture with paint. "Octavius, what happened?"

A shiver zigzags up my spine. He's Tav. Just Tav.

He hugs his stomach. "I'll be fine."

She notices the front of the soda machine and fury twists her features. "Brewster, my office, now."

This might be the 625th time I've been in Headmaster Holland's office, listening to my mother lawyer me out of trouble. It's easier than dealing with a suspension. The headmaster sits behind her dark wood desk with my student folder open. It's about two inches thick before she adds the pages for today's transgression.

Mom reaches an agreement with the headmaster in under seven minutes. It will cost Dad two new soda machines for the school and a small donation to the athletic department, but my record will be wiped clean again.

I don't know why my parents care. It's not like I'll ever go to college. Even if I survive my seventeenth birthday, I'd be going back to the wanshiqi realm.

Once the settlement is reached, Mom asks, "May I speak to my daughter privately?"

I slouch in my chair, dreading what's to come.

"Use my office, I have to step out for a bit." After the deal she just secured, Headmaster Holland is acting all benevolent dictator.

The door clicks shut, and the headmaster's footsteps fade away.

"You're acting out because you can't use your powers, aren't you?" Mom asks.

Sounds good, but I can't jump on it. Then she'll know something is up and dig deeper. "Maybe."

She riffles through her black quilted leather bag. "I don't care how many donations it costs your father. You keep acting human. Don't use your powers until after your seventeenth birthday." She pulls out her compact mirror and lines up her Chanel makeup on the headmaster's desk.

"Seriously, Mom?" I point at her cosmetics.

"I'm meeting your father. Fixing another one of your messes ate into my time for freshening up." Her skin is a deeper olive than mine. She blows on her brush, sweeps it over the apples of her cheeks, dusts the tip of her nose, and traces a heart around her face. The only trace of a heart she still has.

"What's going on with Dad?"

"It's none of your concern." She slides a blood-red nail along her bottom lip, annihilating any color that dared step outside the line.

"I should get back to class." I stand up and brush my hands over my skirt.

"Sit down. I need seven minutes for my eyes." She uses the tone that she reserves for absolute orders. If I don't do it, much, much worse punishment awaits me.

I drop back into my seat. She reapplies her mascara and touches up her purple eye shadow and fills in her eyeliner.

Most girls would love this makeup time with Mommy. I did once. I cling to those memories. Before Pompeii, she would pinch my cheeks to get some color and use petals to redden my lips like hers. The woman sitting beside me is a ghost of who she once was. And she haunts me every day.

A reminder of everything I lost in Pompeii.

"You're grounded this weekend," she tells her reflection in the mirror.

My spine straightens, and my feet press into the floor. "Mandy and I are visiting her aunt in San Francisco." We've been planning it for months. It's my way of saying goodbye, leaving her with one last awesome weekend of us.

"Was that this weekend?" She alters her inflection, acting all innocent.

She knew it was this weekend. It's the only reason she'd waste her time punishing me.

"You should have thought of that before you went vandalizing school property." She puts everything back in her purse, stands up, and realigns the pleats of her skirt. "I'll see you at home."

My frustration festers on the drive home. I stop at every traffic light, yield to each pedestrian, and trace everything back to where my day derailed at the soda machine. This is all Tav's fault.

I stomp through the vestibule and find Grams in the main room. Sunlight streams through the skylight above us. "I will mother a garbage truck before we make that boy lemon bars again." My voice slams into the round walls, almost echoing back at me.

"That sounds painful and anatomically impossible, dear." Grams sits on her spring-green, velvet burnout couch. Its fringe of gold tassels pets the bearskin rug.

"We are never helping anyone again." I toss my backpack on the floor.

She glances up from her Debbie Macomber novel. "Bad day at school?"

"Tav yelled at me. Then Mom went freaking parental."

"Parental?" Grams sounds confused by the term.

"She grounded me this weekend." I throw myself into the armchair across from her.

"She hasn't disciplined you in ages." She dog-ears her page and puts the book on the mahogany coffee table between us. Right beside a plate of her freshly baked chocolate chip cookies. "Wasn't this the weekend you were going to San Francisco with Mandy?"

I cross my arms and sink into the cushions. "Why else would she punish me?"

"Is Mandy upset?"

"She had everything planned." I blow out a breath. "Now she's taking a cheerbaby with her."

"And you're mad." She sips her tea.

"Shouldn't I be?"

"Can't you just pick another weekend?"

"There aren't that many left before my birthday." Even fewer before my death date, but I can't tell Grams that. "It's hard to explain. All these teenage hormones with the mind of a demigod."

"You aren't a demigod. We exterminated them during the Great War."

"You know what I mean." Two seconds later the rest of her sentence catches up with me. "Wait. Demigods existed? And who exterminated them?"

She offers me a cookie. "You never spent enough time on wanshiqi history lessons."

I wave the plate away. "My last class was a couple millennia ago. Remind me."

"Long before you were born, we went to war with the demons. The demigods made the mistake of aligning with them."

"So they're all gone."

"That's what the history books say." Grams's eye twitches the way it does when she's not being truthful.

"But?"

She gives me her mysterious Mona Lisa smile.

I lean forward. "You have to tell me."

"It's not my story to tell. Ask Gramps."

Gramps will usually tell me a truth if I tell him one. It's one of the reasons I refrain from asking him too much.

She clucks her tongue at me. "Now, tell me about what happened at school today."

I loop around the circular room as I catch her up on what happened at the soda machine and in the headmaster's office.

"You covered for Tav?"

There's something unsaid in her voice, and it irks me so much, I rush to explain. "He thought I made things worse with your lemon bars."

"It takes a few days to see the results."

"I don't care." Anger nestles in my throat, branding my words. "He's cost me more than any human should. It was stupid to interfere in human bullshit."

"You're more like the goddess Kali than you realize." Her voice is steeped in chamomile tea and honey.

I stop pacing. "Did you know her?"

"Quite well." Grams's eyes take on that hazy quality that happens when she remembers things from several millennia ago.

"What about the gods? Did they take sides in the Great War?"

"They knew better. We'd proven a good ally in the past."

"What about Kali? Is she still alive?"

Grams gives me her I-cannot-speak-of-this-yet face.

"Is this a qifa thing?" Meaning no one will tell me the details until after qifa. No matter how often I ask, some knowledge remains forbidden. In every reincarnation, I've tried bribery, trickery, even blackmail, but no one will tell me what I am not allowed to know.

"Afraid so, dear." She lifts the plate of cookies as a consolation prize.

Another whiff of buttery chocolate. My stomach gurgles. I snatch one and take a bite. Still, I'm curious about my namesake. "So Kali the goddess?"

"Her fierceness is what most mortals passed on in their stories. She ruled death and time. She understood both, but remained immune to them."

"How's that like me?"

"You've seen what happens when humans die. You know how much time matters and how it can be squandered. Because you've lived through so much, you can be compassionate."

"Compassionate?" The word tastes terrible on my tongue.

"You don't want to feel it. But you do." Her tone is gentle, understanding, kind.

"That's not true," I sputter. "I just wanted to get this stupid project done."

"That's compassion masquerading as selfishness."

I can't accept her explanation. I won't feel compassion. I promised myself that Vesuvius would bury any feelings that could be used against me.

Just thinking about it makes my mouth feel like it's stuffed with clouds that are soaking up all the moisture in there. "I need some milk." I flee downstairs.

Thank you McKim, Mead, and White. For once, I'm grateful those architects put the kitchen a safe distance from the living room. I pour a glass of milk and down half of it. Grams trails in after me.

She sets the plate of cookies on the round oak table in the corner. "Sit." There's no escaping that tone.

I ease into the chair beside her.

"I'll let you in on a little secret." She hands me a cookie. "Wanshiqi doesn't mean inhuman. It means our soul energy, our qi, lasts over 10,000 lifetimes. In our language, the wanwu literally means the 10,000 things on Earth, but it symbolically encompasses everything on Earth. So when we speak of our soul's 10,000 lives—wanshiqi—we mean eternity. We are eternal, but not unfeeling. We get many chances at life, but we don't have to waste them."

"Then why are we so destructive? Mom and Dad wage wars."

"They fan the flames of war. They do not create the spark. It already exists in humans. Your parents simply enhance it." It amazes me how calmly she explains away 25,000 years of their destructive behavior.

"What about Afghanistan? The war the US can't seem to get out of."

Her disapproval winds its way through each syllable. "That was a huge miscalculation by your father."

"I curse people." My voice wobbles. I know what I've done. It can never be undone. Pompeii branded me for eternity. "I am a destroyer."

"You're more than that. Better than that."

My voice hushes around my worst fear. "Maybe the fayuan were right. Maybe I am selfish and immature."

"If that were true, I wouldn't have come here with you."

My chest constricts and I whisper-wheeze, "I don't want to care." It's too hard. It hurts too much. Past pains well up. Ancient emotional scars rip open. I bite my lip and swallow a gasp.

I promised myself I wouldn't care after Pompeii. I wouldn't let anyone reach me again. I wouldn't feel the light emotions—compassion, empathy and love. I've fought so hard across my lifetimes to make that a reality, but love is such an essential part of being human.

It finds a way into my treacherous heart.

CHAPTER TEN

G RAMS HUSTLES ME INTO the back seat of Gramps's SUV without explaining where we're going or why we have to leave at 9 p.m. on Friday night. She doesn't have to. She knows I'll do as she says when she has that look in her eyes. As if what we're doing is vital to the family.

Gramps slides into the driver's seat and gives me a quick nod. The car winds down the hillside in darkness. We hit the main road and the streetlights flash by. Shadows log-roll across the back seat. Eventually, we merge onto Interstate 15. Outside my window, the silhouettes of trees fly by. The stars won't congregate in the sky until we're farther from civilization.

An hour passes in suffocating silence. I can't take another minute of it. "Where exactly are we going?"

Gramps keeps his eyes on the road and doesn't say anything. This is definitely Grams's plan.

"If I knew where we're going, I could enjoy you overruling Mom's grounding more." I keep my voice light, hoping to defuse the tension in the car.

"Somewhere you need to be." The glow of the dashboard lights throws off enough light to see Grams's expression is more serious than an aneurysm.

"At least tell me how long we will be gone." I can't help sounding petulant.

"We'll have you home by Sunday," is all she says.

It's the things she doesn't say that frighten me.

After a night of endless dozing, only to be jarred awake by a seat belt receptacle jabbing my ribs or burrowing into my spine, I give up on sleep. Human bodies were never intended to spend a night cramped up in the back seat of an SUV. At 6 a.m., I'm seriously questioning my *Obey Grams* policy. It's cold, I'm tired, and nothing is worth getting up this early for.

"Morning." Grams's cheery voice bounds over the driver's seat, like an excited puppy licking my face.

My mouth tastes retched. I reach for a Coke to wash it away. "When did you take over driving?" Grumpy gruffness comes through in my tone.

"About four hours ago."

Outside my window, the trees no longer blur past. We've slowed down, trading the freeway for a two-lane highway. "Where are we going?"

Her gaze meets mine in the rearview mirror. "Home."

"We're nowhere near Del Mar."

"Your second greatest feat." Gramps's voice sounds coarsely ground without his morning coffee.

Dread swallows the rest of my sentence. The only word to escape my mouth is "Bodie."

The entire town is maintained in a state of suspended decay. It's like keeping the bones above the grave. Tourists flock there, wandering through the ghost town that still haunts me.

All too soon, Grams pulls onto a road bleached gray by the sun's relentlessness.

"Why?" is all I can ask.

"Some past lessons remain to be learned," Grams says.

I cross my arms, shielding myself with my stubbornness. "I wasn't wrong."

"You see why this trip makes sense?" Grams asks Gramps.

"Wise move, my dear." He smiles at her like she's still amazing him after 100,000 years.

"They killed my father." The memory scorches the back of my brain, leaving a permanent imprint of misery.

Grams grips the wheel and hunches forward. I'd like to believe the road is frustrating her, but I'm pretty sure it's me.

"Our body is just a temporary vessel containing our eternal essence," Gramps reminds me like he's lecturing a student at university.

"If your house burns down, you buy a new one." Grams steers the car onto the rutted dirt road a little faster than she should.

Dust kicks up around the car, forcing us to roll the windows up.

Vibrations rattle my teeth and bobble my head. "I was only nine when I watched Dad bleed out on Main Street."

"A business deal gone bad." Gramps shakes his head, but nothing can nullify what happened.

"I promised Bodie would suffer as much as he did." My voice is low, crawling away from the pain.

"This is a lingering death." Grams's voice catches in her throat, like she's still ensnared by the memories of what the town had been.

"It was a civilized decline. Most moved on to a more prosperous place. I could have conjured an earthquake that leveled the place and everyone in it."

"Have you learned nothing?" Grams's disappointment floods my ears and flames against my cheeks, chiding me into silence. "You need to see what you did to our home."

"It isn't my home." My voice is sharp enough to sever a limb.

Grams sighs and sinks into the driver's seat like I'm wearing away at her spine and her patience. "I remember the day you begged your father to paint your ceiling red. You said that made it your room."

My lips tremble. I won't break. I won't. "I've had hundreds of rooms over the years. It's just a stupid room."

The car lurches to a stop in the dirt parking lot. Grams cuts the engine. "Let's go."

Gramps gets out of the car, reaches for the sky, arches his back, and grunts.

I step out of the car. Despite the sun above, a too-cold-for-May wind ruffles my hair. I zip up my hoodie and slide my hands into my pockets. Grams wraps her sweater coat around her and marches toward the center of town.

I linger beside Gramps in the parking lot, looking at Bodie below us. The harsh landscape has worn down everything that remained. Blistered wood. Rusted machine parts. Buildings slip into oblivion. Weeds and grass creep over nameless yards.

I trudge after Grams. Gramps puts his arm around me and makes me pick up the pace. "Trust your grandmother. She always does her best for you."

I nod, not trusting myself to speak. I know Grams wants me to feel bad, but regret is the road to weakness. I refuse to take it. After the initial horror, there's something to be proud of in all my destruction. My lips betray me, curling upward.

"It's nothing to smile about." Gramps sounds serious for Grams's benefit, but he squeezes my shoulder like he's secretly proud of me.

As I walk, the silence startles me. No rumbling from the stamp mills crushing rocks to harvest gold. No trembling ground underfoot. No clattering wagons kicking dust up along the road. No groups of townsfolk chattering. Not even a braying mule.

"Where are the park rangers?" I ask.

"They've been taken out by one of my stomach bugs." Gramps can kill several people at once, but he always uses the minimum force necessary to achieve his ends. Death doesn't mind someone helping people fall in to his grasp, but he fights dirty if you try to take any of them away.

We pass what's left of the McDowell house. I slip away from Gramps, walk up to a window, and peer through the grime. Strips of wallpaper are shredded from the wall and smeared with dirt. It's impossible to make out the once-ornate floral pattern. Tables are askew with empty glass bottles resting on top of them. The overturned chair will never be righted. Pieces of broken furniture litter the floor. The rusted headboard leans precariously against the wall, its mattress long gone. The bathroom door clings to its hinges, permanently ajar. Dust coats everything that remains, trying to shield it from prying eyes.

"Kali, let's go." Her insistence tugs me along.

I know where she wants me to go: Dad's death spot. With each step, my gut tightens. My large intestines strangle the small. I hated seeing my father die. I've only endured it a few times, but each time, it's excruciating to lose him. It doesn't matter if it was a few lifetimes ago. Just thinking about it shreds my heart.

Gramps leads me down Green Street toward the Wheaton and Hollis Hotel.

I suck air through my mouth. It whistles over my teeth.

"You can do this." Gramps brings me toward Grams.

I hide my face in Gramps's chest, and we keep walking. When he slows, I know we're there.

Why didn't I level this entire place? "Please, Gramps."

He squeezes my arm once more and steps away from me.

"You have to face this, Kali." Grams's conviction can't staunch the wound in my heart.

I open my eyes and stand alone there.

I'm not sixteen anymore. I'm nine years old, and it's 1881 again. The town thrives, even at 1 a.m. Mama would spank me for being out this late, but I had to follow Daddy. I crouch behind a barrel while he enters the Miners Union Hall.

Twenty minutes drags on and feels like twenty days. Finally, Daddy emerges in his dark suit. Several miners follow him out. Their voices tumble across the street.

Daddy swears he's just doing his job, but one miner refuses to see it that way. Farley won't allow Daddy to shut down his section of the mine and cut his hours. He challenges Daddy to a fight. Daddy shakes his head and walks away. The other miners make their way back inside.

All of them except for Farley.

He follows Daddy up Main Street toward the Wheaton and Hollis Hotel. Daddy's on his way home to us. Farley draws his pistol and aims it at Daddy's back.

I scream, "Watch out!"

Two shots rip through the night air. Daddy rears back. Then he slams into the ground.

Farley runs.

I scramble to my father. Roll him over. I can't stop staring at the blood oozing from his chest. Turning his white dress shirt red.

"Daddy." My throat tightens. Dozens of emotions choke me. His death is coming.

I have to do something. My mind races. Grams. She could heal him, but she'll never reach us in time.

"Daddy, I'm going to fix this." The words rush out in a single breath. Fear grips my heart. It won't help me fuel a curse. I struggle to escape its icy grasp. As soon as I do, I reach inside me for a dark emotion. Anger.

But the dark emotions only bring destruction; they cannot save Daddy.

Time is slipping away. That's what I need. A curse to stop time. It's an indirect curse, so I won't need his consent to cast it, but it's a good curse, so it requires the light emotions I've spent ages avoiding. All my love that I've locked away.

He wheezes, "No curses." His pale-blue eyes stare up at me.

It's the only way to keep him here with me. This is the first lifetime since Pompeii that he felt like my father. We are so close to being a real family again. If he dies and reincarnates, it could be millennia before we're this close again. I won't lose him. I can't.

His lips move, but he's so weak, I can't make out his words. I have to lean close to hear him whisper, "You'll die."

"I'll come back." Maybe even be reborn to this version of Mom and Dad. I'll finally fix what was broken inside them.

"You...live." The light is fading in his eyes.

I can't let him slip away. "Daddy, please."

"No." Blood and saliva bubble from his mouth.

I have to find a way to summon all my love for him. I pull up all the memories of us through the centuries. A warmth emanates from my qi. It's delicate and soothing and whispers through me. I start my incantation.

His breath escapes in a weird whoosh. He doesn't take another. I shake him. Pound on his chest. Beg him to stay. But his eyes stare unflinchingly at the night sky.

Time folds in on itself.

Someone comes for us. People pull me away from him. This town takes my father from me.

Mama shoves her way through. The accusation in her eyes flash floods her voice. "What did you do?"

"I couldn't save him." My voice shatters, sending shards of pain everywhere.

Grams wraps her arms around me and rocks me.

I hold on to her. "Bring him back. Bring him back. Bring him back." I chant it until tears choke off my words.

"She can't." Gramps picks me up in his arms. "He's gone, darling."

Grams cannot heal the dead, and Daddy is dead.

There's a rush in my ears like a tornado tearing through me. It's all I hear. I clamp my hands over my ears, but that horrible sound remains inside my head.

Time fragments.

I don't remember how I got home.

Gramps puts me in bed. Grams fusses over me. They confer. Shock. That's what they say. I close my eyes and let them think I've fallen asleep. Hours pass before everyone else goes to bed. Everyone except me.

I may never get back the father I had in this lifetime. Darkness converges on my qi. Shadows swirl inside me, entreating me with their promise: *We can take vengeance.*

Death curses require a fraction of my hate. And I have so much hate inside me. All I am is hate. I whisper my curse. Over and over and over like a vicious prayer. I see it unfolding in my mind.

Farley already snuck out of town with his wife and three kids. He thought he could escape punishment. He has no idea what punishment feels like. But I will teach him.

I make him stop and put a bullet in each of their backs. He watches the life drain out of each of their eyes, unable to help and knowing it is his fault. A sinkhole opens and swallows their bodies. Sucks him in alive. No sign that they ever existed.

It's not enough. The hate cries out for more.

I try to get out of bed, and my knees buckle. My body isn't strong enough for another curse, but my qi is. Hatred fills my lungs to capacity. The loss of my father burns inside me. I let it build and build and build. I don't try to control my emotions; I let them consume me. I give in to my darkest self, reveling in what I can do. Blackness rises from the depths of my qi. I have enough power to fuel one final curse.

Not one of the other miners stepped in to help my father. Bodie must feel as abandoned as my father was.

There are so many reasons people say Bodie failed, but I know the real reason was me.

Standing beside the unblemished dirt, it's hard to imagine some-one dying here. Unless the memory plagues you to this day.

"Why did you do it? You knew he wanted you to live." Grams's eyes are pools of understanding pebbled with uncertainty.

"He's my father." All my love and hurt wrap around each word. I brush the tears from my cheeks. She can't understand. No one does. It's the secret reason I keep dying over and over and over again. To regain the father I had before Pompeii.

"He knew a life-saving curse would be your death." Gramps hands me a tissue.

I wipe my face and blow my nose. "It was my choice." I would do anything to save my parents.

"He had to keep you alive. That's what parents do for their children." Gramps squeezes my arm.

"And I had to avenge him."

Grams swings her arms to encompass the abandoned streets and decrepit buildings. "How does it feel? To know you de-stroyed this town?"

"I made sure all our friends moved on." No one else had to die besides my father's killer. And his family. "I was careful in my cursing."

"You died." Agony, sadness, frustration, and something I don't recognize flicker across her face. Then she points to the barren area, where a fire ravaged most of the town in 1932. "Did you do that, too?"

It's the area where our house used to be. Knowing it existed hurt too much. I needed it gone, the house that would never be our home.

In Bodie, Dad had been a part of my life. He played checkers with me. We talked at dinner every night. He read to me before bed. He was so close to loving me.

I even glimpsed moments of Mom. She liked me enough to let me shop with her. Through the streaked windows of the Boone Store and Warehouse, I can almost glimpse me and Mama inside, buying flour to make cakes. Our underskirts swish and the floorboards creak beneath our feet. I blink my eyes. Dust settles back over everything. Even my good memories of what once was.

If we'd had a few more years, I'd have fixed them. And us.

Farley shattered that possibility.

"I wanted it all gone." My voice sounds like a stranger's. Inside, I'm burning with sadness at the almosts of Bodie.

"You weren't even on the planet then." There's a note of awe in Gramps's tone.

"You'd be surprised what I can accomplish in dengzhong with Hunter's help."

"You left less than 15% of the town standing," Gramps says.

"More like 11%." I wrap my arms around myself, needing to hold on to something.

"All this destruction because your father died," Grams says.

"Murdered. He was murdered." The words tear a hole in my vocal cords.

"And you'd do it again?" Grams tilts her head, waiting for my response.

I raise my chin. "Yes."

"Then maybe you can understand why Tav acted out. His mom is dying, and he thinks you made it worse." Grams releases her words slowly, letting each one sink in.

"That's why you brought me here?" My voice clambers up the nearest building.

"Look what you did despite knowing your dad would reincarnate." She waves her hands around to encompass all that is left of a once-great town.

"I was nine."

"Strictly speaking, you were 3491 years old." Gramps pats my shoulder.

"Tav is what, sixteen years old?" Grams asks. "I'd say he handled things quite well."

"Better than me," I admit.

"And he deserves an apology from you." Grams sounds so wise, and I hate how clever she was in pushing me toward this realization. "So does his mom."

"You want me to apologize to humans?" My gaze goes from Grams to Gramps. There's titanium in both their eyes. I'm going to have to apologize to humans.

"Promise you'll apologize to them," Grams says.

Nuoyan, wanshiqi promises, are not to be broken, even when it requires apologizing to humans. "I promise," I mutter and turn away from them.

CHAPTER ELEVEN

O N MONDAY I GO back to school, avoiding Tav in public places to prevent a repeat of Friday when we combusted like an Iraqi oil field. I duck into the girls' room twice to prevent a hallway interaction, suffering through gossip and hair primping. I refuse to make eye contact with him in third-period English. I know I have to apologize, but that will be after school in private.

Dr. Herger derails my plan by saying, "I'll give you the last fifteen minutes of class to work on your presentations."

The presentation is due this week. I scoot my desk a couple inches toward Tav's.

He shoves his desk against mine and scrutinizes his blank notebook page. "My mom drank tea and ate your lemon bars for breakfast."

They should give her enough energy to get off that couch. "Where?"

"In the kitchen." He lifts his head and sweeps his hair off his forehead. His eyes are liquid mercury. Emotions shift in their depths—gratitude and regret, maybe remorse.

"Do...you need more?" My voice is tentative, trying not to disturb the detente we're settling into.

"Yeah." He gives me a half smile like his face isn't quite sure where we stand. "Thanks."

"Sure."

He taps his pen on the desk. "About last week—"

"I get it." The vehemence in my words makes him sit back in his seat.

Bodie was a fierce reminder of what a child will do to protect his or her parent. The apology I planned for later escapes my mouth in a nervous rush. "And I'm sorry."

"No. I'm glad you pushed your way into our house." His surety surprises me.

"Oh." My stomach has a weird flutter-spasm, like a lone moth is trying to escape from it.

"What happened with Headmaster Holland?" He leans toward me.

I draw swirlies in the margin of my notebook and act like it was no big deal. "My parents handled her."

"Because you covered for me." There's a little awe in his tone.

"You were just protecting your mom." I've done far worse to protect my parents. And I'd do it again. My gaze slips to his lips.

I've never noticed it before, but the bottom one is twice as thick as the top. "Besides, I got to elbow you in the belly."

"True." He rubs his stomach. "Guess that makes us even?"

"Almost, but not quite."

"Fair enough." He gives me a long, considering look. "We really need to get this project done tonight."

I drop my pen and my jaw. "Because I haven't been trying to work on it at all."

He snorts. "So tonight, come over for dinner, and we'll get it done."

"We can try."

"I've already stood you up and thrown you out. What else can I do?"

I can't help smiling at him. "I really don't know."

The hallway is jammed with students passing between classes. My locker door shields my right side from the human traffic. Hunter provides a natural barrier on my left side by leaning against the lockers.

"I got stuck with Sinusitis Stephanie for the English assignment." The words rumble in his throat. Even his grumbling is sexy.

She's allergic to everything and plagued by sinus infections. That's not so bad. Except she likes to talk about it all the time. That's just weird.

I pat his cheek. "Poor baby."

"I have to meet with her in study hall and at the library the next two days."

"Oh this high school drudgery." I press the back of my hand to my forehead and pretend to faint.

His expression only grows more annoyed.

"At least Herger gave you a couple extra days." I force an upbeat note into my words.

"How's Octavius?"

I plank at the name. It takes a few seconds to unsnap my muscles. I pretend to search for something in the back of my locker. "Tav's okay. Too bad you were out last week."

"Why don't we see if we can change partners?"

"Tav and I are almost done." The lie is off my tongue before I even know why I'm telling it.

"I heard you went to his house last week." There's a subtle accusation scratching at my skin.

"His mom was there, too. And I didn't stay long." I skip over the part where Tav threw me out.

My bracelet catches on my jacket, and I shove it farther into my locker. The way I want to shove Hunter away from me right now.

"And then you had an intense fight at the soda machine. Everyone was talking about it."

I can feel his gaze searching my face, so I try to keep it neutral and sound slightly bored by this conversation. "Just a disagreement over diet vs. regular."

Hunter leans closer. "What's going on with this human?" His breath warms my neck.

My heart thunders in my ears. "Nothing." I slam my locker. "It's just one English project."

Hunter's expression tells me he doesn't believe me. "Right." He walks away.

I balance three boxes of lemon bars by wedging them between Tav's front door and my belly. With my free hand, I ring the doorbell.

A few moments later, the locks *slip-slurp* out of place. I clutch the boxes and the door swings inward.

Ms. Ponte stands there in khaki linen pants and a storm-promising gray sweater hoodie. She's wearing a gray crocheted skullcap. Her face has a hint of color. "Sorry it took me so long, I was in the kitchen."

"No problem, Ms. Ponte. I'm hideously punctual."

"Call me Bess."

She's one of those adults. The ones who want to be on the same footing as their kids. Hoping it makes the kids more likely to call in a crisis. My parents always go by their last names with my friends.

"Okay." I shift the boxes, trying to stabilize the stack.

She steps back into the hallway and waves me inside. "Come in. Come in."

I peer over her shoulder, expecting to see Tav, but he's nowhere in sight.

"Octavius had to get groceries. He should be back in fifteen minutes."

I nod, ignoring her use of his full name. "You look good."

She leads me into the living room. No blankets strewn over the couch. No clutter spread over the coffee table. No blinds blocking the daylight. The room is inhabitable again.

She sits down on the couch. "I don't know what was in those lemon bars, but I feel better."

I put the boxes on the coffee table and join her on the couch. "I brought some more."

Her eyes bulge. "I can't eat all these."

"Freeze them. They'll last a few months."

"Thanks." She gives me a gentle smile.

I promised my grandparents I'd apologize to her, but I'm not sure how to begin. I twist my fingers together. My knee bounces up and down like the needle in a sewing machine.

I blurt out, "I'm sorry if I was too blunt when we first met." I weave the lie every teenager tells, inserting *close friend* for *me*. "I had a close friend go through cancer. All the coddling in the world didn't help her."

She pats my hand. "I've been mourning myself when I should have been living."

"We all have expiration dates. Cancer tricks you into believing you know yours."

"I thought it was any day now." Her voice is fragile.

"My friend tried to find something to mark each day as being lived. A gorgeous sunset, a great movie, a laugh with a loved one."

Her eyes are like cashmere. Soft, warm, safe. "That's Octavius."

A ball of cement fills my throat. I don't think my mother has ever felt that way about me. And she's had so many lifetimes to try.

We chat about school until the front door creaks open.

Tav shouts, "Ma, I'm back," and makes his way down the hallway, shuffling into sight with four grocery bags in his arms.

"Kali and I were just chatting." Bess smiles at Tav. It's the first smile I've seen reach her eyes. It transforms her face.

Tav blinks a few times as if he's adjusting to the brightness. "Are you feeling up to dinner tonight?"

"You cooking?" she asks.

"Grilled chicken and veggies." Tav shifts the bags, trying to maintain a grip on all of them.

"I'm in."

"Kali can help me cook," Tav says.

"She's our guest." His mom moves to help him.

I move faster, grabbing the bag that's slipping from Tav's grasp. "I don't mind. We can work on the project while we cook."

"There is some reading I've been meaning to get to." She taps her lip and stares at the stacks of unopened mail on her desk.

On our way to the kitchen, Tav lowers his voice. "I've got a treat for you."

"What?"

"It's a surprise." I can hear the smile in his voice.

Maybe it's soda. I'd laugh if it was.

I follow him into the kitchen and sit at the table while he dances the unload-the-groceries waltz. Then he opens the oven and extracts a plate of coconut chocolate bars. "A peace offering for last week."

I can't believe he did something nice for me. I mean, he's human, and that's how they show remorse. But still. "They're my favorite."

"So I've heard."

"From whom?" Not Hunter. Please not Hunter.

He looks sheepish. "I might have called to thank your grandmother for the lemon bars."

And he took the time to ask about my favorite treat. That's…wow. I'm not sure what to say, so I bite into a bar. Gooey condensed milk and melted chocolate heaven conspire with coconut.

He snags a quart of milk and two glasses for us before he sits down across from me.

I lick the melted chocolate from my fingertips. "Chocolate and coconut—the two best things in the world."

"Three actually. Condensed milk."

"Four, if you count butter." Which I do.

"Are you always this difficult?" He grins, and his eyes lighten, like hundreds of pounds of worry go poof.

"Worse, actually."

He laughs. Not a snort, but a head-thrown-back-and-eyes-closed laugh. I can't help laughing with him. Warmth trickles through me and pools in my stomach. Dear Goddess. Grams was right. I may actually like this human.

The twenty feet between my car and my front door are usually not traumatic. Except tonight when someone steps out of the shadows, blocking my path. I gasp. My blood quickens in my veins. In that split second, I can't tell if it's a human or a wanshiqi. My human instincts kick in, and I throw my cell phone at his head.

He dodges it, but stumbles over a tree root. "What the Hades?"

I recognize Hunter's voice immediately. "Why did you sneak up on me?"

"I was waiting for you to get home." He puts weight on his right ankle and winces.

"Did you get hurt?" I rush toward him.

"Nothing I can't handle." His voice is steady, but he's keeping most of his weight on his left leg.

"Can you walk on it?" Worry frays my voice.

He takes a tentative step, and his face contorts in pain before he can smooth his expression out. "It'll be fine."

"Let me fix it."

"Do you have that kind of energy left?"

I don't. Healing curses require far more energy than hurting curses. But I made him trip, so I have to fix this. I rub my lips together. "I will if you restore me afterward." Hunter has the ability to move energy in and out of things—including me. He can roll me back a minor curse or three.

He nods his consent.

No sign of any of my family nearby. A mending curse requires tapping into my light emotions. The ones I repress daily. It's not easy to reach them. I close my eyes and concentrate.

I need to conjure up all the things Hunter has done for me over the ages. He protected me when we were flowers, he tried to save me when we were crabs, he gave his life for mine when we were pelicans. He's spent centuries helping me prolong my punishment. He's always been there for me in every form. He loves me. And...I love him. It fills me with a gentle warmth. A lightness that I secretly treasure.

I whisper the wanshiqi words for mending, "Zhì yù."

He stretches his ankle out.

"Better?" Acid burns a hole through my stomach lining, like a lit cigarette on skin. Definitely an ulcer, possibly multiple ulcers.

He stares into my eyes. "There's so little brown left now. Do you feel sick?"

"Just an ulcer. I'll be okay."

He shoves his hands in his jean pockets. "Can we talk?"

"Sure." I glance around. "Where's your car?"

"I took my motorcycle. It's hidden beside the garage." He heads toward it and I follow him.

"Beach?"

"Beach." He hands me a helmet. "I'll fix your eyes and your stomach there."

It's only a six-minute ride to Torrey Pines Beach on the back of his bike. The roar of the motor makes it impossible to speak. I don't mind. I wrap my arms around his waist and nestle into his strength. I lose myself in his nearness, breathing in his scent—oceans and stars.

All too soon, he cuts the engine, and the *pssshhh* of the ocean fills my ears. He throws a blanket over his shoulder. The sand hushes his footsteps. I trail after him, breathing in the salt-tinged air. The moonlight silvers everything; the sand pales beneath it. The cliffs take on an otherworldliness they never have in daylight. I move closer to Hunter and slip my hand into his. He entwines his fingers with mine.

When we reach our spot, he lets me go and spreads out the blanket. Before we have a chance to sit, I slip into his arms and offer him my lips. It's easiest to absorb his energy when we have sex, but heavy make-out sessions help, too.

He pulls back before we go too far. "I need to talk."

I look into his sad, turquoise eyes and remember we only have a couple more weeks together. I snuggle into him. "It's too bad we can't meet up in dengzhong." Waiting to reincarnate together would be wonderful. It's hard being stuck alone for years on end.

He hesitates.

I pull back to see his expression, but it's shuttered. "What's up?"

He drops onto the blanket. "Come here." He offers his hand. It's a wanshiqi tradition. Taking it means I trust him.

I put my hand in his and lower myself beside him. "So?"

His chin brushes my shoulder. His dark curls tickle my cheek. "It's our 2304th anniversary."

"It can't be."

He pulls a box out of his pocket. "Thereabouts."

I do the calculations in my head. "It's still three days away."

"This is the only way I can surprise you."

And I was so snarky today, too. I bite my lip. "About this afternoon—"

"Teen hormones." His smile accepts all my faults. It's that simple to Hunter.

"Show me some teen hormones."

He leans in and kisses me breathless. My fingers twine in his curls. I want more.

He pulls back, takes my hand, and rests a tiny box on my palm. "Open it."

All I can think about is his lips. I sway toward them.

"Kali." He laughs as he says my name.

Right, the box. I flip the lid open. On a bed of blue velvet sits a gorgeous labradorite stone set in platinum. It's moss green until Hunter pulls his cell out. I rotate the box under the light and see tree trunks of azure and emerald hidden in its depths. Tiny flickers of amber near the edge.

"Put it on me." Labradorite was the first stone he became after qifa. He spent 129 years living inside that rock. It's a piece of him to keep with me.

He slides it on my left pointer finger and laces his fingers through mine.

I scoot closer to him. "I love it."

"It reminds me of your rainbow eyes." His voice goes husky.

"Is that why you chose to reincarnate as labradorite?"

"It made me miss you less."

He's so close we can share a breath. I close the distance and press my lips to his.

When he kisses me, I can't think. Lost in the possibility of where his mouth will linger next. What his lips will do to my flesh. I paw at his clothes. His skin radiates heat. My core supernovas. The need to be together as only tonggan can. Hunter consumes my mind and I feed from his energy. Our bodies barely survive the encounter.

Forty-five minutes after curfew, I clear the front door and enter the circular main room of my house. Too bad every room radiates off of the main one. The staircase is in an alcove behind the back wall. No way to check my path before I sneak up to my room.

The thick red-and-gold, floral-patterned carpet muffles my footsteps. I make it up the first set of stairs and find Gramps sitting on the stairs above the second-floor mezzanine. Black crumbs cling to his red robe and tartan slippers. Half a plate of Oreos and a third of a glass of milk sit beside him on the steps. "Missed curfew again?"

"Eating sweets again?" He's diabetic in this body. "Grams is gonna be mad." Every time she heals him, he goes right back to the sweets.

"Blackmail is a vile family trait." There's a hint of laughter in his voice. He brushes the crumbs off his robe.

"I was with Hunter."

He points to my hand. "I can see that."

I fondle the ring. "It's our 2304th anniversary."

"Grams and I stopped counting at 75,000."

"But she still wears the ruby ring you gave her."

"Sentimental old broad." His eyes are chocolate fountains, melting with love. Suddenly, his gaze sharpens. "Are your eyes browner?"

Hades, no. I knew my stomach felt too good. Hunter must have given me too much energy when he made the ulcers disappear. I look away. "Must be the lighting."

Gramps is so quiet I'm certain he's caught me. I forget to breathe.

He tenses, and the words drip from his lips. "That must be it."

Something in his tone tells me he doesn't quite believe me. But I let the air out and take another breath. "Can we not tell Mom about me sneaking in late?"

"Your secrets are safe with me." He lifts the plate of Oreos. "Or Grams?"

"Neither needs to know."

I glimpse a white robe above us right before Grams asks, "Know what?" She leans over the railing. "Joe, are you eating Oreos?"

"They're mine." I take the blame and hang my head. "Gramps caught me sneaking upstairs with a midnight snack."

He winks at me. "And young lady, you better start eating better."

I shuffle toward him. "I will."

Gramps hands me the milk and cookies. "Take them to your room."

Grams gives me a dubious look as I pass by her. "Are you covering for him?"

"I'm starving," is all I say.

"Kali." She lengthens the vowels in my name, trying to tug the truth out of me.

I pretend not to hear her and slip off to my room.

CHAPTER TWELVE

Aꜰᴛᴇʀ ᴍʏ ʟᴀꜱᴛ ᴄʟᴀꜱꜱ, I wait beside Mandy's locker. Three-day freeze outs are Mandy's thing. She's been avoiding me since my grounding messed up our San Fran weekend. But now we've reached the end of day four, so it's time for a Kali intervention.

Throngs of people clog the hallway, but I still spot Mandy leading her cheerbabies toward her locker. When she sees me waiting there, she stops like she's going to forgo getting her stuff.

She underestimates me sometimes. I stalk toward her. She swivels, but her cheerbabies are right behind her, blocking her exit.

"Mandy, can I get a second?" I ask.

"We're going to practice." She turns back and tries to go around me.

I block her path. "You don't mind if I borrow her for five minutes?" I stare down her cheerbabies.

A chorus of "It's cool" and "No problem" and "Take as much time as you need" circles around us.

"Thanks." I drag Mandy into the nearest classroom and shut the door, barricading it with my back. "How long are you going to dodge my calls?"

"I've been busy." She crosses her arms and purses her lips and refuses to look at me.

"I know you're upset about our trip, but you know how my mom can be."

"So it's all your mom's fault?" Her tone scales a wall of skepticism.

"I wish I could have gone to San Fran. Did you have fun?"

"I didn't go."

"Oh." I don't want to sound happy, but I am. That was supposed to be our trip. "Maybe we can go next weekend?"

"If something better doesn't come along." Her words reel in resentment. "Guess what I did this weekend?"

I despise the guessing game. And she knows it. "Bought a Louis Vuitton handbag and charged it to Serena's card?"

"I went to visit my best friend." Her tone dares me to explain why I wasn't home grounded—like I said I would be.

Now her mood makes complete sense. "My grandparents had plans before Mom grounded me. They dragged me along."

"Really?" Her breathiness tells me she's dying to believe me.

"I've got marks on my back from sleeping in the car. Worst weekend road trip ever."

"Why didn't you call me?" Her eyes widen with surprise, and her voice deepens with hurt.

"I thought you and your new BFF were living it up in San Fran."

"Pia's not my BFF. She's just…"

"Your cheerbaby?"

She frowns at me. "I don't like that nickname, Kali. She's a friend and a member of my cheer squad."

"Who substituted for your BFF?"

"Wait, are you jealous?" She sounds gleefully shocked.

"Maybe."

Her lips twitch. "Where'd you go?"

"Bodie."

"Get any good pictures?"

"Gramps did."

A smile breaks out across her face. "Did you let your grandparents have any fun?"

Saturday night, Grams, Gramps, and I put on a show for Mandy at our house. In the round main room, Mandy and I sit on the couch with our feet grazing over the bearskin rug. Gramps pulls out some pics he snapped of Bodie. Grams pretends she's a history buff, but she's really recounting our lives there. Mandy wants to believe us. So she does.

Humans. They always doubt their instincts. I want to scream at her sometimes. Tell her I'm as bad as everyone thinks, but I can't because she makes high school more bearable.

By the end of the night, Mandy forgives me. I wave goodbye at the door, and my cell rings. It's Hunter. Weird. He was supposed to be in the wanshiqi realm all weekend.

"What's up, love of my lifetimes?" I can't help looking down at the labradorite ring he gave me.

"Can you come over tonight?"

"I've got three hours until curfew. On my way."

The fifteen minutes while my car skims over the roads to his home feels like fifty. Exceeding the speed limit and blaring the stereo don't make time pass faster.

When he opens the door, I throw myself into his arms. Kiss him, wrap my legs around his waist, and prepare for some serious sexing.

Except Hunter's kiss fizzles out. His hands support me, but don't grope me. I've unbuttoned half his shirt buttons; he's not undoing any of mine.

"What's wrong?"

"I need to talk to you." His voice is so heavy, it exerts a gravitational pull.

"Sounds serious." My feet hit the hardwood floor and my arms unlock from around his neck.

He slides his hands into his back pockets. "We need to talk about Octavius."

"Tav is just my English partner. For one assignment."

He squints at me like he's trying to calculate the square root of 3267. "Not the current one. The Octavius from Pompeii."

"Oh."

I walk into his living room and drop down on his white leather couch. Facing the glass wall, all I see is absolute darkness. Everything closes in. The air thickens and I can't seem to catch my breath. I fight to control the fear rising in me.

I stare at the grain in the wood floor and take short, shallow breaths. That's all I can manage. My eyes skim over the room to the built-in shelves and cabinets in the wall beside me. I need something to anchor me. I count the books on the shelves and force a little more air into my lungs.

Hunter sits on the couch beside me. "The lishihui were furious when you trapped Octavius in Pompeii."

"I noticed." I gesture at our surroundings. "How many centuries have they been punishing me?"

"At first, they thought it was temporary. That your curse couldn't last more than a few human lifetimes."

"I figured he'd be able to escape eventually," I lie. Evil like Octavius has to stay buried.

"No one knows how you did it, but he disappeared with Pompeii." His words make my skin tremble.

I look down at my labradorite ring. Hunter's the only one I can share everything with. He's my tonggan. But I've never told anyone this truth. It's too risky.

He reaches under my chin and lifts my head so that his turquoise gaze holds mine. "There's a new urgency to the search for Octavius. The lishihui want him found and freed."

All the moisture evaporates from my mouth. My tongue skims the roof of my mouth, trying to stimulate the saliva, but it doesn't help. Because if Octavius escapes... No, I can't think about what he'd do to me.

"What went on in Pompeii, Kali?"

"You've heard the story." My voice creeps toward him.

"From your parents and the lishihui archive, but never from you." Hunter shakes a curl out of his eyes. It flops back there. "Tell me why you did it."

"Because I'm evil. Selfish. Immature. I like causing trouble. I'm unbalanced." Those were all the things my parents testified to.

"I've watched the holographs from your trial. You never defended yourself."

"I couldn't." My voice comes out like a wounded bird begging for help but unable to trust anyone.

When I tried to tell my parents the truth about Vesuvius, they got agitated. Suddenly, their eyes lost focus. They dropped to the floor and their bodies convulsed. Muscles spasmed, locking and releasing in some unknown rhythm. Seizures.

Their eyes. I'll never forget their eyes. They stayed wide open, but they couldn't see me. It felt like an eternity before their muscles calmed down and the focus finally returned to their eyes. When they came out of it, they didn't remember anything I said about Octavius or what had happened to them. It was like their qi couldn't take the truth. I was petrified of what would happen to them if I testified, so I didn't.

Grandfather and Grandmother denounced me without ever asking for my side. They severed their business ties with Dad. I never told Grams or Gramps what really happened. They asked, but I couldn't tell them. If they believed me, they'd try to help, and it could destroy Mom's and Dad's qi.

"I've helped you stay human all these years. You can trust me." His voice ripples over me and makes me want to do everything he asks.

I learned long ago no one is immune to Octavius. When I think of him, everything I buried in Pompeii rushes back. Oh Goddess, I don't want to feel this again. Invisible bats attack the inside of my belly. A wave of nausea crests in the back of my throat.

If Octavius is freed, Hunter needs to know what will happen to me. To us. The words tangle on my tongue. "Octavius hated that you were my tonggan."

Hunter moves close to me. "His tonggan disappeared five thousand years ago."

"Do you know how?" I have my suspicions, but I've never been able to confirm them.

"His father claims she became a part of a meteor and wandered deep into space."

"Nice story." Fear whittles away at my lungs. "Octavius wanted to be matched with Livia." That was my name in Pompeii. It's too hard to say *me*. I need to keep some distance. It's the only way I can talk about it—another name, another lifetime.

My gaze darts to the window, afraid to see the disbelief in Hunter's eyes, but the window is filled with blackness. No ocean. No sand. The unbearable emptiness chokes me like the poisonous air in Pompeii.

He squeezes my hand to assure me he is here. But he hasn't always been. My heart cramps at the memory of missing him. It's a sharp pain that radiates out into my chest.

"During your qifa, I was alone, and Octavius came after me. He wanted power over me."

Hunter doesn't interrupt. He gets that once I start, I won't be able to stop. He sends a pulse of reassuring energy into me.

"He made the people of Pompeii hate Livia." I hear my words, but it sounds like they are spoken by another person.

"With his abilities?"

"He's not a dream weaver like everyone thinks," I whisper. "He manipulates memories. Permanently."

The most precious thing wanshiqi have are our memories. They are part of our qi. Manipulating them alters our qi. Screws with who we are at our very core. Everyone thinks my parents turned cold and cruel because of our punishment, but I know it was what Octavius did to them to get to me.

"Memory manipulators are very rare and very dangerous." Hunter rubs his lips, trying to process everything I'm telling him. "Falu requires them to register with the lishihui so their powers are monitored."

"Falu doesn't apply to him." I learned from experience—Octavius is above all laws.

Doubt paddles across his features before he can drown it in concern.

The words come faster, needing to get out. "He attributed every evil in Pompeii to Livia. When a prominent citizen fell ill, he made people think she did something to him. Bread went missing and she was to blame. The drought, even the animals dying, he made people believe it was all her doing." I grip Hunter's hand. "The humans fell under his sway. He used his power on my parents. They were all convinced Livia had to be punished."

"Did you report him?"

My shoulders slump. "I tried, but his dad was head of the lishihui. He must have buried my reports. You were gone. Grams and Gramps weren't around back then. I had no one to help me."

Hunter's voice is measured, but his forehead is a mess of lines. "What did he do to you?"

I try to shut out the pain, but it's all there. Locked inside the memories no one shares with me. "Public floggings. Scalding my feet. Breaking my fingers. Fire ants. Every day, he devised a new way to torture me." My voice vibrates like Vesuvius.

"Your parents let this happen?"

"They participated in it." A sob escapes, and hot tears race down my cheeks. "He made them think I was a demon that took on their daughter's form. They believed that I deserved to be punished."

"Kali, no," he half-whispers. Maybe it's sadness. Maybe it's the dawning horror.

I can't speak, so I nod.

Hunter pulls me toward him. I want to collapse into him, but if I do, I won't be able to finish, so I pull back.

Hunter's palms soak up my tears. "Do they remember it?"

"He altered their memories. I don't think they can remember what really happened. They never knew it was me."

"But you knew it was them. Is that why you buried the city?" Understanding fills his voice.

"Octavius wouldn't stop." The physical pain wasn't the worst thing he did. The words scrape the back of my throat. "He tried to make me forget you."

"That's subject to annihilation by falu."

I hiccup. "Only if he was caught." And his father would never let that happen. No one could know what Octavius did without it threatening everything his father had built as head of the lishihui. A bad seed is traced back to its tree. Just ask my parents.

"Octavius had to know that after my qifa I'd find you. I wouldn't let you go easily."

I look down at my hand entwined with his. "He said…" My voice cracks, and it takes a moment to come back together. "He'd twist your memories. Before you could help me, he'd make you hate me."

Hunter presses his palms to my cheeks and looks into my eyes. There is so much love and acceptance there. "I could never hate you."

"You don't get it. He's that powerful." My voice rises on an ocean of unspoken emotions. "He twisted my parents' memories forever. He would do the same to you. I couldn't let him hurt you. I had to stop him."

"What did you do?" His voice is hushed, knowing how Pompeii ended.

I wish I could get a deep breath, but my chest is so tight right now. I can only afford a sip of air. "I cursed myself to have untainted memories. It gave me a brain tumor."

Hunter gathers me in his arms. He sends pulses of soothing energy into me. Tiny reminders that I'm okay.

I press my cheek against his chest. "When Octavius tried to alter my memories, he fought my curse. I clung to my thoughts of you. I couldn't let him take them away. But it made my brain tumor grow rapidly. The pain nearly killed me."

Hunter squeezes my shoulder. "Does anyone else know?"

"No."

I sink deeper into his arms and listen to the thudding of his heart.

"That final curse, the one that ended Pompeii, do you remember what you said?"

"I don't." That's a lie. I know every word I spoke to banish Octavius and his precious city to an eternity devoured by darkness. Lava and ash were crucial. Add to it my qi exiting my body. And my curse solidified in a wanshiqi trap. But there is danger in knowing what I did and how I did it. I have to keep that knowledge tucked away.

In his arms, I find the peace only a tonggan can give. Exhaustion creeps over me. I yawn. "He's still trapped."

"For now? Yes."

"What do you—" My words are cut off by a flash of white light. It fills the window, demanding Hunter's immediate attention.

The light pulsates, encoded with a message only Hunter can hear.

"What is it?" I sit up.

"I'm so sorry." He brushes my hair back and kisses my forehead. "I have to go."

All the lights in the room blink off, plunging me into primordial darkness. The darkness of Pompeii. Of death. I scream. When the lights flicker back on, Hunter's gone.

CHAPTER THIRTEEN

IN POMPEII, OCTAVIUS PINS me to my bed. I struggle, but I can't get out from under him. The weight of his body wrings the air out of my lungs. I fight for each breath, but tiny gasps are all I can manage.

There is no escape.

His coal-black eyes plunge into my qi, trying to incinerate my memories of my tonggan. I won't let Octavius win. I conjure up every emotion, every thought, every second of Hunter.

Kodo drummers beat out a song of almost defeat in my head. The throbbing mass inside my skull grows. I can feel my death coming, but I can't give up. "No. No. No."

Octavius frowns. If I didn't know better, I'd swear regret flared in his eyes. Then he backhands me.

My head bounces off the bed. Stars form before my eyes. I wish I could escape into those galaxies. But Octavius won't allow it. He shoves smelling salts under my nose. I recoil into the bed and return to myself.

The entire time my father stands there, watching.

"Daddy, help me. Please, help me."

My father steps toward us.

"It's not your daughter, remember. It's a demon playing tricks on you." Octavius's voice is so compelling, his words alter my father's memories and restructure his reality.

Daddy's face twists with revulsion. He thinks I'm one of the demons he's fought for centuries. My own father forgets who I am because of what Octavius can do.

Octavius's voice dips and rolls over my father. "Go join your wife on the boat."

My father leaves the room. The front door slams a few moments later.

I'm alone with Octavius.

He brushes the tear off my cheek. It's an oddly tender gesture from a terribly cruel man. "Daddy's never going to help you."

I barely have enough air to speak. My voice comes out breathy and small. "I'm never going to be yours."

"Livia, didn't you hear about my original tonggan?" His coal-black eyes burn with such intensity. I want to look away, but I can't.

"She disappeared," I whisper-wheeze.

"She disappointed me. Don't disappoint me." His breath sets my cheek on fire.

It's getting harder to think, but I know one thing: Tonggan are born and find each other. We complement each other. That's what I've been taught for centuries. "We only get one tonggan." My voice sounds threadbare, on the verge of ripping beyond repair.

"According to who?" He laughs without joy and props himself up on his elbows, so he can stare down at me.

I take a gulp of air. My brain clears. I cling to the rules of our world, praying they will somehow save me. "Falu says—"

"Falu says. Falu says," he mimics me. Then he sighs like I've been disappointing him for centuries. "Why do you always follow the rules?"

My mouth is so dry. My tongue feels too big. Clumsy. "We have to."

"No, we don't." His eyes are blacker than black. "Look at everything I've done to you. Your precious falu couldn't protect you from me."

He's right. But I haven't lost all hope. Not yet. I've sent reports to the lishihui. Someone has to receive them. Someone has to help. They have to.

"Why do you make me do these things?" He binds my wrists.

The rope doesn't chafe anymore. There are layers of scars there now. He drags me to the hook in the ceiling. The one he installed to torture me. He loops the rope over it, leaving my body dangling.

My toes scrape the floor, trying to gain a foothold. They can't. He made sure that I'm helpless. Again.

Octavius circles around me. "Why don't you fight back?" Frustration creeps into his voice like he wants me to do something to save myself.

Desperation wells up inside me and forces the words out. "You don't have to do this."

He stops in front of me. His eyes meet mine. "I wish I didn't."

For a split second, I know he's telling me the truth. I scramble to hold on to it. "Then don't. Please. Find another way."

"It's what I have to do." There's such finality in his tone. My heart responds, beating twice as hard. His hand strokes my cheek. "You are so sweet." He says it like he almost regrets trying to destroy me. "Loving your parents, caring for your human friends and following falu. You have been so very good. And where, where has it gotten you?" He pauses, waiting for my reply.

I don't want to answer. But he'll make me suffer for my silence. My tongue scrapes over the roof of my mouth. My voice wobbles. "Here."

"Being good has gotten you here." The emphasis he puts on *here* sends shivers rippling down my spine.

I've fought him for so long. But at this moment, I realize he's right.

He always wins because he knows what I will do: Follow the rules.

All my light emotions—my compassion for humans, my love of my parents, and my respect for falu—have been my undoing. He has used them all against me. They've left me weak and helpless. I have to stop following the rules. I have to silence every light emotion inside me. I have to stop being good.

The ground trembles slightly beneath us. Vesuvius refuses to rest. Tremors are the norm here. But in that moment, it's like she senses what's happening and cries out for me. It's comforting that something cares. And then I realize that's the only way I can beat him. Me and Vesuvius.

I just need a little more time.

I'm pretty sure Daddy will reincarnate if his human body dies, but I still can't bear to cause my own father's death. It'll take Daddy twenty minutes to be out at sea. I only have to hold on for twenty more minutes. But those twenty minutes will translate into 1200 seconds of torture.

Unless I can keep Octavius talking. My thoughts race to keep up with my heartbeat. "Why do you have to do this?"

"You would never understand. Everything changes after qifa." Octavius yanks my hair back, exposing my neck and reminding me how powerless I am. "This can end. All you have to do is give in to your darkest thoughts."

I don't know why, but he needs me to break falu and be like him. "No." I can't do that. Not yet.

"So be it." His face shutters like it always does right before the torture begins.

I forget the throbbing of my scalp when his knife slices along the ravines between my ribs. All I feel is the awful burning. I pant through the pain, but it never eases. The pain transitions to a stinging agony. I can't stop trembling. The blood seeps up around my ribs, striping my dress. Saturating it in red.

Octavius spends the next 1120 seconds cutting, burning, and twisting my flesh. Every time the pain becomes unbearable and I black out, he brings me back to consciousness. Each time, I grow colder. It could be the blood loss. It could be my impending death. But more likely, it's the fear. Fear of what he will do to me. Fear of what he will make me do. Icicles of fear form on my bones. This fear will freeze me from the inside out. Making me more powerless than I ever have been.

I can't let the fear win. I search for a flint to spark my anger.

He can't break my bond to Hunter, so he's going to break me. Torment me and force me to become like him.

I do.

It's the only way to stop him. All the anger, all the frustration, all the pain—I surrender to every dark emotion inside me. The inky blackness obliterates all lightness. Darkness rises in me. Burning me with its strength and melting the fear. It feels so good. Powerful.

My final curse unfurls. Vesuvius rumbles. The room shakes with the force of what I've unleashed on Pompeii. Octavius stumbles to the door to see what is happening.

I use the last of my strength to lift my head. Through my window, I see my father's boat embrace open waters. I take a deep breath. Poisonous gases burn my nose, scalding my lungs. Relief chokes me to death as lava and ash bury the entire city alive.

I wake up screaming. No coherent words. Just screeches soaked in blood puddles of pain.

Grams rushes into my room. "What's wrong?"

"I had no choice." The burning ash still chokes me. "No choice. No choice." A coughing fit racks my body.

"Shush. You're safe. I'm here." Grams climbs into bed and rocks me.

The past clings to me. The air incinerates my lungs. The coughing won't stop. It's impossible to breathe. An awful mechanical noise fills the room. It sounds like a machine dying. It's me. A clammy coldness bursts over my skin.

"Let me help you."

I nod, and she presses her palm to my breastbone. She whispers ancient healing words. The past loses its grip on me. The air doesn't pollute me anymore.

I take a few shuddering breaths and realize I'm not in Pompeii. Dad didn't leave me to Octavius. I didn't die before the hot stones rained down on us. I'm not powerless. I'm not Livia anymore. I'm Kali.

But it did happen. Two hundred lifetimes ago, it happened. And now Hunter knows.

I bury my face in Grams's terrycloth robe. It's soft and warm and safe. I breathe in the lilac scent of her qi.

She strokes my hair, murmuring, "You're safe. You're all right."

But I'm not. There are things that are done to you that leave a permanent scorch mark on your qi. Those things have been done to me. I've done those things. Too much destruction to ever be all right again.

Grams's voice wraps me in her love. "Gramps and I are here for you."

"Thanks." I sniffle. "It's a stupid nightmare."

She rubs my back. "Darling, you've woken up screaming like that in every reincarnation since Pompeii."

"There was so much poisonous gas and ash." I shut my eyes. Grit my teeth. The memory still lingers in my room.

"I've always wondered how you escaped."

The muscles in my shoulders instinctively tighten. "I died before my curse buried the city alive."

"What about Octavius?"

I pull away. "I couldn't save him."

"Did you want to?"

I don't trust my tongue to form the words to lie to Grams, so I just look at her.

She must see the truth in my eyes because her expression softens with sadness. She cups my face in her palm. "Were you insane?"

Octavius's family said I was. They brought forward Octavius's reports that I was recklessly cursing the humans. He blamed me for all his crimes in Pompeii. They swore the rapid use of my power led to the brain tumor that made me incapable of controlling my powers. My parents testified to it all. Why else would I disobey falu and use my powers on a law-abiding wanshiqi like Octavius?

"No," I whisper.

"I didn't think so." She gently brushes my hair from my face. "What happened in Pompeii?"

"I can't. Please, Grams, not tonight."

"Someday, you must." She rocks me until I drift off to sleep.

CHAPTER FOURTEEN

THE NEXT MORNING, I remain under the covers on my four-poster bed and stare at my phone. My calls to Hunter go straight to voicemail. I can't tell him about the dream. I don't know what to do with myself. I pull the duvet over my head and pretend I'm still asleep. Half an hour later, I force myself to get out of bed.

The hot shower doesn't relax the muscles in my neck. I wrap a scarf around it, hoping the warmth will ease the tension. It starts to help until I enter the dining room. The chestnut-paneled walls and antique coffered ceiling remind me of the grandness of our palazzo in Italy. This room usually relaxes me, but not today.

My parents sit at the rectangular dining room table with Grams and Gramps, pretending this is a normal family breakfast. All of us haven't eaten breakfast together in ten years. I slide into my chair, and Anna drops off my food—scrambled eggs, toast, bacon. Milk with a dash of coffee and sugar.

Before I take my first bite, Dad clears his throat. "How'd you sleep last night?"

Grams's smile encourages me to share.

I sip my coffee. "Not well."

"Pompeii?" Mom's voice is soaked in disappointment with a sprinkling of disgust.

Grams must have told her. There's no way Mom could come up with that on her own.

"Something like that." I fork my eggs.

"Consciences are the worst part of being human." Dad uses his diplomatic voice.

"That's why qifa is so important." Mom bites into her dry toast. "You remember that last day in Pompeii?" she asks Dad.

"The entire city leveled when we returned." He sounds almost proud.

"Why couldn't you make sure Octavius escaped?" Mom's accusation hangs in the air.

My neck muscles spasm. I drop my fork. It clatters against my plate.

Rage gurgles in my belly, foaming up to my mouth. "Why don't you remember Pompeii?" I stalk out of the room.

I drive to Hunter's, but he's not there. I can't stop thinking about Pompeii. Octavius. My parents. It's a thousand canker sores on my qi, festering and aching. No matter how many miles I put between my parents and me, the pain won't stop. I have no destination in mind, just an absolute need to keep moving. My car crisscrosses the city until I end up in Tav's driveway. I want what he has inside that gingerbread house—a family who loves and protects and trusts.

Before I know what I'm doing, my feet take me up the front steps, and I knock on his door. It's Sunday morning, and we did our presentation already. I have no reason to be here. I should slink back to my car and make my getaway, but Bess opens the door.

Her jeans are dirt-stained and her long-sleeved blouse is rolled up to the elbows. Her skin has a touch of color, like she ventured outside and enjoyed it. A pink scarf adorns her head.

"Good morning." She acts like it's the most natural thing in the world for me to be here on her doorstep.

I shuffle my feet. "How are things?"

"Good. Doing a little gardening with Tav."

I back up. "Sorry to intrude—"

"Come in." She tugs me down the hall, past the pictures that form a timeline of Tav. She's with him in every single one. "We could use another set of hands."

I follow her to the backyard. The screen door squeaks open.

"Ma, remind me to oil that tonight." Tav prunes swirly-shaped bushes. A baseball cap keeps his hair out of his eyes.

"Hey," comes out of my mouth in an I-don't-know-why-I'm-here way.

He jerks and almost slices half the bush away. "Hey. Were we supposed to meet?"

I shake my head. I have no reason to be here. I should go.

Before I can bolt, Bess links her arm through mine. "Kali's here to help us with the yard."

The rock bed is full of weeds, the bushes need serious reshaping, and the lawn begs to be mowed and de-dandelioned.

"Is America's Next Top Model away again?" He refuses to call Hunter by his name.

"Hunter's with his dad." It's my go-to lie when he's in the wanshiqi realm.

"After the A on your English presentation, I can't wait to see what you do with the landscaping," Bess says.

Tav picks up a set of work gloves and tosses them at me. "How do you feel about weeding?"

"I'm very supportive of it." Though we've had people to do this for us for ages. Today, however, I'm willing to do anything to escape my thoughts. Attacking the unwanted growth around the rocks and bushes eases my mind. Repetitive action is calming for anything in human form, even a wanshiqi.

The sun warms my skin. The breeze cools my neck. We pass an hour working.

Bess gets up and stumbles, but she catches herself.

Tav rushes to her side. "Are you okay?"

Her smile is tired. "I think I overdid."

Tav tries to help her inside, but she waves him away. "You kids finish up out here."

Tav watches her go inside. His face tightens with fear.

"How long has your mom been sick?" My voice is softer than dandelion fuzz.

"She was diagnosed when I was eight. She did a couple rounds of chemo and radiation. We thought we'd beaten it. She was in remission for five years." He recounts her medical history with a forced calm. He picks up the clippers, and his face falls. "Then the cancer came back last year."

I yank at the weeds peeping through the rock bed and toss them into a garbage bag. "Where's your dad?"

The clippers slice faster. "Gone."

"Dead gone or dead-beat gone?"

"Probably both." His voice flattens like a bug beneath his Converse sneakers.

"Grandparents?"

"I never met my dad's parents. Mom's are dead."

"Any other family?"

"None worth mentioning." He hacks away at the bush. "Why'd you stop by today?"

I spray the dandelions with the chemical he gave me. It's supposed to stop them from coming back. "I needed a break from my parents."

"Must be nice to have people to get away from." Longing shadows his words.

He has no idea how lonely it is to be with my parents. "Sometimes alone is okay. Just not all the time."

"She's not going to die." His eyebrows leap together in defense, like I aimed a blow at his third eye or something.

"I didn't mean... I was talking about my family, not yours."

He goes back to pruning the bush with a renewed relentlessness.

I know what it's like to have no one you can confide in. I've spent almost two millennia that way. "If you ever need someone to talk..."

"I'm good."

I ignore the *stop now* in his tone. "But if you do..."

"I'm guessing the prom queen and Adonis don't get you."

"Adonis, I mean, Hunter does. Mandy's a good friend."

"Uh-huh."

"Is it so ridiculous that I might like talking to you?"

A grin creeps across his face. "I'm an excellent listener."

"But not a stellar talker."

"Only when I have something important to say." He moves on to the hedges.

I wander across the lawn, spritzing the dandelions and ending their existence. I can't help comparing me and my parents to Tav and Bess. Tav and Bess get one go-around together. One chance to be mother and son. It's dangerously close to the end. I keep going and bringing along the wanshiqi I love, but we never get as close as Tav and Bess are.

None of this is fair.

None of it.

CHAPTER FIFTEEN

O N MONDAY AT LUNCH, I can't help glancing around the dining hall for Hunter. My gaze starts at the doorway, slides over dozens of round, wooden tables with matching chairs all the way to the other side of the room and back again. In a sea of students, he's nowhere to be found. Mandy prattles on and on about cheerleading. I am only half-listening until she starts in on the upcoming cheer competition in June.

I won't be here then. My death date is coming faster than I realized. There's so much I still need to do. My stomach tightens, pushing all the tension up to my throat, which suddenly feels too narrow to fit a word through. I sip my soda and try to swallow that sensation away.

Tav slides into the chair beside me. "Hey."

"Hey." I take another sip of soda and clear my throat. The words come easier this time. "You know Mandy?"

Tav lifts his chin in an upward nod of acknowledgement. "Hey."

Mandy mumbles, "Hi." She forks a carrot and loses it halfway to her mouth.

She's usually quick with a smile and coordinated. I give her my what's-going-on face, but her gaze drops to her plate.

Tav leaves Mandy alone like he's used to her weirdness. He leans toward me. "Sunday was fun."

"I'm still recovering."

A slow grin spreads across his face.

Mandy's fork clatters against her plate. "What? You two?!" she squeals.

A few sophomore heads turn our way. I give them death stares until they look away. "Don't be dirty. I helped him with yard work. My calves are killing me."

Mandy's cheeks flush to crimson-crush red. The exact shade of her favorite lip gloss. "He made it sound... I mean anyone would think..."

"You remember Hunter, my boyfriend?" Mandy knows I'd never cheat. Or she should know that about me.

Her voice is saturated in embarrassment and deep fried in remorse. "Sorry, that was stupid."

"Mistakes happen." I try to keep my voice light, but my arms cross.

She gives me a tiny, tight smile. The kind of smile that tells me something is wrong. "I got to go."

Three-quarters of her plate is full of food. "You haven't finished your lunch yet."

"Cheer stuff." She rushes out of the dining hall, leaving me alone at the table with Tav.

"That was awkward."

"It always is." He sounds resigned.

"Why?"

"I make her uncomfortable." He taps his fingers on the table like he's playing a song I can't hear. His hair falls across his forehead and into his eyes.

"You guys know each other?"

"We were friends in elementary school," is all he says.

"And now you aren't?"

"Pretty much." His tone tells me to stop pushing.

Still I ask, "What happened?"

"Life." Something flickers in his eyes. It's too quick for me to figure out.

I give up, knowing I'll get the real story out of Mandy.

He brushes his hair out of his eyes. "You want to come over this weekend and work on the front yard with me?"

"Sorry. I've got plans."

"I thought the Roman god went away on weekends."

"His name's Hunter, and my plans are with Mandy."

"The pillow fight sleepovers that guys dream about." His eyes go all woolly.

I have the sudden urge to touch his face and see what change that would bring about in his eyes. I shake it off, grab my plate, and get out of there.

When Hunter reappears in my physics class on Tuesday, his eyes are a murky teal. Dark circles creep under them. He tosses too many everything's-fine smiles at me.

Something's wrong.

I can't ask about it here. The entire day I pretend okayness. By the time the bell rings, I'm exhausted.

I trail him out to the parking lot. "What's going on? Why'd you have to leave so abruptly on Saturday?"

He unlocks his dark-blue-colored Porsche 911 without looking at me.

"Hunter?"

He's already inside. I slide into the dove-gray leather seat and slam my door. "What in Hades is going on?"

"Pompeii." He pulls out of the school parking lot.

10,062 questions burst through my brain.

Before I can ask one, he says, "The lishihui are drilling holes in Pompeii, trying to locate and rescue Octavius."

Goddess, no. I'm pretty sure a hole won't let him escape, unless they find the exact spot where I imprisoned him. "Is that why you asked me where Octavius was?"

"Yes."

A terrible thought slams into my brain. Could Hunter be helping the lishihui? Would he betray me like that? A wave of fear pummels my body. It yanks every grain of certainty out from underneath my toes. Tumbles me into the depths of doubt. Terror floods my nose. Can't breathe, can't think, can't escape.

"I'm trying to lead them in the wrong direction." He grips the steering wheel.

My breath comes out like spray from a shaken soda can. "Why would you do that?"

"If he's as powerful as you say, you and I can't fight him." Hunter's face is grimmer than a reaper. "I need to know where Octavius is buried."

"Pompeii."

He slams his palm on the steering wheel. "How can I protect you if you don't trust me?"

"I've told you more than anyone else—more than Grams and Gramps. Don't you get it?" I stare at Hunter, but he looks straight ahead as we speed north along Camino Del Mar toward Highway 101. We hit downtown Del Mar, and houses, shops, and pine trees pass by us on this two-lane highway.

"I've done everything, everything, to protect you." His voice sounds like a wounded warrior, fighting for me despite how much I hurt him.

"And I'm doing this to protect you." They can't get the info from him if he doesn't have it. They'll have to come after me.

His face tightens and his features sharpen. "They don't know you did it on purpose. They still believe you lost control of your powers."

He shouldn't have any insider information on the lishihui. It's got to be gossip. "You can't be sure—"

"I'm sure."

The certainty in his voice sets off a low-level ringing in my ears. I'm missing something. Something bad. "How?"

"My dad is on the lishihui." He stares straight ahead at the road, not daring to look at me.

The ringing grows louder and my head feels floaty. My vision gets speckled. It's that last moment before everything changes. I can feel it slipping away or maybe that's me slipping away. Hunter touches my hand, and I suck up his energy. My head clears and everything crystallizes.

Wanshiqi spend ages accumulating enough power to merit a seat on the lishihui. It's the highest honor until you become a zhangzhe. Once a seat is bestowed upon a family, it is coveted and passed down for eternity.

My lips form the only word they can. "When?"

"After Pompeii."

"How?" My voice comes out like I'm galaxies away from him.

"He took your father's seat."

My lungs shrivel inside my chest. His father gained my father's power because of me. My birthright became Hunter's. "Why didn't you tell me?"

"I couldn't."

He's kept so much from me. My human heart *thumpbumps, thumpbumps, thumpbumps,* sending anger coursing to my extremities. My fingers curl into furious fists, nails digging into palms.

"You couldn't change anything. It would just add to your guilt to know you'd lost your father's seat." Hunter tries to rationalize everything away.

He may be right, but it doesn't stop the emotions from swirling inside me. My body is burning with betrayal. I feel like Vesuvius come to life. "So you're part of the lishihui?" The lishihui that are led by Octavius's father. The lishihui whose fayuan damned me to this existence.

"Not yet."

"But one day you'll inherit your father's seat." Bitterness twists my voice. "My father's seat."

Once a seat has been given to another family, it can't be regained unless that family falls from favor. Hunter's downfall is the only way for me to regain my position with the lishihui.

It's not that I want that seat. I never wanted it. But the seat was supposed to be mine, and now it never will be. Because it's his. "You'll be one of them."

"You were destined to be one of them, too."

"That was centuries ago." Everything changed after Pompeii. I changed after Pompeii. "Pull over."

"What?"

The words rumble in my throat. "Pull this damned car over."

The trees and houses continue flying by, but not as fast as my emotions are flying around inside me.

"I don't want to use my last curse to get out of this car." My voice comes out serrated, cutting into him.

He shifts and guns the engine. "You can get out when we reach Cardiff-By-The-Sea."

I grab the wheel. "Pull the car over."

Everything goes blue.

CHAPTER SIXTEEN

I FEEL MYSELF WAKING up. I have no idea where I am, but something soft contours against my back. The *whoosh* of the ocean fills my ears. Grains of sand cling to the crevasses between my fingers. I blink my eyes open to the blazing blue sky above me. I glance toward the water and recognize this stretch of beach.

Cardiff-By-The-Sea.

I move, and my muscles spasm, clench nerves, and shoot pain everywhere. "What did you do?"

"You grabbed the wheel." Hunter leans over me and brushes the hair off my forehead. "I had no choice."

"Did you steal my energy?" My voice is raspy. Not sexy-raspy, but hurt-raspy.

"You'd be dead if I did."

"I'd feel better if I was."

"I threw an energy bolt at you."

Normally he gives me his energy gently with my consent. "You tasered me?" I cup my temple. It doesn't stop the pain from shooting around my head in a halo of agony. I struggle to sit up. Pain rockets from the base of my brain to my big toe.

"I'm sorry."

He tries to help me up, but I push him away. The sand's not stable enough. I'm not stable enough. My legs wobble and my knees collapse.

He catches me. "Let me help you."

I don't have a choice right now. I need his help. But I still hate what he did to me. Tonggan can only use their power on each other without consent once before both have reached qifa. We reserve it for emergency circumstances. Most never use it. He's wasted his today. "Was it worth it?" The hurt in my voice is mirrored in his eyes.

"When you grabbed that wheel, you could have killed us both." His forehead wrinkles up like a Shar-pei puppy. "I saved us."

"Are my eyes browner?"

"A little."

Something tells me it's a lot. All my doubts from the car return: Hunter's betraying me. "You're helping the lishihui?"

"No." He tightens his grip on me. "I wouldn't do that to you. Just listen to me."

"I can't." My gut is screaming, run now, run fast, run far. I twist away from him. "Let go."

A smattering of people litter the shore. The nearest couple stares. A jogger slows his pace to watch us.

Hunter releases me. "I can explain. Give me ten minutes."

The need in his voice isn't enough to keep me here. I force my feet to move. One foot then the other. My muscles cramp and cry out. Three steps. Four. His betrayals beat against my skull. I've barely made it five feet when I stop. There's one thing I need to know. My voice simmers in anger. "What did Octavius's father promise you?"

"Excuse me?" He closes the distance between us quickly. A storm brews in his eyes.

"It had to be pretty good to betray me."

Clouds flood the sky. The air crackles with energy. My accusation infuriates him enough to impact the weather.

"I never betrayed you." His voice is gravelly. "I've always been on your side. Always."

The clouds menace the sun.

"Bullshit." Tremors weaken my legs.

The clouds darken and lock the sun away.

"I can't do this." I'm trapped in a cone of uncertainty. A piece of me wants to believe him, but all I can hear are my worst fears echoing in my ears. I curl my hands into fists to hide how much they're shaking. I'm shaking. Everything inside of me is shaking. "I need to be alone."

"We have to talk." His voice is low, compelling me to listen.

The natural attraction of a tonggan ripples over me. I take a step toward him without meaning to. I dig my nails into my palms, fighting it. Fighting him. "Now, you want to talk?" I choke on indignation. "I want to think. Alone."

He doesn't move. The clouds thicken overhead. Everyone else abandons the beach. It's just Hunter and me there now.

"If you don't leave, I will."

"You can barely walk." Doubt straddles his words.

"I can curse."

"You have no idea how much energy you have left."

"I'll risk it." I'd do anything to get away from him right now.

"I can't just leave you here."

"I'll be fine. I'll call Mandy."

"We have to talk, Kali." His eyes beg me to listen, but I can't.

"Just go." My neck spasms. The muscle contracts around itself and tugs my head toward my shoulder. The burning pain brings tears to my eyes. "Now." I yank off my labradorite ring and toss it at his feet.

He bends down to pick up the ring. "You have no idea how much you're risking." His words singe my skin.

"Neither do you." The whisper scorches my throat.

He walks away.

Once he's gone, I drop back into the sand and wait for my body to approach normal. The clouds clear out with Hunter, revealing a beautiful blue sky overhead. The sun warms me.

The rush of the waves fills my ears again. I watch the sea foam fizz over the sand, and the sand chase the waves back out to sea, abandoning the shore. So certain of the water. So unafraid of its depths. So unaware of what will happen next.

It's a while before I pull out my phone and call Mandy. She answers her cell on the fourth ring, breathing heavily into the phone. "Call you back in ten?"

I hear the heart-slamming music of cheer practice in the background.

"I need a ride." I try to sound calm, but my heart is already in pieces, and my voice cracks when I say *ride*.

"Where are you?"

"Cardiff-By-The-Sea."

"Hunter problems?"

"Big blowout." I burrow my toes in the sand. It's cool and comforting and clings to my skin.

"I'm on my way." She yells to her cheerbabies, "Becca take over and stretch them out." She asks me, "You need me to stay on the line?"

"Just text me when you get here."

"Okay." She rushes to add, "Whatever happened, we'll get through this. You'll be okay." Then she hangs up.

I wish I could believe her, but it feels like I'll never be okay again.

Hunter kept things from me. My human heart feels it all—hurt, betrayal, doubt. It's worse than Mom and Dad torturing me in Pompeii. They were compelled. He did this of his own free will.

I think back over my lifetimes, trying to figure out how I missed his betrayal. I can't remember him pushing me to talk about Pompeii or Octavius before. Well, maybe in my earlier reincarnations when we first reunited. Then he let it go.

But power is a seductive thing. Wanshiqi spend eternity accumulating it.

I lean forward, wrap my arms around my knees, and let my hair fall over my face. A blanket of blackness. He knows my secrets. My plan to die. My never wanting to end my punishment. My curse on Octavius. If he tells the lishihui, he will ruin everything.

Tears sting my eyes. No one can see, so I let them fall. My arms absorb my tears. I almost slip into the chaos of helplessness. But I'm not some silly teenage girl who lets a boy get the best of her. I'm Kali the destroyer. That's why my parents gave me the name. It's my choice to live up to it.

I lift my head and dry my face. I use my phone to check my eyes. Brown bleeds out of my pupils, rimming the bottom of them. Hunter rolled me back one or two major curses and a couple minor curses. I should put in my contacts before Mandy arrives, but I don't. He's given me an unintentional gift—enough energy to curse and protect myself.

I only get one opportunity to use my powers without Hunter's consent. He squandered his chance today when he forced energy into me. I've got to make this count.

I need time away from Hunter. At least until I figure a few things out. Three days. I need three days of Hunter seeing no Kali, hearing no Kali, speaking no Kali.

Rage is the perfect fuel for a banishment curse. It's so easily coaxed from my core, darkness swells, eclipsing any light left in my heart. A blistering, hot fury spirals through me. The words hum in my ears, begging to be spoken. And I do.

CHAPTER SEVENTEEN

I SLIDE INTO THE passenger seat of Mandy's pink-and-cream-striped Mini Cooper. The cream interior is oddly comforting, and for a moment, I'm just a teenage girl getting picked up by her BFF.

"What happened?" Mandy asks in a tone that is aimed between concerned and soothing.

"We had a blowout."

"Chernobyl or Three Mile Island?" She leans in for a hug.

I hold on to her. The truth catches in my throat. "Chernobyl."

She gives me a reassuring squeeze. "We'll figure this out."

I desperately want to stay in her Rainbow Brite hug and believe her. But I can't. And I don't like being this way. This human. So I pull away and put my seat belt on, stuffing all the emotions back down inside me.

She starts driving. "Another girl?"

"No." I wish it were that simple. I fiddle with the radio until she shuts it off.

"What did he do?" Her voice is almost demanding.

"Kept stuff from me." It's the understatement of a hundred centuries. He lied to me. He profited from my downfall. And he's probably still betraying me. My chest throbs. I cross my arms, protecting what remains of my human heart.

"The can-I-really-trust-him conundrum."

"Yeah." I stare out the passenger window as we drive past houses and palm trees. They're the same ones I drove by with Hunter before everything changed.

"Betrayal makes it hard to believe anything." It comes out more personal than an observation because it's hard-won knowledge for Mandy.

"It's not the same as you and Ryan."

"You're right. Ryan cheated. But I get how it feels to have someone withhold info and betray you." Her fingers tighten around the steering wheel the way she wanted to squeeze the truth from Ryan.

I have no idea how to process what Hunter has done. "How'd you deal?"

"I called you." Her expression softens, and her grip on the wheel loosens. "You let me sleep over. You told me I deserved better. You came up with a plan to expose him as a cheating scumbug."

"And that helped?"

"Immensely." She winks. "The Cheetos, too."

Hunter's my tonggan. We're forever. Or at least I thought we were. My heart shrinks and tightens. It's an awful pain in my chest. I can't think beyond today. I just have to get through this moment, then I'll deal with the next one. "It's different."

"You're right." Mandy's face puckers in seriousness. "You'll sleep at my house tonight. We'll eat Chili Cheese Fritos. And I'll plot his downfall."

I laugh but it sounds more like a groan. "You wouldn't plot to bump into him without cushioning his fall."

"I can be mean." Her voice hardens, as if she's resolving to be.

"Uh-huh." I glance at the notebooks covering the back seat. "Still doing Serena's homework for her?"

"Just until she's feeling better," she says quickly.

"I rest my case."

Three hours later, I'm in Mandy's cupcake-colored bedroom—sugary-pink walls and vanilla-cream carpeting—plotting Mandy-style. We sit on the rug, surrounded by bags of chips, canisters of Pringles, and boxes of cookies. We eat junk food on paper plates, which I'll smuggle out in my backpack along with all the wrappers, so her fitness junkie mom doesn't catch us.

I've talked as much as I can about Hunter, so I focus on Mandy. "Why were you weird with Tav at lunch yesterday?"

She dodges my question by stuffing sour cream and onion Pringles into her mouth.

I wait until she's done chewing. "Did he do something to you?"

Her face is doused in regret. "He should have."

"Why?"

She stuffs a few more Pringles into her mouth.

I grab the Pringles canister. "Tell me."

She stares at the rug, refusing to look at me. Her voice is hesitant and soft, like she doesn't want to disturb the past. "We were best friends in third grade. Inseparable. We played at each other's houses...until his mom got sick. His house got so still. It was like the house was holding its breath, waiting for the bad thing that was coming."

Before I can say a word, she rushes to add. "I didn't want to be there anymore. My parents tried to explain, and it just scared me more. I loved Bess. I didn't want her to be sick. I didn't understand how long it would take for her to get better." She looks up with eyes full of remorse.

I reach for her hand and hold on to it. "That must have been awful."

"Tav wouldn't come to my house. I missed him so much, but my parents kept telling me to make other friends. That I was only a kid, and there was nothing I could do to help."

"They were right."

"They were wrong." Her voice shakes like a 6.0 earthquake hit it.

"You were only eight years old."

"So was he. And I left him alone to deal with it." She pulls away from me and wraps her arms around herself like there's a fault line opening up inside her.

"You didn't know what to do. How could you?"

"He did." Tears gather in her eyes, tremble on her lower lashes, and slip down her cheeks. "He took care of his mom. And he did it on his own because his best friend was a coward."

I hand her a tissue. "Have you seen Bess since then?"

She blots her tears and blows her nose. "I've run into her at school events. She's always friendly. I don't know how to explain what I did. The more time passes, the more awkward I get."

"Have you apologized?"

"They must hate me."

"You are so unhateable." It's what drew me to Mandy from the start. She's the most accepting person I've ever known. "If you aren't ready to talk to him about the past, at least stop being so weird with him now."

Mandy dries her eyes. "I can do that." Her voice is solemn.

If she hasn't talked to them, Dear Goddess, she doesn't know that Bess's cancer is back. I take her hand in mine because what I have to say requires human contact. "Sweetie, she's no longer in remission."

Mandy gasps. Her face crumples like a used tissue. I hold Mandy while she cries her way through it.

In English class, Hunter stares at my chair, but can't see me or hear me, even when I'm answering Dr. Herger's questions. Banishment curses are like that.

Unfortunately, I'm experiencing the backlash of Hunter refusing to accept the banishment curse. My severe headache will morph into a migraine if he keeps fighting my curse and trying to find me.

I delay lunch in the noisy dining hall and linger in the student lounge. Mandy stays with me on the couch.

Tav sees us and comes over. "Where's your Italian Brad Pitt?"

"Wasn't my turn to watch Hunter." I rub my temple and wish Hunter would just give up on talking to me today.

Mandy giggles. "Good one, Tav."

He does a double take. He smiles tentatively at her and sits down across from me. "Troubles in happily ever after?"

Mandy glances at me.

"Everything's okay," I lie.

I guess it's not too convincing because Mandy adds, "They'll be fine. They've been together forever."

She tries to be normal with him. I should be happy that she's taking my advice, but her sudden comfort with Tav annoys me. Then again, the pulsating in my head makes everything annoying.

He unwraps a Snickers bar. "A month forever or a year forever?"

A wanshiqi forever. The blood pounds against my skull.

"Eighth grade, right?" Mandy asks me.

We're always together. We just don't make it official until it's okay in human years to be dating. "Yeah."

"What about you?" He leans back in the chair like he's going to stick around to talk.

She licks her Dorito-coated fingertips. "I haven't found the right person yet."

"Me neither," he says.

I glance up at the ceiling tiles. I hate triangles. Maybe it's because wanshiqi society is based on twos—tonggan. Three feels threatening. Someone is always left out. Right now, it's me.

"So what's on tap for your girls' weekend?" Tav shifts toward Mandy.

Mandy leans toward him. "Secret road trip."

Tav's voice dips. "To?"

"San Fran," she says softly.

"Why?" he asks.

I can't help feeling like I'm intruding on their time together. "Why not?"

"Just curious." He puts his hands up in a sign of no offense.

A sharp pain lances through my temple. Hunter is nearby and refusing to cooperate. If he comes in here, I can't explain to them why he can't see me. "I need to hit the girls' room."

Mandy asks, "Want me to come with you?" But she doesn't make a move to get up from the couch.

"It's fine."

I pass Hunter in the hallway. He pauses as if he can sense me.

I hold my breath. He heads for the student lounge. I can't go back until he's left. I end up in a stall, texting Mandy. Waiting to hear that he's gone.

CHAPTER EIGHTEEN

I TEAR MY fitted sheet off the bed, trying to find that one position that will let me drift away into a dream. But I can't sleep when I'm fighting with Hunter. And this fight, it's tearing me apart.

I slip out of my room and pad downstairs to our sprawling kitchen in need of something chocolate. I flick on the lights. The white cabinets reflect brightness at me, and the cork floor hushes my footsteps.

No point bothering with a bowl. I grab the half-gallon of Edy's double fudge brownie and the can of Reddi-wip from the fridge, slide onto a stool at the island, and think about Hunter. Ever since I left Mandy, he's all I think about. He's between shades of gray.

I need to talk to Grams and Gramps about Hunter's lies, but I'm so afraid that they won't be able to explain away what he's done. And they are my last hope.

Gramps's voice rumbles behind me. "Trouble sleeping?"

I jump. My mouth is filled with whipped cream. One word, and it will spew everywhere. I use my spoon to point to my bloated cheeks.

"Take your time." Gramps shuffles over to the stove. "Hunter called me."

I gulp down the Reddi-wip and play dumb. "Why?"

"He's having trouble reaching you." Gramps sounds confident that there's more to the story, but he doesn't push me. He pours milk into a saucepan and leaves it on the stove to simmer while he measures out the Hershey's cocoa.

"I needed some space." A banishment curse of space. Hunter shouldn't be able to talk about me yet. "What did he tell you?"

"Nothing. He was so upset he couldn't even bring himself to say your name." He adds a dash of cayenne pepper to the hot chocolate—his secret ingredient. "What happened, Kali?"

"His father took Dad's seat on the lishihui after Pompeii. Hunter never told me. I feel like I don't know him anymore. Maybe I never did." I stare down at the ice cream. While I was talking, I carved the wanshiqi symbol for betrayal into it.

"You've never cared about politics before." Gramps continues making the hot chocolate. He's too calm. The calm of someone who digested this information long ago.

I choke on my ice cream. "You knew about it, didn't you?"

"Of course." He makes those two little words sound so reasonable.

"Does Dad know?"

"Who do you think nominated Hunter's father for the seat?" The whisk makes a constant clinking sound against the pot as Gramps mixes up the hot chocolate. "We needed a trusted friend to take your father's seat, or it would revert back to his father."

To Grandfather. I stare at the patterns the gray makes in the white marble counter and swear it's a wolf's head. Maybe it's the mention of Grandfather that conjures that image up. "Why didn't you tell me?"

"You had enough to deal with back then. Hunter just did as I asked."

"You asked?" My voice chases my frustration to the ceiling.

Gramps's expression is eulogy serious. "It was my decision to keep this from you."

His confession should make what Hunter did hurt less, but it doesn't. Because tiny, awful doubts have taken root inside me, and I can't just pluck them out. "Do you still trust Hunter's father?"

"Augustus hasn't given us a reason to doubt him."

I wait for a wave of relief to rush over me, but it's barely a trickle. I still feel wronged and betrayed. "Hunter kept this from me for centuries."

"Have you told him everything?" He pokes at my duplicity.

There are things only I can know about Octavius and Pompeii. "I can't."

"Yet you expect him to tell you everything?" Gramps levitates his bushy eyebrows.

Tonggan are about reciprocity. If I have secrets, Hunter is allowed to have secrets. My wanshiqi soul has no right to be upset, but my human heart refuses to catch up. It still aches over how easily he lied to me all this time.

"How do I know he's not betraying me?" It's a terrible doubt that lingers like a cough after bronchitis.

"You can trust him or you can test him. But you can't sentence him without evidence."

"Rules of fayuan."

"You never did testify to what happened in Pompeii." Gramps traps me in his ancient gaze. I feel like he can see all the locked doors inside my qi and has enough patience to open them over our lifetimes.

I look away. "The evidence was overwhelming. Nothing I alone could refute."

"The hardest thing is the truth, especially when no one is willing to believe it." There's too much understanding in his voice.

My eyes sting. Treacherous tears threaten. I can't fall apart. I walk over to the fridge and pretend to look for another snack. I have to quiet everything he's stirred up inside me.

He gives me a few moments. Then he comes over and kisses the top of my head and hands me a mug of hot chocolate. "We're more alike than you realize."

"You mean besides the millennium-old sweet tooth?" I'm so shaken up, I can't even manage a Mona Lisa smile right now. I rest my cheek against his plush, red bathrobe.

"I didn't want to be separated from my parents." His voice is low and hushed, an unexpected confession. "In my day, qifa meant a complete separation from your past. I never saw my parents again. I moved forward with my tonggan." His expression shifts through loss, excitement, and resignation.

"Do you miss your parents?" My voice is softer than the marshmallows floating in my hot chocolate.

"You always miss your parents. Don't believe your father. He can't admit how much their siding against him hurt. Then he'd have to realize what he did to you." There's an eternity of sadness in Gramps's eyes.

It echoes in my own qi.

"His parents embodied the worst of the wanshiqi. All they cared about was power." His brow sinks toward his eyes like there's more that he isn't saying. "Did I ever tell you about Cleopatra's fall?"

I shake my head, confused by the topic change.

"Your father's mother burst with pride that day." He pads back to the island and sits down on a stool, preparing to tell his tale.

I join him. "Why?" Dad's been taking out empires for millennia.

"Your grandfather, Xia, had a fondness for using his power to shift his qi into and out of physical shells. Xia spent several nights as Julius Caesar bedding Cleopatra. Then he went back inside a mountain like nothing happened." Gramps's voice sticks in neutral, neither judging nor approving.

"I take it Grandmother found out?"

"She'd made peace with his desire to dally with humans as long as he told her who and when." Gramps gives me a sideways glance. He must see the disgust on my face because he adds, "I don't understand it, but it worked for them. When he didn't tell her about Cleo, your grandmother knew that human woman was special to him."

"How could his cheating not bother her?" If Hunter slept with another girl, I'd curse them both.

"Every tonggan defines their own relationship rules."

I hesitate to ask, but a part of me needs to know. "What about you and Grams?"

"She's the only one for me." His love fills every syllable.

I can't help thinking how much I want what they have. Never what Grandmother and Grandfather share. "Grandmother must have been terribly hurt."

"She craved vengeance." His eyes take on a faraway look, like he's gazing through the mist of memory. "She fanned your father's interest in Roman politics. He influenced Caesar to name his grand-nephew his heir. Should have been the end of it once Caesar died. But Cleo was tenacious and interfered in your dad's carefully laid plans for the Roman Civil War."

"So Dad removed Cleo from the game?" I sip my hot chocolate.

Gramps nods. "He's perfect for the lishihui. His parents groomed him to take over his father's seat." I catch a note of disapproval in his words.

All this talk of lishihui seats reminds me of Mom's seat. "Who took Mom's seat?"

Gramps graces me with his enigmatic smile. "It reverted back to me."

"What happens when the lishihui are in session?"

"I can't vote. But no one can challenge me for the seat until I return to power."

He's never shared so much with me before. I don't know when this moment will pass, and I can't help pushing for more. "Was Atlantis really you?"

Gramps chuckles. "One of my defining moments."

Pompeii is a tiny blip on the map of what my family is capable of. "Was it overrun with demons? Did you bury them at sea?" I lean forward, anticipation stealing over my voice.

"Something like that." His expression is unreadable. Not a blank page, but a page filled with ancient language that I can't interpret.

"Come on. Grams says you know more about the Great War."

"We'll swap stories someday. Pompeii for Atlantis."

I look away. "Someday."

When I finally fall asleep, I dream of the Aztecs. Not the rhythmic drumming, the energetic rattles, or the sweet flutes playing at the festivals. Not the vibrant markets with the people trading obsidian and feathers. Not the times of peace and prosperity. No, my mind rewinds to 1520 and the Spanish Conquest.

Except my memories are schizophrenic.

Mom gropes Hernan Cortes, who is Hunter's twin.

When I pull them apart, he says, "Trust me."

"How can I?" Revulsion twists my voice.

Mom strokes his cheek. "He's so handsome. How could you doubt him?"

Ew. Ew. Ew.

The scene shifts.

I stand in a crowd before our leader, Heuyi Tlatoani Moctezuma II. Except he looks like Dad. He promises, "We will drive the invaders from our border. We will prevail."

He shakes his maquahuitl. The obsidian blades embedded in the club catch the light, magnifying his power. The weapon contains the spirit of the sun god. The sight of it in his hand works the crowd into a fevered adoration.

They rally around my father's battle cry, chanting, "Death to the invaders. For Huitzilopochtli." They will do anything in the name of their sun and war god.

They shove past me to get closer, to glimpse their savior, to show their faith in him. I stumble, trapped in the flow of their feet.

Someone grabs me. It's Gramps.

I feel a flicker of relief until he pulls me toward the temple and says, "Time for the sacrifice."

"No. Gramps. No." My feet slide across the ground. Dust whirls around me. My stomach churns, and a wave of acid crests against my throat. I taste something bitter and awful. I twist and pull, but his grip on my wrist is inescapable. "Please, let me go."

His fingernails bite into my skin. He bares his teeth. They are filed to points. "We have a feisty one here."

Atop the temple stairs, Octavius brandishes his blade.

All the air inside me evaporates.

At his feet lays Grams's body. He holds up her bloodied heart in offering to Huitzilopochtli.

My heart skitters in my chest, knowing it's next and trying to escape its cage.

"Every battle has its casualties." Gramps shoves me up the steps toward Octavius.

I open my mouth, but the scream refuses to come.

CHAPTER NINETEEN

I WAKE UP TANGLED in my sheets and down comforter. My skin is clammy hot, the room darkly familiar. I kick the bedding away and curl up against the headboard. My skin pulsates like at any moment my blood will break free of me. I flick on the lamp beside my bed and look down at my wrist expecting to see Gramps's nail marks embedded in my skin.

My wrist is untouched.

It was only a nightmare. A nightmare my mind crafted especially for me. They say what you try to escape in your waking hours comes for you at night.

They're right.

I hold my head in my hands, trying to pull myself together. Everything Gramps told me last night is crawling around in my mind. I'm not okay with Gramps keeping things from me for my own good. Or his ability to sway Hunter to do the same. I'm hurt and betrayed by what Gramps did. That's the only explanation for what he did to me in that dream.

And Hunter. Hades. I'll never get the image of him making out with Mom out of my head. That would be the ultimate betrayal. So why do his lies still feel so awful to me? I don't know. And that scares me.

I pace around my room. What was the whole Aztec thing? Mom caused their downfall, but that's not how things actually went down. I rub my forehead and wish I'd dreamed of unicorns and fairies. Or even just the typical naked-in-school anxiety dream.

But I didn't and it bothers me.

I even pulled Octavius into the nightmare. Was that my lingering fear of him, or does he represent something? I don't have any good answers and all this ambiguity feeds my doubts.

My thoughts move faster and faster. I can't focus. Can't hold on to a thought and complete it. My thoughts spiral. I'm losing control of my own mind.

I can't. I can't. I can't.

There's a weird *whooshing* noise in my ears, and my vision tightens and tunnels toward darkness. Everything disappears.

I wake up on the floor, clutching a pillow. My skin isn't pulsating anymore. My mind has returned to me. My clock says 5:06 a.m. I need to do something. Anything.

School.

I have school today. I shower. Brush my teeth. Do my hair. Get dressed. My human routine is all that feels stable right now.

I can't look at Mom. I head down the stairs, skip over the main floor, and sneak into the kitchen. Grams reads her newspaper at the round oak table. I grab a yogurt and try to slip away.

She folds her newspaper, sets it aside, and pats the table. "Your mom and Gramps are both gone. Have a little breakfast with me." Her words are like milk coating a fire of Indian spices in my gut.

I drop into the chair beside her.

She traces a finger over my cheekbone. "Your dark circles are reappearing. More bad dreams?"

"I'm swearing off late-night chocolate."

Her lips compress. Concern sneaks into her eyes. "What's bothering you, Kali?"

My hard-fought calm is too fragile; I will lose it if I talk about Hunter or Gramps. I have to talk about the other parts of the dream. "Why did Mom destroy the Aztecs?"

"Your mother gets all caught up in her cause and forgets there will be ramifications." Grams gives me her she's-my-daughter smile.

"You still think it was an accident?" I never have.

Her voice gently navigates me around the truth. "She meant to incite a battle. She never meant for it to go as far as it did."

"I remember the night Dad insisted that the foreigners be driven out." He despised Cortes and Castillo for interfering in Aztec power struggles.

"Your mother always hated the human sacrifices. Then the leaders selected me for sacrifice. She did what any loving daughter would do. She brought in outside assistance."

"By stoking the greed of the Spaniards until conquest became their sole desire?" My mouth tastes of vinegar. The bitterness of living through Mom's bad decision.

"That, and she seduced Cortez and Castillo. She thought they'd be a good influence on Tenochtitlan." Grams sips her tea. "She was also fighting with your father at the time, if I'm not mistaken."

"Why do they always take their problems out on humans?" The exhaustion in my voice is overtaken by frustration.

Grams clears her throat. "Bodie, dear?"

I ignore the reminder of what I did. "You got killed in the resulting battle. Not a human sacrifice, but a sacrifice to Mom's cause." The memory rages in my mind. "Gramps spread smallpox. He brought about the fall of the city."

"No one likes living without their tonggan." She heaves one of those immortal sighs. The kind that takes an eternity to taper off.

"Can anyone?" My voice is a feather in the wind, unsure I want the answer.

Her eyes narrow like she's x-raying my heart and concerned by what's inside it. "Do you want that?"

I feel my face collapsing. I can't stop it. Tears blur my eyes. I grip my hands and hold on to all that I have left: me.

"Whatever Hunter has done, he's worth forgiving." Grams reaches over and squeezes my hand, reminding me she's here, too. "He loves you more than you realize."

I let my tears fall and hope she's right. I can't summon up the surety that I once had about Hunter. The realization softly suffocates me.

No chiseling into my skull. No alarm ringing in my ears. No carving knife slicing into my cerebellum. Hunter's not in school today. I don't know if I'm happy or disappointed. I thought a few days without him would make things clearer, but my emotions are murkier than ever.

All I can do is stay busy and ahead of the emotional storm raging inside me. I douse myself in my human friends and ignore my wanshiqi woes.

I make my way down the crowded hall to Mandy's locker.

Her scrunched-up face and twitching fingers warn of impending explosions.

"Did you know the seniors are having a bonfire this weekend?"

I was hoping to avoid it. "We're juniors."

"I'm head of the cheer squad. I have to be there." She uses her this-is-how-things-are tone.

"To cheer on their beer pong game?" Sarcasm slices through my words. "Are you backing out of San Fran?"

Her head tilts, an unbalanced scale tipping toward the importance of her social status over our BFF adventure. "Justin invited me."

He's the quarterback of our football team, and it's his party.

Her brown eyes beseech me to understand. "We've got our whole lives to do San Fran."

She's wrong. We only have this weekend because of my death date.

Before I can reply, Tav stops beside us. "What's going on?"

"San Fran or lame bonfire in town?" I ask.

He doesn't hesitate. "Bonfire."

I do a double take. "What?"

"I don't want to go by myself." He adjusts his messenger bag and tosses his long hair out of his eyes.

"So don't go." It comes out more surly than I meant.

He drops his mercurial gaze to his sneakers. "Mom made me promise to socialize more."

"We can't leave Tav alone." Mandy's voice wraps me in lollipops and cupcakes. I want to barf from the sugar overload.

Frustration ferments in my belly. I feel it bubbling up to my voice box. I'm going to say something awful. And I can't stop myself.

Tav brushes his elbow against my arm. The sudden contact distracts me.

"You should go. I'll deal with the bonfire alone." His words are exactly what I want to hear, but his voice is deadened with dread.

My frustration slips away. I feel myself giving in. Compromising. The two of them will be my downfall. "Fine."

He bumps my arm again. "Fine for real, or fine we'll pay for this later?"

I snort. "For real. As long as Friday Mandy does what I want."

"Sounds fair." A laugh lingers on his lips.

"I never agreed to let you two plan my weekend." Mandy sounds miffed.

I'm not sure if it's because Tav and I came up with the new plan, or if she's still annoyed at me for trying to get out of the party.

I widen my eyes and play on her guilt. "Wouldn't a friend who cancels at the last minute make up for it?"

Tav holds his chin, reminding me of a Taoist sage. "A good friend would."

Mandy looks from me to Tav. "I guess I'm outnumbered." She sounds like she'd rather go down fighting than surrender to us.

A smile tugs at the corners of my mouth.

Tav smiles back at me.

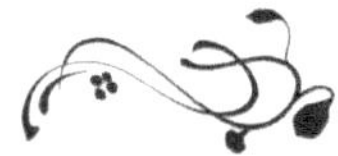

Friday night, getting past the bouncer at the underground party is easy—a little confusion curse and he reads twenty-one on our IDs and Mandy doesn't even notice. The warehouse is so dark I don't have to worry about swapping my contacts. It's like a rave had sex with a circus and birthed this place. There are mini-stages scattered throughout the place. Three barely dressed dancers twirl fire around their heads. I throw my head back and see little people performing tightrope acrobatics ten feet above us.

Mandy's first words to me are "This is AWESOME."

"Something to never tell your grandkids," I shout over the throbbing beats of the music.

She gives me a smile brimming with the future. "I can't wait for college."

"It'll be even better." A bittersweet feeling settles in my chest. I hope it is for her. Maybe I'll find her in my next incarnation. Except she'll have no idea who I am or what I meant to her. My heart tightens and cramps like an overexerted muscle. I rub my chest, but it doesn't help.

We meander through the crowd, and her eyes widen, like a child bewitched by all the lights and colors. "Nothing can top this."

"Cool." The tightness in my heart eases. I focus on what this is—a night to remember.

I make my way to the makeshift bar and order drinks. Mandy sips on a Grasshopper—a mint chocolate concoction—for an hour. I suck down my rum and Coke. We'll cab home.

We spend most of the night dancing in the corner. Backs to the wall to prevent the sneak attacks where guys hump you from behind. It works well until a fight breaks out.

I don't need any wanshiqi abilities to tell me this is bad. My human senses scream, *get out.* The crowd rears and bucks. People go down, dominoing toward the fire dancers. It's going to be an inferno in ten minutes.

Mandy's eyes are closed, and she's moving to the music. I grab her arm, hoping to make it to the nearest exit before the crowd explodes. "Mandy, we have to get out of here."

She blinks and looks around like she forgot where she was. "What's wrong?"

A beer bottle smashes into the wall above her head. She stares at the beer dripping down the wall, and fear trickles over her face.

"That's what's wrong. Stay close. I'll get us out." The exits are too far away. Too close to the fire dancers and the flames they can't control.

People scream and shout. The music cuts out.

I'm going to have to curse my way through the bedlam. A rescue curse requires light emotions. I reach inside and grab my concern for Mandy. My affection for her. I think of all the time we've spent together.

A lukewarm droplet touches my qi. It's not enough. I need more love. I concentrate on my feelings for Grams. How many centuries I've loved her and believed in her. A gentle warmth spreads through my qi. I close my eyes and picture Mandy and I becoming transparent and slipping through the wall itself. We are ghostlike in our escape.

Four minutes later, we're solid again and on the street three blocks from the party. Ten minutes later, we are in a diner perusing the menus when the fire trucks wail by us.

Mandy's bewildered expression tells me she'll take any explanation I can spin.

"Too many drinks, huh?" I ask.

"I just had one."

She's right, but I lie. "One an hour for four hours. Let's get some food in you."

Confusion swirls across her face. "It didn't feel like I had that many."

That escape curse should leave her disoriented. "I bet the past half hour is a blur."

"Sort of."

"That's the liquor."

She leans in and drops her voice low. "How…how did we get out of the club?"

"We were near an emergency exit." I don't mention that I created it.

Her expression shifts as she absorbs my lie. Then she nods like she's accepted it. "Wow, your eyes look so blue."

"It's the lighting." Good curses always sap my energy. I slip away to the ladies' room to put in new contacts and hide the signs of my cursing.

CHAPTER TWENTY

THE NEXT MORNING, SUNLIGHT sneaks through Mandy's blinds and tugs me from my dreams. I can barely roll over in her bed to check the clock. Every muscle aches and burns. The shortbread mouth and throbbing brain are part of my cursing hangover.

One minor curse got us into the underground party, but I needed an unexpectedly larger one to get us out safely.

I turn back and face Mandy. She is snuggling her teddy bear with her hand tucked under her chin. In a deep sleep, she looks like a little girl after a big celebration. I hope she treasures our crazy night for years from now. It's silly that it matters to me because in the blink of a wanshiqi existence, Mandy will be gone. It's on me to remember her for eternity.

I study her face, memorizing the tiniest details: her long, dark eyelashes with blonde tips, a perky little nose with a smattering of freckles, the silver scar that is hidden in the hairline near her left temple. I should be used to being the one who will carry a memory forever, but today it stabs me in the gut.

Only tonggan are there to share the memories of eternity. Loneliness licks my heart. Fear clings to my qi. I shiver and burrow deeper into her puffy, pink covers.

Mandy's eyes open. "Are you watching me sleep?"

"Maybe."

"You're so weird."

"I didn't take pictures. You're so welcome."

She shakes her head at me and rubs the sleep from her eyes. "Last night was crazy."

"Fun crazy?"

"Great escape crazy. I need today to recover."

"What about cheer practice?"

She puts the pillow over her head. "Can you call me in sick?"

"Yeah." Time with Mandy is short. I'll snatch it any way I can.

Mandy and I walk up the path to the front door of Tav's gingerbread cottage. Her heels clack on the paving stones. Mandy fidgets with her bracelets. It's the first time she's seen Bess since finding out the cancer's back.

"Just be normal." I aim for soothing, but my voice veers toward irked.

"Normal." Her tiny smile is quicker than a hummingbird in search of nectar. There and gone before we reached the front porch. "Do you think.... What if Bess.... I mean..."

I stop and turn to face her. "You've got this." My words are firm because she needs them to be.

Unease flickers in her eyes.

"I'm right here." I take her hand.

She holds on tight. "Okay."

We step on to the porch, and I ring the bell.

When the door opens, Bess stands there in yoga pants and a cotton, long-sleeved shirt with a turquoise silk scarf wrapped around her head.

"Mandy." Bess's tone wraps a ribbon around her name and ties a bow. "It's been too long."

Mandy smiles like she's repenting for a dozen sins. "It's great to see you again."

"We've missed you." Bess extends her arms for a hug.

Mandy drops my hand and leaps into Bess's arms, nearly strangling Bess with a hug.

Mandy has to feel how thin Bess is, but she doesn't say anything. When she lets go of Bess, concern crosses Mandy's face, but she quickly summons up her usual smile.

I look over Bess's shoulder and into the hall. "Is Tav ready?"

Bess's posture shifts from benevolent nurturer to protective mama. "Are you driving tonight?"

"Yes." I shake the keys in my hand.

"No drinking." She uses her parental voice.

"I never drink when I'm driving." I don't like slaughtering innocents unless I have no other choice.

Bess's face is bathed in skepticism.

"She'll be stone cold sober the whole night," Mandy swears.

"I'm counting on it." Bess's voice promises retribution if I'm not.

I keep eye contact long enough to convey that I'm telling the truth. "Tav is safe with me."

He comes up behind his mom and catches the end of my sentence. "Am I?" He drops a peck on his mom's cheek and squeezes past her.

We start down the porch stairs.

"If anything changes, and you need a ride, call me." Bess's words and her worry trail us to the car.

"I promise." Tav shouts, "Shotgun."

From the back seat, Mandy gives me directions to Justin's house in northern Del Mar. It's exclusive—not one of the Ocean Beach fire pits that is routinely patrolled by beach police. We park a few streets over per Mandy's instructions.

On the walk to the house, Mandy gives us the rundown on the party. She acts like Tav and I should be grateful to be invited. All this social hierarchy really matters to her. She doesn't realize how little most of our classmates will matter over the course of her life.

I can't help rolling my eyes when she's not looking. Tav smirks at me.

Mandy gets us buzzed through a wrought-iron gate and leads us along a trellis-covered slate walkway to the backyard. It's a semi-secluded stretch of beach, wedged between cliffs of rock that jut out into the ocean. Unreachable at high tide.

Coolers are situated every ten feet along the beach. I peer inside the first one and find soda and beer—two dozen brands with labels in Korean, Japanese, and Spanish. There's a huge punch bowl on the patio table. It's filled with purple party punch, which usually includes an assortment of hard liquors mixed with a variety of fruit juices. I grab an Orange Miranda soda. Mandy eyes the party punch.

"Pace yourself. Remember last night?" I say.

"I'm fine." She bristles like an angry porcupine. Her gaze shifts from me to Tav. Her expression tightens. She looks away. "Oh, there's Justin. I better go say hi. I'm sure you two will be fine together."

Tav grabs a Hoegaarden beer. When she's out of hearing range, he asks, "She used the bad *fine*, didn't she?"

"Definitely."

Mandy leans toward Justin to pour a cup of party punch. Her blonde locks skim over her bare shoulder. He's the perfect alpha male—all muscle and arrogance with a dash of intelligence.

"We'll make sure she only has a couple glasses." I'm not sure why she's acting like this, but it looks like tonight I'm the good BFF.

He looks at the wall of rocks. "Bet we could catch a fantastic sunset from up there."

"Probably." I glance back at Mandy. She touches Justin's arm for the third time and closes the space between them. "But we should stay down here with Mandy."

"Raincheck?" His easy smile makes my heart double-dutch.

"Raincheck." I take off my sandals and move farther along the beach. "Mandy feels awful about how things ended between you two."

"It was too much for her to handle." His words don't mask the disappointment in his tone.

"It was too much for any kid to take on." He's stronger than most humans I've known.

He lets his hair fall over his eyes, and his voice drops to sandstorm quiet. "She's my mom. She'd have done it for me."

The way he loves his mom is how I love my parents: unconditionally. The way Bess loves him—I want that so badly for myself. I stare out at the waves breaking on the beach. "Can you forgive Mandy?"

"I already did. She kept acting weird so I left her alone." He glances at me. "She's been different lately. Your influence?" His gaze is intense, focusing solely on me.

"I just told her that she had to live in the now and not in the what was."

"Wise words."

"She wants to be in your life."

He looks back at the patio where Mandy is dancing with Justin and his friends and her cheerbabies.

"I don't fit in with her crowd." He shoves a hand in his pocket and sips his beer.

"Neither do I. We just carve out a space for us to be friends. You can do the same."

The sun weakens in the sky. The sand isn't as warm as when we arrived, but it still feels good under my bare feet. It lures me away from the party. Away from the people I'll never be like.

I head toward the ocean, and Tav follows me. Just for tonight, I wish I didn't know everything I know. I wish I wasn't a wanshiqi. I wish I was a normal teenage girl.

Silence lingers between us. It's not awkward at all, and that surprises me. "You can go dance, if you want."

"Can I?" His voice carries a hint of laughter.

"I'm not big into parties. It's more Mandy's thing."

"My mom made me come here, remember?" He brushes his arm against mine.

I can't help smiling. "I guess it's best we stick together."

"I'm not complaining."

"Neither am I."

"So are you going to tell me what happened with Prince Charming?" His voice is hesitant, like he hates interrupting this moment.

"Not tonight." Tonight, I want to feel like I'm a normal girl.

Tav and I sit down in the sand and watch the sunset. Oranges and yellows fade to reds. Pinks and purples shadow them. Beckoning the sun to sleep. Soon, all that's left is the light of the bonfires behind us flickering in the distance.

Darkness seeps around us. Separating us from everyone else. I run my fingers through the cool sand. He digs a hole with his bare heels.

The music and voices of the party fade away. It's just Tav and me on that beach. He smells like limes and cedar.

"What are you thinking?"

He slowly fills in the hole he dug. Just when I think he won't respond, he says, "Mom keeps insisting that I have a life outside of her. It's like she knows something I don't." He tries to keep his emotions from hijacking his expression, but fear and frustration slip into his voice.

"She just wants you to be a teenager."

"That's impossible."

"For a few hours, you can." We can. I touch his arm. His skin is unbearably soft. I can't help caressing it.

The breeze tugs a strand of my hair free and presses it to my cheek. He tucks it back behind my ear. His fingers are so warm. I sway toward him.

He moves closer. I smell the sweet beer on his breath.

"Tav?" My heart thuds in my ears.

"Yeah?"

I put my hand on his chest. His heart hammers away beneath his skin, beating in rhythm with my own. "I don't think this is a good idea."

"Neither do I." He closes the distance between us.

CHAPTER TWENTY-ONE

Tav's lips are softer than I expected. Softer than the sand beneath us. He tastes of candy canes. I wrap my arm around his neck and pull him closer. For a moment, I forget about the wanshiqi, forget about betrayals, forget about holding back with a human.

Forget that I'm not a teenage girl.

All I can think about are his lips on mine. I lean back into the sand and bring him with me. The darkness cradles us. I can barely hear the voices and music from the party over the roar of the ocean and the squeal of my heart.

"Get your hands off her." Hunter yanks Tav away from me, shoves him back into the sand, towers over him.

There's a rip current of emotions pulling at Hunter's features. Shock wrinkles his forehead, anger clenches his jaw, and hurt flames in his eyes. I know what this expression means. If he hits Tav, it will be a deathblow.

I scramble to my feet and leap in front of Tav. "Hunter, don't! You'll kill him!"

Now his face looks more furious than hurt. "Get out of my way."

"No! It's not Tav's fault."

"It's both your faults." Hunter's voice slices to the truth.

Hunter shoves me to the side. I try to block him, but stumble over something. I catch a glimpse of it as I fall back—Tav's beer can. I expect to land in the sand, but someone catches me and pulls me close.

"I've got you." Tav's breath warms my ear.

I tremble, not with fear, but something far worse. Desire.

"Don't. Touch. Her." Hunter's voice is so menacing, the sky rumbles.

A kiss might not mean much to humans, but to Hunter, it's an absolute betrayal of thousands of years of loving me. A betrayal of our tonggan bond.

I right myself and step closer to Hunter. "I'm sorry. I was upset. I made a mistake."

"A mistake?" Hunter asks in his do-I-look-like-a-dumbass voice. "I saw what your hands and lips were doing."

"We had a moment. A moment I shouldn't have let happen. Tav's a nice guy."

"That's such a bullshit thing to say. Nice guys don't kiss someone else's girlfriend."

"Nice guys don't upset their girlfriends," Tav murmur-mutters.

While we were talking, clouds gathered near the cliffs. Lightning echoes from cloud to cloud, drenching the sky in light, and casting shadows across Hunter's face.

Hunter is a ball of energy ready to explode. I have to protect the only person he might hurt. I quick-glance at Tav. "Stay out of this. Please, give us a minute."

Tav moves two feet back, but he doesn't leave.

Thunder screams above us. Hunter takes two steps toward Tav.

The words rush out of my mouth. "Tav, go back to the party."

"Are you sure you're okay?" Tav asks.

"I'm fine here with Hunter."

Tav heads toward the group at the bonfire.

I press my hands to Hunter's chest. His muscles are hard and unyielding, just like his expression. "Please, let's talk."

A wildfire of emotion burns in Hunter's eyes. "Now you want to talk?"

"I shouldn't have avoided you the past few days." My voice drops to a cemetery softness—a guilty repentance. "It was a lot to understand about your family and the lishihui."

"This is how you understand?" He gestures at Tav in the distance. "By kissing him?"

"Forget about him. This is about you and me."

"Then why do you keep protecting him?" Hunter's tone is devastatingly calm, but lightning cuts across the sky and stabs the ocean.

"I can handle your anger. I deserve your anger. I'm the one who betrayed you. Us. Tav's just a human kid that got caught in the middle. He doesn't deserve to die."

"You care about him."

"No, I mean, it's…"

"Wanshiqi never care for humans. It's not who we are." Doubt scurries across his face. "Or at least who we are supposed to be."

"I've never been a good wanshiqi."

"You risked our eternal tonggan relationship for a human. And you only have two weeks left here, Kali. Two weeks. It doesn't make sense."

"I don't make sense. I'm selfish and immature, just like the fayuan said. I haven't learned much in nineteen centuries." I hurt Hunter. I will hurt Tav. All I bring is hurt. My parents were right. I am Kali the Destroyer.

"Was it worth it?" Hunter stands there, waiting for my answer.

Sorrow blurs my vision and truth burns my tongue. "No."

When I think about what I've done to him, I want to drop to my knees and apologize until my throat is raw, but there's too much anger and hurt in his posture.

"And you still did it." His voice is hoarse.

"We need to talk. Really talk. About everything."

"I can't talk to you now." The hurt in Hunter's eyes may take centuries to undo.

"Tomorrow?"

"I won't be here."

The rumble of thunder subsides, and the realization hits me: If I lose Hunter, I lose everything. "Please." I reach for him, but he sidesteps my touch. "Don't do this to us."

"You did this to us." The venom in his voice makes my hands tremble. "I need some time alone." His voice is so distant, it reminds me of when universes separated us.

"How much?"

He turns and walks away from me. Each step takes him farther from me. Shadows swallow him. The tightness in my stomach reaches up and wraps around my throat, making it impossible to speak.

I want to run after him. Beg him to stay. But that is not how wanshiqi handle these things.

CHAPTER TWENTY-TWO

THE NEXT MORNING BRINGS two killer headaches. Mine is from thinking all night; Mandy's is from drinking too much party punch. Aleve won't help mine, so I drop two in her outstretched palm. She downs them with a glass of water and slides onto a stool at the island in her kitchen.

"At least your parents don't get back until tonight."

"Shhh." She rests her elbows on the cement countertop and drops her head in her hands. "You don't have to yell. And turn the lights off."

The sound of my bare feet against the tile floor echoes through the kitchen. She groans and falls forward, presses her face against the cement counter.

I flick the lights off. "Better?"

"Tiptoe, please."

I make my way back to the counter and whisper, "Okay now?"

She raises her head. "Less hellish."

I put a plate of toast in front of her. She smears a bit of jam and nibbles on it. I give her a cup of coffee and wait. It takes two slices of toast and a cup and a half of coffee to make her almost human again.

Her first words are, "I can't believe you kissed Tav."

"Me neither." I crack open a few eggs and drop their contents into a frying pan. They sizzle in the butter.

"Hunter saw everything?" Her voice is tentative like she's afraid her words will hurt.

They do. "And I have no idea how he will forgive me."

"He loves you." She says love like it's a cure-all.

I'm not sure his love is enough to overcome what I've done. I grab a spatula and start mixing up the eggs.

"Why did you do it?"

"It was just a moment." One moment over 2,300 years. "A mistake." Wanshiqi make mistakes, especially before qifa. But this is a colossal mistake.

"Come on, Kali."

"I didn't mean to. Tav's just a friend."

"Umhm." She tilts her chin down and to the side and looks at me with coy eyes. "So when are you planning to stick your tongue down my throat?"

"Mandy!" I drop the spatula, and it clatters on the counter.

"You get that you are bullshitting both of us, right?"

"I get that Tav and I can never be." That he's human and I'm wanshiqi. Our lives were never meant to intertwine. I screwed up. More than anyone can possibly understand. "I just wanted to escape everything for a moment."

"I knew he wanted you." She sounds like she didn't want to be right.

"It was the sunset and the beach and the sand." I close my eyes at the clichés.

"You underestimate your power over boys."

"I only want to have power over one boy—Hunter." My voice frays with frustration.

Her expression is remote, like she's gone to survey the mess I've made. "Tav's got that emo boy thing. I can see the attraction. You're so goth inside. Hunter's so not. I never understood how that worked."

I slam the spatula on the counter. "So you think we don't work?"

She puts her hands up to ward me off. "I'm just saying you are the opposites-attract couple."

"I guess we aren't Justin and you." My tone slides into snide.

She turns pinker than the peonies in her mother's garden. "Well maybe if you weren't monopolizing all the guys, I wouldn't have to turn to Justin."

"All the guys? I've had one boyfriend since middle school." My mind catches up to my mouth. "Wait, are you... No. You can't be interested in Hunter?"

Mandy sprays coffee at me. "Hunter? No way."

"Tav?"

She mops up her coffee spritz. "It's been nice hanging out with him again."

"You like Tav?" How did I not put this together? Maybe I didn't want to see it.

"It's not that crazy." Insecurity stalks each syllable.

"For the head cheerleader?" The same girl who was afraid to be seen walking into a party with him.

"He's a good guy." She huddles around her coffee cup. "It doesn't matter. He kissed you last night."

Thoughts tumble through my head, but the words that could make this okay aren't there.

Mandy sniffs the air. "Is something burning?"

"The eggs!" I grab the spatula and flip them over. They're charred on the bottom. I toss them in the garbage.

I crack four more eggs and start over. This time I'll be more careful. "It was a mistake. Tav knows that," I tell the pan.

"But he wants you." There's something I've never heard before in Mandy's voice—jealousy.

"I can't be with him." It's impossible to explain all the reasons why, so I tell her the one that will make her feel better. "I'm the kind of girl Tav kisses once. You're the kind of girl he kisses forever." The words are fiery red peppers dancing across my tongue. Saying them stings. Afterward, it burns more.

Her eyes are like hot fudge topping, all sweet and soft. "You're just saying that."

"I never just say anything."

"I don't want your leftovers."

"I never had Tav." I can't. "Why didn't you tell me you liked him?"

"After what I did, I never thought it was possible." Her voice trembles like a blade of grass in a windstorm.

"You need to forgive yourself. Bess and he did a long time ago. Give him a month, and he'll have forgotten all about me. He'll be yours by the end of the summer."

I imagine them walking along the beach. Mandy splashing him. Tav tossing her in the water. His lips brushing hers. The way they did mine.

I'll be gone.

A memory to them.

The pain in my heart burns my eyes. My vision blurs. I blink and the oven and pan are back in focus. Then they blur again. I wipe my face on my shirt, but the tears keep coming. Faster and faster.

Mandy leaps up and throws her arms around me. "I'm sorry. It will be okay."

I hold on to her. And let myself cry for everything I've lost and will lose.

Hunter banishes me, not with a curse, but with his actions. In the car, I try his cell and get his voicemail. I text him from his lobby, but there's no reply. I bang on his door; he doesn't answer.

I let myself into his apartment. He's nowhere to be found. No note. No sign of where he went or when he'll be back. If he'll be back.

How did this happen to me? I'm better than this. I'm better than human. I can't be this person. I can't be a person.

In his living room, I drop on to the couch and stare at the beautiful ocean view, but it feels empty, devoid of Hunter. I wander back to his bedroom. The room smells faintly of him. I need more. I climb up on his bed and smell his pillow. Oceans and stars. Universes away from me right now. I curl up in his sheets, wrapping them around me. I close my eyes and pretend it's Hunter holding me.

CHAPTER TWENTY-THREE

H OME IS WHERE WHAT remains of my heart gets torn out. Mom meets me at the door. Her refined slacks and blouse can't disguise her mood. Her hair is stretched back in a ponytail. Her eyes burn like a hundred fire pits.

"Where have you been?" She reaches for my chin. "Have you been cursing again?"

I jerk my face away and slip past her. I steal into the main round room. I want to get up the stairs and into my room.

"Don't ignore me." She grabs my arm and shoves me into a chair. The spring-green and cream-colored room feels so much bigger when she towers over me.

"Where are Grams and Gramps?" I look for them, but they aren't there. Oh Goddess, no. I'm alone with her.

"You are the worst wanshiqi. I can't believe I am stuck here because of you." Her venomous words sink into my skin.

I've spent centuries excusing her behavior, swearing it was a side effect of Octavius tampering with her memories. I kept telling myself it wasn't her; it was him. I've prolonged my punishment and kept us human, hoping to bring back that feeling of family that humans have. I've tried so hard to fix what was broken in her in Pompeii. But in this moment, I can't help feeling that deep down, this is how my mother really feels about me. That thought is a serrated blade jabbed through my stomach. Pain rushes over me and steals my breath. For a moment, I can't speak.

She watches me like one of her human toys. I won't let her see how much this hurts. How much it has always hurt. Sarcasm spews out. "Don't hold back on my account, Mom."

In her eyes, snakes writhe, coil, strike.

Great. Probably another war erupting in Pakistan.

Her hands are fists at her sides. She would love to knock some sense into me, but instead she picks up a knickknack and throws it at the wall. It shatters, and pieces scatter across the floor. "Why can't you be a good daughter?"

Words collide in the back of my throat like a bad pileup on the Five. Not one of them survives.

"You're just like your father." Her viciousness splatters against my chest and summons my cruelty.

"If I were, I wouldn't be here."

She stares at me without seeing me. It's the way she looks at Dad. Right now, I'm just a piece of him that she can torment. A piece that can't escape her.

He's done something. Something that she is taking out on me. It's wrong. But there's nothing I can do. She has to have her say. Tear me apart to make herself feel better.

Her laugh slashes through the air, sending shockwaves in every direction. "You smile like him, you know."

"What did Dad do?" My tone is etched with exhaustion. Hunter's absence has left me unable to deal with her drama.

"This isn't about your father." She paces the round room, moving past the couch, by the fireplace, behind me, and circling around again.

"It's always about Dad." The biggest emotions wanshiqi experience are related to our tonggan in some way. Something familiar flickers in the depths of her eyes. I saw it last night in Hunter's eyes. Pain and jealousy. "He has a girlfriend, doesn't he?"

She drops onto the couch across from me. "He did."

"What did you do?"

"She's gone."

"Permanently?"

"She's still alive. Though I may have twisted up her heartstrings." Her frown dissolves into a radiant smile. It scares me how fast her emotions can shift. "But oh how she hates him now."

I've never understood my parents' twisted tonggan bond. "Mom …"

"He knows better."

"You're divorced in this life."

"Human laws don't apply to us," she scoffs.

"Is Dad okay?"

"It's forbidden to harm a tonggan."

According to falu, anyways, but that didn't stop Octavius. I'm no longer certain it would stop her.

I don't know what happened to the mother I once knew. The mother she was before Pompeii. All that's left is this woman, and I'm terrified that one day I could become like her.

I have to be the mediator, holding out the burning olive branch and letting Dad cut off my hand. I knock on the front door of his beach house. No one answers. I don't know why I'm at his house. It's not like he wants me here. It's not like he wants me anywhere.

I spy his car in the garage. He could be out back. I have a key. I fumble through my purse. It's been ages since I used it, but I never took it off my key chain.

I unlock the door and step into the foyer. There's a hint of him in the air—the oak and cinnamon scent that is intrinsically him. The open floor plan lets me see into the living room, through the sliding glass doors, all the way out to the Pacific. Dad's on the balcony, probably pretending Mom didn't get to him. My father is the greatest actor. He pretends everything away.

In the living room, pictures of me and him and our sandcastles line the wall. He added the one from a few weeks ago. I don't understand why we have to be this way. We have all this time together, and we squander it.

I cross the living room, slide the door open, and step out into sunlight. Dad has his back to me. He leans over the wooden railing, sipping his drink, and staring out at the ocean.

"She send you to check on me?" The flatness in his voice worries me.

"I decided to stop by."

"How badly did she lay into you this time?"

I put my purse on the table. "Same as always."

He turns toward me. His eyes are scorched with regret. "Kalifornia, please let this end."

"I'm sorry." I don't know what to do. I've never seen him this upset. I take one, two, three steps toward him. His arms open, and I walk into them, trying to remind him that I'm here. I know what it's like to survive one of Mom's attacks.

"We can't go on like this anymore," he says in a quiet voice that should be reserved for dead things.

I've hurt him more than I realized. All I wanted was a chance to fix what Pompeii did to them. What Octavius did to us.

"We need to go back. It's time." He pats my back.

My throat is brimming with regret. I nod, pretending to agree, but I'm not ready to let my family go. Not yet.

"What happened in Pompeii?" he asks.

I freeze. He's always been so certain of his memories. He never asked me why I did it. I've tried to tell him a few times, but his mind shuts down, and the seizures come for him. I can't bear to see my dad in that kind of pain, so I stopped trying to tell him.

"I need to know."

"I can't." I won't hurt him like that again.

"If we free Octavius, everything will be better."

He has no idea what he is asking.

He cups my face with his hands. His pale-blue eyes bore into mine. "Sweetie, we can fix this."

Something is wrong. My father rarely hugs me. He never asks me about Pompeii or calls me sweetie in any of my lifetimes. He's being kind. He's being thoughtful. He's reaching out to me.

And underneath his cologne, something is missing. There's no cinnamon and oak. Instead, I catch a whiff of licorice.

My pulse speeds up like my blood recognizes him before I do. I step back. "You're not fooling anyone, Grandfather." My father's father has taken over Dad's body.

"Are you all right? Sit down, sweetie." My father's expression is the perfect blend of concern and hurt. But it's not him. It's Grandfather.

"Dad never calls me sweetie." My blood is absolutely certain. It pounds against my temples and pulsates into my fingertips.

"Clever Kali. I forgot how cold your father is." Grandfather gives me a sly smile.

"You took over his body." Grandfather can shift his qi into any form at any time, even if that form is already inhabited by another qi or soul. I don't know what that means for Dad. Fear pinches my heart. "Did you hurt him?"

"Almost two millennia, and that's your first question." He shakes his head in dismay.

The words rush out. "Is he okay?"

"Your father is strong. He'll survive this."

"Survive?" An immortal surviving doesn't make me feel better. Whatever he's doing to Dad, I want it to stop. Now. "Let him go. You can take me instead."

The man who looks like my father chuckles. "You never grasped the big picture."

Suddenly Mom's anger at Dad's new relationship makes sense. "You stirred Mom up."

"Of course." His eyes twinkle like silver starlight for a second. Then they are back to Dad's icy blue.

Grandfather is dangerous—ancient and powerful. He abandoned Dad and me to preserve his standing among the zhangzhe. He has no sense of family. Power is all he cares about. If he's here, he wants something from me. I don't know what it is, but he'll do anything to get it.

I've got to stay calm. Find a way out of here. I have to warn Grams and Gramps that he's here. They'll know what to do. My purse is too far away. It's a one-story drop to the beach.

His lips curve into a bowl, perfect for cherries. "Your father won't remember me being here in his body. The entire time will be a blur."

"He's going to be furious when he finds out." I edge away from him along the railing.

"He made a mess of things. I'm here to help clean it up. It's what any good father would do for his son." His smile makes me shiver despite the sun above and the seventy-degree weather.

Grandfather's never been a good father. "You didn't help with Mom."

"I got her to realize how much she still wants him, didn't I?" He arches a manicured brow.

I rest both my hands on the banister. If I go over the side of the balcony, I might be able to make a run for it. But I need to know what Grandfather is up to. Why he suddenly reappeared in our lives after two millennia.

I press my palms against the banister to ground me and try to make my voice sound stable. "Why are you here?"

"Because you need me." His voice is confident. It slides over my skin, and I shudder in fear.

My father's family is the forerunner to mercenaries. There is always a reason for everything they do.

My face must betray my thoughts because he asks, "Have you no understanding of wanshiqi ways? I thought your other grandparents would educate you."

"Don't talk about them. Ever."

He tilts his head. "And if I do, what can you do? Curse me?" He chuckles again, like I'm a ladybug taking on a hornet's nest.

"Maybe."

"With those eyes? Oh my dear, you wouldn't survive it. Then again, maybe that's always been your plan." His gaze slides over my face, appraising me. "I've watched you over the centuries. Your control has gotten better. How peculiar that you haven't been able to reach seventeen."

He's baiting me. So why do I feel like I've already been caught?

"I can understand why you'd like to prolong your mother's punishment. Your father, however, has so much left to do."

"And I'm holding him back?"

"Yes."

"Why are you here?" I hate the quiver in my voice.

My grandfather can manipulate anyone. He's had a hundred millennia of experience. My mouth goes drier than the sand dunes below us. I see the answer in his eyes, before he says the words.

He's here for me.

CHAPTER TWENTY-FOUR

THE BLOOD RUSHES IN my ears, drowning out Grandfather's words. As he moves closer to me on the balcony, something inside me screams, *don't let him get you.* Fear clings to my qi. I don't have time to summon my lighter emotions to save me.

I have to escape him.

I suck as much power as I can from my human body. Kuai, kuai, kuai. A speed curse races off my tongue. Fast enough to elude Grandfather's grasp and leap over the railing, but so weak it slams me into the sand on the beach below.

My body throbs, but I can't stay here. I push onto my hands and knees. My head spins and my neck stiffens. I can barely stand. The curse pulled too much energy from my human body.

Grandfather looks down at me. "Nicely done."

His smile tells me it isn't enough. I'm not strong enough to escape a zhangzhe. A cold sweat breaks out across my skin, making my teeth chatter. My stomach churns like the ocean. Another wave of dizziness crashes over me.

One thought propels me: I have to warn my family.

The beach is miles of sand, leaving me out in the open too long. My car's back on the road. It's my only chance. I stumble under the deck and press my spine against the back of the house. My brain is foam-like. Fuzzy.

When I try to step away from the house, I nearly topple over. I brace against the wall to remain upright, sliding along it toward the path that leads to the road. Each movement makes the ground topsy-turvy.

"Kali, Kali, Kali. You'll never get away now." The boards creak above my head. Grandfather knows exactly where I am.

"That's enough, Xia." Gramps's deep voice rumbles above me on the balcony.

"I knew you'd show up, Joe." Grandfather sounds annoyed by the intrusion.

Grams comes around the side of the house toward me. "He's not here alone."

"Yuan." Xia says Grams's name like it's a virus.

"What are you doing here?" Gramps moves across the deck above me, creating flickering shadows in the sand.

"Fixing the mess your granddaughter made." Grandfather makes it sound like he's cleaning up a juice spill, not commandeering my father's body.

Grams wraps her arms around me. I feel her strength as mine dissipates. She's all that is keeping me upright.

"I've got her," she shouts up to Gramps.

Grams lowers me to the sand. She smooths my hair out of my face. Her palm is so cool against my forehead. She peers into my eyes. "Kali, you cursed."

"I had to." My voice is barely there.

"She's burning up. We need to get her home." A note of fear resonates in her words. I'm sicker than I thought.

"I'm not done with her," Xia snarls.

"Yes, you are." Gramps's voice visits a thousand plagues upon Xia.

I can't see what's happening on the deck above me. Shadows flicker in the sand. I can only see bits of movement through the slats in the deck. I hear scuffling and the cry of an injured bird. Then silence.

I collapse in Grams's arms.

I wake up in Grams's study with its gilded molding, gold leafing, and ivory walls. A delicate chandelier and wall sconces radiate light down on me. A couple layers of blankets cover me on the couch, but I'm still shivering like I'm buried in snow at the North Pole.

Grams and Gramps speak in hushed voices. I catch snippets of it. Temp of 102. Something about the brown in my eyes. Grams can still heal me because I'm sick, but not death sick.

"Let me take the fever away." Her voice is insistent beside me. "Please."

As soon as she has my consent, Grams presses her hand to my forehead and whispers healing words over me. She pauses and frowns.

"What is it?" Gramps stands beside her. His expression is shadowed and difficult to decipher.

"Viral meningitis." Her words are hushed by the severity of my illness.

"You shouldn't have cursed." Lines of worry crackle across his forehead. He rubs at them.

"I had to...eyes...take me." The words aren't forming right. What I meant to say was if Grandfather got a hold of me, he would sacrifice me. I saw it in his eyes.

"I'm going to need some herbs." Grams rushes to her sunshine room.

I fight to stay awake, but my body betrays me, and I slip into sleep again. When I wake up, the room is hazy. I tell my eyes to focus, but they refuse to listen. I try to sit up, but I can't.

Gramps lifts me up.

Grams presses an elixir to my lips. "Drink this."

It smells of sappy pine and rotten salmon. I shrink back, but Gramps holds me in place.

"You have to drink the whole thing in one shot." There's enough urgency in her tone to get me to toss it back.

It's awful. I gag and cough, but I keep it down. Gramps lays me back on the couch. Grams tells me to rest. I'm not sure how long I sleep. I don't dream. I disappear. When I wake up, my head's clear again. The room's back in focus.

Grams and Gramps help me sit up. Grams stays close to me on the couch like she knows I still need her. "Feeling better?"

I lean into her and smell her lilac scent. "Yes, thanks."

"Good."

Gramps lowers himself onto a cream-colored Louis XV chair. His fingers curl around the armrests. "We need to talk." He uses that tone that tells me the family is in trouble.

I rub my lips together. "Is it safe here?" I don't smell any other wanshiqi, but I want to be sure.

"It's just the three of us here." The certainty in his voice is enough for me.

"Is Dad okay?"

Gramps nods.

Relief trickles over me. "How did you beat Grandfather?"

They exchange a look. The kind where their eyes communicate everything in a way that only they can understand.

Grams edges closer to me as if her proximity can blunt the blow of her words. "Hunter and a few of our allies helped take down Xia."

Hunter was ten feet away from me and never said a word. Something inside me breaks. Shards embed in my gut. I can't stop them from impacting my voice. "He didn't stay to see if I was okay?"

"He helped get Xia to leave your father's body." Gramps gives me his where-are-your-priorities face.

I should be grateful Hunter helped after what I did. I recede into Grams's arms.

"He's watched Xia for a while." Gramps's face is locked in neutral, not giving anything away. Even his eyes are guarded. I can't read anything there.

"How long has Xia been here?" It creeps me out to think he could have been Dad before.

"He's been lurking around your father for months. Now we know why—he wanted to impersonate him." Gramps gives me the truth.

It sets off a low-pitched ringing in my ears. "How long has Hunter been helping you?"

"He'd do anything to protect you." Grams's voice reminds me of warm tea and honey.

Guilt comes quicker than anything else. After everything Hunter has done for me, I doubted and blamed him. And I'm the one who betrayed him. What kind of tonggan am I?

"We need to talk about Xia." Gramps's voice drops to a deathbed confession quiet.

I sit up and grip the blanket. I tell them what he said to me and end with, "I think he wants me to turn seventeen and free Octavius."

Grams laces her fingers through mine. Somehow, she knows I need an anchor.

"Octavius has been imprisoned for almost 2000 years. Why is everyone suddenly concerned about him?" The words explode from my mouth, releasing the frustration and fear inside me.

Another look passes between them.

"They want Octavius free so they can groom him to take over the lishihui." Gramps's expression darkens. It frightens me. "His father wants to step down as head of the lishihui."

"They can't." If Octavius ever got that much power, he would destroy all of us.

Gramps tells me the awful truth. "Anyone who helps Octavius will be rewarded by his father."

And now it makes sense. "Grandfather turned on us. Not just during my trial, but today, and every day in between."

"He was richly rewarded for it." Disgust twists his mouth.

"What does he want now?"

His eyes lock on mine. Millennia of knowledge are in their brown depths. "Power. It's always about power with Xia. Whatever he says he wants, it's part of a bigger plan he's executing."

I hold my head in my hand, trying to contain my thoughts. All these centuries I've spent dying, I was caught up in keeping my family together and never thought about what was going on back in the wanshiqi realm. Now, somehow, I'm at the center of it all. The hub that may unintentionally destroy the spokes.

"I have to talk to Hunter." My throat aches with need.

"He won't be back for a while." Gramps appears so steady and reasonable.

I can't be either right now. I lift my head and look into his eyes. All my desperation and despair spills out. "Please, I need him."

Grams squeezes my shoulder, reminding me that she is here with me. "We'll try to get a message to him."

"And Octavius?" Gramps pushes us back there.

"He is a danger to all of us if he escapes." The steadiness in my voice sends chills racing down my spine.

"Is that why you imprisoned him in Pompeii?" Grams prods at my darkest truth.

Panic seizes my heart. I fight to keep my voice level. "It was an accident."

"Livia wasn't the kind of girl who had accidents." The gentleness in Grams's voice pinches my qi.

"You don't know what I was like. You were gone. Off living your own life." I can't stop the hurt from raking over my words.

"Do you remember Marcus the baker in Pompeii?" Grams asks.

My mind tumbles back to Marcus. His pale-green eyes warmed every time he saw me. He'd chuckle and offer me the best loaf of bread in his shop. He'd sneak me salves for my cuts and burns. He was the only person who showed me kindness. He didn't fall under Octavius's control. He was disemboweled for it.

Emotions clutter my throat. I don't trust myself to speak.

Grams strokes my back. "That was me."

I choke on the word. "How?"

"We suspected Octavius was using his powers on you. Gramps sent me to spy. Hunter's grandfather moved my qi temporarily into Marcus's body and Marcus's soul was stored in a nearby animal. Octavius didn't know it was me. He just knew something wasn't right about Marcus."

"How did you resist Octavius's powers?" He was so strong.

"Zhangzhe are immune to the powers of regular wanshiqi. One of the perks of being ancient."

She was there in Pompeii. Suddenly, centuries of anger erupt inside me. My body is hot, not with fever, but with fury. My voice splinters. "Why didn't you save me?"

"I had to reincarnate after Marcus died. I should have had time to tell Gramps everything before I went to dengzhong and took my next form. He would have stopped it."

"So what happened?" I can't believe they left me to be tortured.

"Gramps was sequestered for months in a special zhangzhe meeting. I couldn't warn him." Bitterness sours her voice. "I passed the message to Xia, but he never told Gramps."

My vision tunnels. I sway. Suddenly, Gramps is in front of me, holding me in place. He won't let me keel over. "Breathe, Kali. Breathe."

I try, but the realization squeezes all the air out of me. Grandfather let Octavius torture me. He could have stopped it. He could have saved me. He didn't. I always knew Dad's family wasn't like Mom's. But up until this moment, I never realized they were monsters.

Memories of what was done to Livia burst through my mind like an out-of-control kaleidoscope. I feel it all over again—the burning flesh, the splitting of my skin, the welts rising up, the sting of bee venom.

I hear an awful, agonizing sound. It's the air scraping against my bronchi.

"Just try to breathe." Grams presses her palm to my chest. She can't heal this kind of injury. It's not my body, but my qi that was damaged. No one can heal that.

Gramps and Grams hold me until I'm able to take one breath, then another, then another.

"You didn't leave me?" I rasp.

"Never." Grams's eyes are dewy with regret.

"Why didn't you tell the truth about Pompeii?"

Gramps rubs his lips, like he doesn't want to tell me, but he will. "We don't think Octavius was acting on his own. We just don't know how far up into the wanshiqi hierarchy this plot went."

I'm not important enough. I'm not on the lishihui. I haven't even gone through qifa. I'm an ant in the wanshiqi realm. "Why me?"

Gramps walks to the window and gazes outside. "You were a pawn in a power struggle."

My tongue is sandpaper. I can't speak without tearing into the roof of my mouth.

All these centuries Octavius remained the monster of my nightmares. But he was the instrument of my torture, never the source of my agony.

My memories yank me back to Pompeii the day after Marcus died. A day Grams tried to prevent from happening. A day Grandfather wanted me to experience.

My mother heats the tar over the open flame in our kitchen. Octavius whispers something in her ear.

My wrists and ankles are bound to the table. My dress is cut open so my entire back is exposed.

"Please don't, Mom," I whisper.

She doesn't hesitate to drizzle the molten tar on my back. It singes. I bite my lip until I taste blood, but the burning continues. Melting each layer of my skin. My screams fill the room. The agony seeps into my qi. Throbs at my core. Every time I pass out, Octavius revives me.

"You can make this stop, Livia." His eyes entreat me.

My mother hums a victorious tune. She's certain that I'm the demon that Octavius warned her about. She doesn't see what she's doing to me. She never did.

"Kali, where did you go?" Grams's voice tugs me back into her study.

The tar is gone, but it still burns.

"Do you know what Mom and Dad did to me for Octavius?" My voice carries centuries of pain.

Grams's eyes tear up.

"We do." Gramps's voice is gravel shredding my skin.

"How long have you known that Octavius is a memory manipulator?" Everything inside me is engulfed in flames, but my voice comes out calm. I barely recognize it.

"We figured it out a few centuries after Pompeii. When we saw your parents' inability to hear the truth about Pompeii." Gramps studies my face.

Grams reaches for me, but I pull away.

There are no words left in me. My reality has shattered so much I'm not sure there is enough glue to put it back together anymore.

Suddenly, nervous laughter fills the room. It's a high-pitched, hysterical laugh, and it's coming from my mouth.

Everything I thought I knew. Everything I based my decision to die upon, it's all wrong.

Nothing is what I thought it was.

Nothing.

CHAPTER
TWENTY-FIVE

L AST NIGHT, MY GRANDPARENTS sliced through the layer cake
of family secrets. Today, I'm still trying to digest the piece
they served me. I am at school because it's the only bit of normal
I have left. While some of my classmates secretly text, I pay
attention in English class, so I don't have to think about Pompeii
or Octavius or Xia or Hunter's empty desk.

The day still goes by too fast.

During the last period, Mandy and I sit around the coffee table
in the student lounge and work on homework. I watch time tick
away on the clock. My muscles tense. When the school bell rings,
everything, everything, everything will come crashing in on me.

Mandy shakes her pen and makes quick circles on her paper. But no ink comes out of it. "Can I borrow a pen?"

"You need to be more prepared."

Her features fold in confusion. "Are we talking about pens?"

"Yes. No. I don't know." I rest my forehead against my palm.

"I can ask someone else." She starts to get up.

I slam my pen down on her notebook. "Just take mine."

"Things will get better with Hunter." Her gentle tone is like a hammock rocking each syllable.

Darkness swirls in my depths. Harsh and raging words fly through my mind. I clench my jaw to stop them from lunging at her. She's not the one who turned my world upside down and shook it until I vomited. It's Grams, Gramps, and Xia.

"Maybe you should text him again?" she suggests.

"I've tried." I grit my teeth. This isn't about Hunter. My entire world imploded last night, but I can't explain my wanshiqi worries to her.

"He just needs some time."

I hate when Mandy tries to be the voice of reason. She's human. She's never the voice of anything except raw emotion. I bite my lip to hold back a curse.

I don't trust myself around her. Around anyone, actually. I shove my stuff into my backpack. "I have to get out of here."

Her eyes widen, and she shrinks away from me. "Did I do something?"

"You're the only person that hasn't." I stomp away before she can ask anything else.

I'm halfway to my sanctuary, the closet, when someone steps in front of me. I bump into his chest.

His shirt muffles my, "What the Hades?" It smells of cedar and lime. Of Tav.

He steadies me. "Sorry."

"Watch where you're going." I squirm until he releases me.

"Having a cranky day?" He tries to tease me, but it doesn't work.

"Get out of my way."

He doesn't move. I step to the side, and he mirrors my movement. I go the other way, and he does the same thing.

"What are you doing?" I grip my backpack straps to stop from shoving him.

"Trying to talk to you."

"Not today." Something primal comes out in my voice.

He steps back. "I'm sorry about the beach. I'm not the enemy."

He got between me and my tonggan. My mind latches on to one thought: It's his fault Hunter's not here. I have to deal with all this wanshiqi drama without my tonggan because of Tav.

The shadows inside me whisper, *we could make him disappear.*

All I have to do is let them take over. A part of me wants to give in. I fight that urge, and the words burst from my lips. "You've ruined my life. Go away."

Hurt flares in his eyes. He turns and leaves.

I would wait forever for Hunter, but I've only got two weeks before my death date. If I keep to my plan. The revelations about Grandfather's manipulations make me doubt my decision. I thought I understood what was at stake. I knew I was making the right decision in my gut. I was staying with my parents in human form until I could fix what Octavius broke inside them in Pompeii. My death was the only way to keep us all together. To fix what Octavius broke in us.

Now I'm not so certain. There are much bigger stakes in the wanshiqi realm. I'm mired in indecision. My mind keeps turning over what I know and trying to figure out what is best. My head aches from thinking. But I don't have enough information to recommit to dying or to alter everything and live through my birthday.

The only thing I'm certain of is if Xia wants me to live and to free Octavius, then those are the two things I should never do. But what if he's playing a game with me, and he really wants me to die and leave Octavius trapped? Then my dying is what he truly wants. The indecision is paralyzing.

I can't believe how much Grams and Gramps kept from me. If I knew what they knew… What would I change? I don't know, but I might have done things differently. I'm not ready to talk to them about it yet. There's too much to deal with all at once. So I compartmentalize my pain and tackle it one thing at a time. It's how I've survived all these centuries—shutting down and dealing with what I can when I can.

For now, I will stick with my original decision—dying in two weeks.

I spend three hours on Hunter's couch, staring out at the beach below and turning to the door every time I hear a noise in the hallway. I've never needed him more than I do right now, but he's not coming back. Not now, anyway.

I don't want to face everything without Hunter. I head to his closet to borrow one of his shirts. Slip into the sleeves. Wrap a little piece of Hunter around me.

Home doesn't feel like much of one, but all I have right now are Grams and Gramps. I'll process their revelations at some point. But not today. I can't. Today is about Hunter.

When I get home, Grams is waiting in the main room, perched on her couch. Sunlight trickles through the skylight warming her auburn hair. Before I can say a word, she looks up like she sensed I was there, closes her book, and puts it on the table.

"Darling, I know you feel hurt and betrayed and angry. You must be doubting everything and everyone right now." Centuries of love fill her voice. Her gaze tells me she will accept any response I give her.

I feel it all. And something I hate more than the lies. "I'm scared."

She gets up and hugs me. "Gramps and I will do everything we can to protect you, and Hunter is on your side." The genuineness of her tone creates a crack in my wall.

"And my parents?" I mumble into her shoulder.

She pulls back and holds on to my shoulders. Her eyes are oceans of uncertainty. "I don't know. Their choices may be a side effect of Octavius tampering with their memories."

Yesterday's revelations were an avalanche encapsulating me. Each one buried me deeper. This is just a snowball. I've been keeping my parents out of the loop since Pompeii. Nothing has changed.

But everything has changed.

"What am I going to do?" The quiver in my voice radiates into my body, and I tremble.

Grams finger-brushes the hair off my forehead. "One thing at a time. Like you've always done. First, you are going to fix things with your tonggan."

"How? He's not even here."

"He will be soon, and you will have to give him a tonggan daoqian." Her voice is so smooth and certain, but worry tightens her mouth.

It's the ultimate apology and requires my taking on all his pain. "What if he doesn't forgive me?"

Grams caresses my cheek. "Trust yourself. Trust him."

CHAPTER TWENTY-SIX

THE NEXT DAY, HUNTER strolls into English class five minutes late. He won't look at me. He ducks out of class before I can talk to him. He skips lunch. He refuses to answer my calls or respond to my texts.

During study hall, I sneak out to hide in his car, but it's already gone. I can't miss this chance to talk to him. I won't. I leap in my car and drive to his apartment.

In his building's elevator, worry catches up to me and wraps me in a bear hug. When the elevator doors spring apart, the long corridor to his apartment stretches before me. Today, it feels longer than the one to dengzhong. Each step brings me closer to knowing if my tonggan can forgive me.

I raise my hand to knock on his door, but my fist freezes in midair. It's a few minutes before I can do it. The knock vibrates through my knuckles. An odd almost pain. Three knocks. Pause. Three knocks. Pause. Three knocks.

I know he's in there.

The door swings open. Hunter lounges around the edge of it.

I look straight into his turquoise eyes, so he can see the regret in mine. "I'm sorry for the banishment curse."

He shifts. Muscles ripple under his gray T-shirt.

"I was desperate, and I needed time to think." I bite my lower lip. I'm doing this all wrong. I'm apologizing chronologically instead of by magnitude. "I'm really sorry about Tav."

He arches an eyebrow.

"May I please come in?" The words rush out on an exhale. What if he says no? My heart stutters, refusing to beat properly until he responds.

He moves aside. No invitation to enter; no request to leave.

I slink past him and make my way into the living room. I don't know what to do, so I drop down on his couch. My heart pounds in my ears. Uncertainty encircles me. My knee bounces up and down. I stare out the wall of windows, waiting to face him.

Hunter slowly shuts the door and pads into the kitchen. I hear the fridge door open. Ice clinks against glass. Liquid trickles over it, making the ice cubes pop. It feels like hours pass before he stands in front of me with a drink in his hand.

"I shouldn't have sided with Tav over you, but he's only human. You could have killed him." I lace my fingers together. A prayer to humans. An act of supplication to him. "I'm sorry."

"You think that's the worst thing you did?" He gives me his Kali-are-you-kidding-me face.

"I never should have kissed him." I bow my head.

"No, you shouldn't have." His voice is cold and deep, like the frigid waters of the Arctic Ocean.

"I know you were there to help Gramps fight Grandfather. You protected me, even after everything I did. Thank you."

He recedes to the window and looks down at the water below. His face is half-turned from me. I want to touch the dark curl on his forehead and wipe away the frustration cluttering the corners of his eyes.

"I've always been here to help." His voice is calm, but clouds form on the horizon.

I lean forward on the leather couch, desperate to close the distance between us. "I know."

"But you doubted me. You betrayed me." The hurt in his voice is ten lashes to my back.

I gasp. The weight of what I've done to him chokes me. "I was stupid and wrong. And selfish and awful. I screwed up." I rub my forehead. I need to give him as much truth as I can. He deserves that. The darkest realization rips through my vocal cords. "I'm damaged, Hunter. Really damaged."

"I thought Grams healed you. You're okay now?" He pushes away from the window, takes a step toward me, and stops.

"I'm not talking about my body. What happened in Pompeii destroyed parts of me. I'm not sure I'll ever be who I was before Octavius." My voice shakes with the knowledge of how much is wrong inside me.

He sits next to me. Stars and oceans—he always smells of them. The heat from his body is more than I can bear. I slide my hands under my thighs to stop myself from touching him. How could I ever compare what I have with Hunter to Tav?

He needs to understand. I stumble over the words. "I wanted to be like Tav. Human. Facing a single existence. I didn't want to be what I am. But it's not a choice. I can run and I can hide and I can pretend. But I will always be wanshiqi. I will always love you."

I close my eyes against the rush of desire. The need is stronger than before. Maybe I'm weaker.

"You missed me." Hunter's words caress my neck.

"Yeah." It comes out softer than a breath.

"Take your contacts out."

I do as he asks.

He looks into my eyes. "You've been busy cursing again."

I nod.

"I could fix that." He sips his drink.

"Today is about you, not me."

He lets the silence envelop us. I stare out the window. The golden sand and blue sea below feel so far removed from us, like a picture of what was lingering on a wall.

I drop to the floor and kneel in front of him. "I was wrong to banish you. I was wrong to kiss a human. I was wrong about so many things."

"Kali," he says my name with such sadness. "You aren't strong enough for a tonggan daoqian."

I smile up at him with all the love in my heart. "I owe you this. This and so much more."

Apprehension scrunches his eyes and thins his lips. "It's too much for you."

"It's my decision." The air flutters in and out of my chest. "You deserve better than I have given you. I failed as your tonggan." My heart beats faster, echoing in my ears, and making my words sound so far away. "I love you. You are my tonggan. Always and eternally."

I look down at his feet. The skin is tanned and smooth. "I'm sorry." I bend to kiss them. My lips graze each foot, siphoning his pain away. "I'm so sorry."

The pain comes faster than I expected. It hits me in the belly, doubling me over. I drop to my hands and knees, trying not to flatten against the floor. He needs to see that I will fight for him, accepting his pain as my own. I will suffer for what I've done to him.

Tears blur my vision. This is nothing—one night of suffering for the centuries of suffering I've caused him.

Fire burns my esophagus. My throat swells. I can't breathe. I hear a mechanical wheezing, like a dying factory. It's me. I have to absorb what is poisoning my tonggan even if it risks poisoning me.

My vision pixelates. The hardwood floor presses against my cheek. Hallucinations come for me. The floor morphs into moss beneath my cheek. Ants, fire ants, march over my skin. Biting. A distant buzzing grows louder and louder. Wasps swarm and sting. I swat at them, but I can't escape. Because none of it is real. All of it is real.

The pain won't stop until it's burned itself out or Hunter forgives me.

A scream tears through my qi. An acute puncturing. Energy trickles out of me like blood after a gunshot wound.

CHAPTER TWENTY-SEVEN

Gentle arms lift me, carry me, hold me. I feel safe, but I refuse to open my eyes just in case this is another hallucination.

"Hunter?" I whisper.

"Shh. You need to rest."

I clutch his T-shirt. "But…"

"I forgive you." His voice warms my qi.

The words slip from my lips like a prayer. "I love you."

"You shouldn't have given me a daoqian," he murmurs in my ear.

This feels so real. I want to believe it is. "I had to make amends."

"I know." He tries to shift me onto something soft.

It feels like his bed, but I can't bear the absence of him. I cling to him until the fabric of his T-shirt rips.

His voice shakes with laughter. "Kali, you have to let go."

"No."

"I'll stay with you."

"I'm afraid I'll open my eyes, and this will be another hallucination."

His lips are warm and welcoming, promising this is real. "Open your eyes."

I look around. I'm in his bedroom. Hunter's above me, unbuttoning my blouse. Those eyes. That face. He's mine.

His fingers caress my skin. Tiny bursts of energy electrify every inch of me. I suck them up. Grateful for what he can do to me. I slide my hands under his T-shirt and try to get it up over his abs.

"You're impatient even when you're weak." His voice tenderizes my heart.

"I need you."

He nuzzles my neck. "You have me."

"Please."

His eyes are lakes. Fresh water. Pebbled shores. I've undone all the damage I caused.

He tugs his shirt off. His skin warms my skin. The heat of him sweeps through me, bringing me back to life.

His mouth is on mine.

When he deepens the kiss, a memory engulfs me. The first day we met, we were flowers. A little girl picked us and kept us in her room. She never understood how our stems came to be intertwined.

It was the beginning of us.

Sunlight glows behind the blinds, intruding on my world of sleep. I roll away from it and into Hunter. His fingers sweep over my throat, sending tingles along my collarbone.

"I missed you." My words don't begin to capture the pain of tonggan separation.

"Me too." He kisses me like he'll never let me go.

It's a few minutes before he has enough air to ask, "How are you feeling?"

"Better." The agony of last night has faded to a terrible memory.

"I gave you a boost of energy."

"Is that what you call it now?" I wink.

He laughs and my heart smiles. "Well, we did that, but I sent lots of tiny bursts of energy into you, too."

"Thanks."

He reaches into his nightstand and pulls out my labradorite ring. I put my hand out and he slides it back on my finger.

"I'm sorry I threw that at you. It was childish."

He kisses my forehead. "I hurt you."

He understands me better than anyone else. "But you were protecting me."

"Always." He strokes the gulley of my spine. "When I was gone, I found out more about why the lishihui want Octavius back."

"Tell me everything." I pull away from him, tuck the sheets under my armpits, and prepare for a discussion that is probably going to upset me.

"You remember wanshiqi lore?"

The complete topic change startles me. "What in Hades does that have to do with Octavius?"

"Give me a few minutes. I'll get you there."

"Fine, but there's a few hundred thousand years of lore. Can you be more specific?"

He pushes his back against the mahogany headboard, letting the sheet slide down to his hips. I can't help staring at his tanned chest. Those sculpted abs. I bite my lip to stop from kissing them.

"Trouble focusing?" Laughter and desire are tangled up in his tone.

"I'll get to your abs later."

"Can't wait."

The way he looks at me makes my cheeks kindle.

"Remember the story of the five kingdoms?" He switches to his scholarly voice. "Wanshiqi lore says five of the zhangzhe were of such power that they formed the core of our world. They united the five kingdoms and were called the wuwang. Before them, our realm was rife with war. Afterward, they reigned in peace. Without them, we are nothing. With them, everything remains in balance."

"It's just a legend."

"Legends are always rooted in reality. They existed." His expression intensifies.

"Of course they did." My entire world is shifting. Why not add some legends to it?

He runs his hand through his hair. He's trying to condense hundreds of thousands of years of history into a five-minute explanation.

"What happened to them?"

"Xia, Shang, Zhou, Qin and Han still exist. And Zhou's been exiled." He watches me closely like he's waiting for me to process what he said.

Zhou is as common a wanshiqi name as Joe is to an American kid. And it's also Gramps's name. "Joe is Zhou? You're telling me Gramps is the Zhou of the wuwang?"

"Yes."

I sit up straighter. I always knew Gramps was powerful, but not this powerful. My mind whirls with the possibilities. "Which means Grandfather is the Xia of the wuwang?"

Hunter nods.

I grab his hand. He's all that's certain in my ever-changing world. My stomach tightens. "Octavius's grandfather is Shang?"

"Yes."

There are two names left. "Your grandfather is Qin."

He squeezes my hand. "Yes."

"So Han is?"

"No one knows. She disappeared long before we were born. But they need her. She was the deciding vote of the wuwang. The wanshiqi realm was at its most stable under her rule. Without Han, it all started to fall apart."

"Wanshiqi don't die." I need to know that fact remains true in my unraveling reality.

Hunter's head tips back and forth. "Not in a traditional sense. We always exist. We change form. We hibernate. And sometimes when we are ancient, we forget."

A chill relay races up my spine. "Forget?"

"She's out there somewhere. But she may not remember what she is."

I'm still not seeing the connection. "What does Octavius have to do with the wuwang?"

"The lishihui suspect he knows what happened to Han."

"Like he did something to Han, or he knows where Han is?"

Hunter pulls me into his arms and strokes my hair. "Both."

Wuwang are even stronger than zhangzhe. Han was one of the wuwang, so Octavius shouldn't have been able to harm her. The past few days, however, have made me question my certainty about wanshiqi rules. "Is there any way Octavius could use his memory-altering powers on Han?"

"It shouldn't be possible."

"Which means there's a slight possibility Octavius harmed Han." That my enemy took on one of the most powerful beings in our realm and won. My mouth goes drier than the Sahara in summer. "Where is Han's tonggan?" He should be there when she forgets. He helps carry all the memories of their existence together. An eternity of memories is too much for a single wanshiqi to possess.

"Han never had a tonggan. She alone carried all the memories of each of her lifetimes." Hunter rests his chin on the top of my head. It's oddly soothing.

"That's a crushing burden."

"She was the most powerful of all of us." He says it like she was equipped to handle it.

"How could this happen to her then?"

"Forgetting is an escape. A relief. The danger comes in not remembering."

If Han refused to remember, she would have no idea what she was capable of. She might not know how to defend herself from another wanshiqi. Hunter must read the fear on my face.

"It's highly unlikely Octavius got to her."

"But it's possible." My face cramps with confusion. "Gramps said the lishihui wanted Octavius back to lead them. Now you're saying they want Octavius back to help find Han. Which is it?"

"Depends on who you talk to. There are factions within the lishihui with very different motives for getting Octavius freed from Pompeii."

"But they all want the same thing—Octavius's return." My blood pounds against my skull, trying to escape the realization: When the lishihui are united, things happen. Octavius will return.

And when he's freed from Pompeii and put in charge of the lishihui, my family is in serious trouble. Octavius would love nothing more than to see us imprisoned.

I shudder. Imprisonment means extricating our qi from its shell. The qi cannot take form. It cannot move. It cannot escape. Imprisonment makes Octavius's torture of me seem bearable.

Hunter and I dance around his kitchen in domestic simplicity. The gray granite tile floor and black marble counters are masculine and minimalist. So much sunlight streams into his apartment through the wall of windows, we don't even need to turn on the kitchen lights.

I scramble the eggs, while Hunter makes the bacon and coffee. He's in his plaid boxers; I'm in his blue button-down shirt with the sleeves rolled up. He slides across the back of me on his way to the sink. My body responds immediately. Contact and closeness stir everything inside me. I can't help leaning into him.

"We have to eat first," he murmurs against my neck before he drops a quick kiss.

"It's been a while."

"Twenty minutes is a while?" he teases.

"It is for me." For once, I'm giving in to our bond, reveling in it.

Hunter gets the mugs out, and I stare into the frying pan. The eggs form into semisolids. It's the state of everything in my life. Transition incomplete.

Fear seeps into me, icing over everything it touches. I'm burning cold.

"Kali?" Hunter's voice butters my pain.

I turn the burner off. "Eggs are ready." My voice cracks and panic oozes out.

Hunter wraps his arms around me and radiates warmth into me. "We'll figure things out. We'll be okay."

My brain is submerged in all the things I've learned. I lean my head back on Hunter's shoulder. "I've been fighting to keep my family together for so long. But we're not together." I whisper the words that hurt the deepest. "We're broken."

Hunter kisses the side of my head and rocks me. "Families aren't perfect. Grams and Gramps did what they thought was best to protect you. You did what you thought was best to protect your family."

"And my parents?"

"They've always been an enigma to me." His voice is more neutral than Switzerland.

A nervous giggle bubbles up inside me.

"Confounded me for centuries." He tickles me until I'm laughing as hard as he is.

When I turn to face him, he gently pushes my hair back and holds my face between his palms. "Don't worry, we'll figure things out. And if not in this lifetime, in the next."

I want to believe him. I've survived hundreds of lifetimes with that philosophy. But deep in my qi, I know this life is different. This is the life where every decision matters.

CHAPTER TWENTY-EIGHT

A FEW HOURS LATER, I walk into the main room of my house to talk to Grams and Gramps about everything, from Hunter accepting my daoqian to Gramps being one of the wuwang to Octavius's involvement in Han's disappearance. Now that I've fixed things with Hunter, I'm ready to hear what they have to say and figure out what we do next.

I have on yesterday's clothes, but once I explain all of Hunter's revelations, well, they'll understand why I spent the night at his place and skipped school today.

I wander the entire length of the main floor calling, "Grams?"

No one responds.

After I check all the rooms on the main floor, I go downstairs to the kitchen. Empty. I head upstairs to their bedroom, but she's nowhere to be found.

In my room, a note sits on my desk, propped up against the books. *Kali* is written in Grams's handwriting across the envelope. Suddenly, I can't move. I don't know how much time passes before I walk to the desk and pick up the letter. My fingers shake, making it harder to slide her note out.

Dearest Kali,

Gramps and I need to find answers to your questions and ours about who is behind everything that's happened to you. There is much we don't know. Trust in us. Trust in Hunter. Trust in yourself.

All our love,

Grams

I sit in silence on the floor, rereading those lines and trying to understand. My heart whispers, *they left me.* Just like they did in

Pompeii. Hot tears sting my eyes. I don't fight them. They drop onto the letter, dissolving the ink into blurs of blue.

I try to bury myself in teen drama at school, but no one is available. Hunter's back in the wanshiqi realm again. Tav's not around either. At lunch, Mandy drones on and on about a new cheer routine. She thinks her squad has a chance of winning the regionals. She doesn't ask for much from me. Just an occasional nod and smile. A "really?" and a little later a "that's awesome."

Lunch ends and I go back to class. Outside the window, the palm trees and blue skies promise a good day. They lie.

"Kali?" Dr. Herger says my name like he's said it a few times already.

Everyone in English class stares at me.

I guess I'm supposed to answer a question. Another question. "Yes?"

"Care to weigh in on the most important Transcendentalist?"

This I know. Grams told me all about her friendship with Emerson and Fuller. "Margaret Fuller."

Dr. Herger raises an eyebrow. "Not Thoreau or Emerson?"

"They were important, but she was overlooked."

"Interesting point. Perhaps you've found the topic of our next paper." Dr. Herger sounds academically excited.

The entire class groans.

"Ms. Brewster has inspired me. Pick your favorite movement in literature and tell me who was the most important person in it and why. A thousand words due next Monday." He taps his fingers on his desk like he's inputting it into his calendar.

The looks coming my way aren't friendly. I don't care because the bell rings, and I'm free.

Mandy grabs me outside class. "Did you hear about Tav?"

The worry in her tone twists something in my stomach. "What happened?"

"He's finishing the term from home." Mandy's voice trembles.

"He was here on Monday." Three days ago.

"Do you think Bess got worse?" Mandy nibbles on her bottom lip. "Should we call him?"

The lemon bars should be helping Bess. "I'll skip study hall and go check on them."

"Tell him…just tell him I'm thinking about him." Her cheerbabies call out to her, but she lingers next to me.

"I'll text you the details, and you can stop by after practice to tell him yourself."

Her eyes brighten. "I can do that." She takes off down the hall.

Three days. What could have happened? Bess has to be fine. Maybe it's Tav? No. I'd have heard if he was injured or hurt. I check my phone. No messages. No texts. Nothing.

Dread laps at the walls of my stomach. Something is wrong. Something I know nothing about. He tried to talk to me on Monday, and I acted like he was utterly disposable.

I was utterly wrong.

Tav doesn't respond to my texts or my knock on his front door. I stand there on his porch, trying to figure out what to do. Finally, I meander back to my car.

"You looking for the Pontes?" A gray-haired woman peers over her hedges at me.

"Yes."

Her face sinks under the weight of what she knows. "He took her to the hospital yesterday." She tsks and shakes her head as if the movement will invalidate the reality of what happened. "That cancer won't let her be."

"The cancer?" Dizziness sends my world spinning. I lean back against my car, needing something solid. This can't be happening. Bess should have had weeks of healthiness.

"She gets better and the boy gets hopeful. Then she gets worse."

"Do you know what hospital she's at?" The words stumble over each other in their rush to get out of my mouth.

The old woman's cheeks scrunch up, swallowing her eyes. "Mercy Memorial, I think."

CHAPTER TWENTY-NINE

THE SOLES OF MY shoes slap against the hospital floor, making a hollow sound that echoes in my ears. I turn down another hallway. The air reeks of lost hope and life unlived. I finally find Tav on the third floor near a vending machine. He stares at the rows of candy bars as if this is the most important decision of his life. He pushes his hair back and sees me. Emotions skip across his face. Fear. Relief. Annoyance.

I close the distance between us. "Hey." With that tiny word, I try to convey how sorry I am and how concerned I am.

"Hey." His is an exhausted whisper.

I reach over and punch in the number for his favorite—a Snickers. "Protein helps."

The bar *clunk-thumps* into the bottom bin. He reaches down to retrieve the candy bar.

"I'm sorry." I lower my voice in respect for all that is wrong around us.

"For what?" His words come out clipped and cold.

"I was a total bitch on Monday." And he had to endure two days alone here. "You should have called me."

"You made it clear you didn't want me in your life."

I wince. I hate apologizing, especially to humans, but he deserves one. "I was upset and hurt. I lashed out at you. I'm still your friend, even when I'm being awful."

He looks up at me like he's trying to read the truth in my eyes. "Okay." He unwraps the bar and takes a bite.

We're back to quiet again, but I can't bear the silence. "Mandy's worried about you. Why didn't you call her?"

"Because she's so reliable in a crisis." His sarcasm startles me.

"She is now."

He gives me a I-can't-take-any-more look.

"What happened to your mom?"

His shoulders swallow his neck for a second. "Nothing. Everything."

It's too hard for him to explain it all, so I ask for it in pieces. "Why'd you bring Bess in?"

"She coughed up blood."

That's bad. Really bad. "What's the doctor saying?"

Tav leans against the wall like he desperately needs the support. "Not much."

"They never do." Cancer follows a path like no other. "Can I see her?"

"They took her away to run more tests." He stares down at the tips of his Converse sneakers.

I touch his arm—a gentle reminder that I'm here. "Let's take a quick walk."

"I should…" His voice trails off. There is nothing left he can do. He just can't say it.

"Five minutes." I wrap both arms around his and try to give him the support he needs.

"Five minutes." He lets me drag him to the elevator.

Outside the hospital, the sunlight grows palm trees, green grass, and perfect flowerbeds. It's the most beautiful lie to all those inside the hospital battling their own decay.

"She's really sick." There are so many fissures in the foundation of his voice. It reminds me of an old house about to give way.

I wrap my arms around him. It's like hugging a surfboard. "You don't have to be strong all the time."

"I can't." Anguish ignites in his tone.

I tighten my hold on him. "Let it out. She won't know."

"I can't lose her." He caves around me, clinging to me as though I'll slip away at any moment.

I've never faced the permanent loss of a parent. I always knew I would meet mine again. He won't.

I wish I could take his pain away. I want to give him what I never had: more time with a parent who loves me.

The realization bursts through me—If I use my last curse to help his mom, I can give Tav everything I ever wanted. I can't stop her death, but maybe I can stall it and give her a few more years with her son.

Tav's tears wet my neck. I tighten my hold on him. Humans need to be held when they come undone.

"I can't lose her. I need her. She's my mom." His urgent whisper fills my ear.

I feel the same need in my qi for my parents. It's up to me to make it happen for him. "You won't."

He pulls back and wipes his face on his arm. "It's not that simple." Anger colors his words.

I cross my arms. "Are you done fighting for her?"

"I'll never stop fighting for her." Red splotches mottle his neck. "You don't understand. You don't know what we've been through."

He walks away from me without looking back. He doesn't have to. I know he needs someone to fight. Someone flesh and blood. Someone who could handle his anger.

He needs someone like me.

I feel unbearably human, so I leave the hospital and head to Hunter's. He's not home, so I let myself in and drop down on the sofa. Staring out at the dusk-tinged beach, I try to create a curse to save Bess.

Before I figure it out, someone knocks on Hunter's door. When I check through the peephole, I see an unfamiliar middle-aged man with silver hair, wearing an expensive gray suit.

"Can I help you?" I ask through the door.

"I've come to finish our conversation." His voice is authoritative, demanding.

"You have the wrong apartment. We've never met before."

He lets out an elegant sigh. "It's just another form, Granddaughter."

I unlock the door and smell licorice, the twisted scent of Grandfather's qi. "Whose body did you take this time?"

"Some LA millionaire." He waves his hand dismissively, like he didn't just steal a human being's body and completely derail his day and possibly his life.

"What do you want?" Suspicion stalks each syllable.

"Invite me in and you'll find out." A glimmer appears in his brown eyes. A shimmer of silver. Then it disappears.

I don't want to be alone with Grandfather again, but he has knowledge that I need. I step out of the way, and he walks into Hunter's apartment.

He drapes his trench coat over the couch, unbuttons his gray suit jacket, and takes a seat in Hunter's leather chair. "I came to offer you a trade."

"I don't trade with people I don't trust." Grandfather is the king of treachery.

He chuckles. "I don't trust anyone."

"So how could we trade?"

"Like all untrustworthy parties—with a show of good faith." He says it like the answer is obvious.

I can feel disbelief dropping my jaw and raising my eyebrows. He's never been good or given me a reason to have faith in him.

"Information, dear." A smile skims across his lips. "I'll share a memory with you."

That requires more intimacy than I want. Our memories are stored in our qi. He'll have to touch my third eye and transmit his memory into me. For a moment, our qi will be connected. I scramble for an excuse to avoid it. "Memories can be tainted."

"Not mine. Being ancient has its perks." He brushes lint off his suit.

"Not for Han."

The slightest crease appears between his brows before he can smooth it out. "Poor Han." He says it like he isn't the least bit sorry for her. "All that power wasted on one who never wanted to wield it."

"What power did she have?" No one has been willing to tell me about it.

"That's a future trade." He sounds thrilled to have something else I want.

"Forget it." I don't want any more dealings with Grandfather. "What do you want to trade now?" When the devil wants to deal, you need the terms first.

"The location of Octavius."

The remnants of daylight disappear outside Hunter's window. Darkness rises.

The words rush out of my mouth. "I can't help you with that."

"Come now. No need to lie to your grandfather." His voice conjures up warm milk and old friendship.

I don't fall for it. "All right. I won't help you."

"I do enjoy when you show a little backbone. It reminds me of your father." His voice is somewhere between playful and manipulative.

His compliment makes me uncomfortable. I lace my fingers together, finding assurance in my own touch. "There has to be something else you want."

"Perhaps there is another trade we can make." Grandfather takes his time thinking it over. When I cannot sit there another second, he says, "I would like you to live through your seventeenth birthday."

"I thought you wanted me to stay here on Earth."

"Where you are is immaterial to me." He rests his hands on the arms of the chair. He's so calm as if he didn't sacrifice me to Octavius all those years ago. Just the thought of what he let Octavius do to me sends blood burning to my neck and cheeks. A fight or flight reaction. This time I fight.

The words bungee-jump from my mouth. "How could you let Octavius torture me in Pompeii? You could have warned Zhou. You could have stopped Octavius. You could have saved me."

"Trade-offs and collateral damage."

"I'm your granddaughter." Rejection clogs my throat.

"I've kept you alive." He says it like I should be grateful.

"Because you need me alive."

He glances out the window. "Being human is degrading your father and destabilizing your mother. Don't you care about them?"

Rage kindles in my belly. "Everything I've done has been to protect them."

He tilts his head and gives me a considering glance. "Maybe you care for too many. Your parents, your grandparents, your tonggan. Even your humans. They make you vulnerable." His warning cuts through my qi.

Suddenly, I hear ocean waves crashing inside my ears. My breath quickens. "Are you threatening them?"

"I decimate without warning." It's the most honest thing he's ever said to me.

I steer the conversation away from those I love. "If I live to seventeen, what do I gain?"

"Qifa." He beams at me.

"No, from you in this trade."

"Ah." He sits back in the chair. "I can ease your family's transition back to the wanshiqi realm. There are many ways their return can go wrong. I can make sure it goes right."

One of my biggest fears is what our return will do to my parents. "Can you make sure their powers and prestige are restored?"

He gives me a nod.

I drop back onto the couch. It's a tempting offer. But there's one more thing I need from him. The one thing I haven't been able to fix in two millennia. "Can you fix their memories from Pompeii?"

"You mean remove those false memories Octavius gave them?"

"Yes." It's all I've wanted for them.

"I have someone who can do that."

"Will…will my parents remember that they loved me?" My voice comes out so soft, I'm not sure I even said the words out loud until he answers me.

"They will."

Relief rushes over me. But this is Grandfather, so I have to ask, "How?"

"My methods are mine alone."

"I don't trust you."

"Hence, the show of good faith. I'm giving you this memory without securing anything in return." He rubs his hands together. "You wanted to know what is at stake with your punishment ending. I can show you why it matters to the wuwang so much."

I hate that he's the one who is willing to tell me. Why didn't Gramps? My heart pumps twice as hard, as if my brain needs more blood to understand. "Does this involve Octavius, too?"

"You've always been so focused on Octavius. He was just a tiny piece of a much bigger plan." He sounds like I've been disappointing him for centuries.

"Why did he torture me—was it for the lishihui or the wuwang or some other zhangzhe?" It's something Gramps isn't even sure of.

"Finally, you're thinking bigger." He claps his hands together and stands up. "The memory will help you understand."

With Grandfather there are always strings attached. The kind that strangle or shackle in seconds. It takes all my courage to stand. My feet refuse to budge. He moves toward me.

"This has to be consensual," he reminds me.

He will tunnel into my head. The way Octavius wanted to in Pompeii. Bile scalds my throat and lacerates my tongue.

I take a step toward him. He presses his right pointer finger into my third eye. My skin tingles. Energy ripples along his finger and shoots into my mind. Images play inside my head.

I see everything through Xia's eyes. He's at a wuwang meeting. He takes the form of a crow perched on the back of Shang's chair. I hear Xia's thoughts. He hates that he must be in bird form. Being number two to Shang is an affront to everything he's done over the millennia.

"When will you return?" Shang's a shadowy figure in Xia's memory. Cloaked. Xia never looks right at him. His qi smells of burning wood. It stings my nose.

"After all the grandchildren reach qifa." Han has taken the form of a Chinese woman. She smells of mint. Of promises kept. Of words remembered.

"That could be tens of thousands of years." Zhou's voice is over-starched, chafing at the possibility of Han leaving. His white hair and beard make him look like an ancient wizard.

"Shang can rule for a while. It has been his deepest wish for too long." Han's voice reminds me of a flute—majestic and sad at the same time.

"Where will you go?" Qin takes the form of a hawk sitting on Zhou's shoulder.

"I won't be here but I won't be far." Han gives Zhou a gentle smile.

"As you wish." The balance of power shifts again. Xia's alliances remain fluid until a choice must be made. And when that time comes, he will choose himself like he has always done.

I blink, and I'm back in Hunter's living room. Grandfather leans over me. Sometime during the memory, I must have collapsed onto the couch. His eyes are brighter than the stars. Knowledge festers there.

"Do you understand now?"

My mouth is parched. The words are so hard to say. "This isn't about me."

"On the contrary, this is all about you. You're the last grandchild of the wuwang to reach qifa."

"It could have been any of the grandkids." My voice trembles like a cliff about to slip into the ocean.

"You've always been a pawn, my dear. Birth just made you the most precious pawn in the wuwang power struggle."

"If I don't reach qifa…" The consequences ripple beyond my family to the entire wanshiqi civilization.

"Han doesn't return."

"So everything, everything, that happened to me was to keep Han away permanently?" Horror dawns in my voice. "That's why you let Octavius torture me, so I would use my powers on him and be punished for it. You wanted to make sure I wasn't allowed to undergo qifa."

"I thought you'd break months before you did." There's a gruffness to his voice.

The realization creeps over me. "Dad and I are nothing to you?"

Xia reaches toward me. I shrink back into the couch. His finger grazes my third eye. "I've told you more than Zhou ever did, yet you doubt me. Choose your alliances with more care."

Gramps kept this from me. It's earth-reversing-axis important. Xia showed it to me. Xia. Something inside me withers away.

Grandfather interrupts my thoughts. "No one anticipated what you did in Pompeii. You formed a wanshiqi prison." He lets out a whistle. "No one's done that before or since. Some of the lishihui fear you can do it again. They'd prefer you never undergo qifa and reach your full potential."

"The lishihui fear me?" My voice scrambles up the wall.

"That was an incredibly powerful curse for one so young." His eyes are intent. "Could you do it again?"

I'm not sure if he wants me to or not. "I don't think so." I lie because I don't want him to know that I can. Then a thought occurs to me. "How could you know I would keep dying in every lifetime and delay my qifa?"

"Free will keeps things interesting for us. If we decide everything that will happen, there's no sport in it. Though there were times we nudged you along."

"When?"

"That club fire. I thought for sure you'd curse bigger and save more people, not just your friend and you. I overestimated your humanity." He sounds happy that I let those people die.

"Is this all one big game to you?" Who he is horrifies me.

Grandfather towers over me. "There are many games of all sizes going on around you. Learn to play, and you might make it through them." His voice slithers around me like a boa constrictor.

"With all your power and knowledge and abilities, this is what you do with your time?" I can't keep my disgust out of my voice.

"Power is everything to us." He says it like I'm a child who needs to learn how the world works.

"But Gramps isn't like that." He's better than that. Isn't he?

"We were kings. Now we rule all the wanshiqi. All of the wuwang crave power. We just have different ways of acquiring it. Zhou and Qin are the opposite of Shang and I. The light to balance the dark, more benevolent than dictator."

"What about Han?"

"She was the pinnacle of our pentagon of power. Neither benevolent nor dictator. Above it all."

I sit there trying to understand everything he's shown me and told me. I have to understand the price of this deal. There are only two reasons to die before I turn seventeen: my last curse can help Bess and keep my family together on Earth. But that's just one human life and one wanshiqi family.

In every lifetime, I've made the best decision I could with the information I had at that time. But this information Xia gave me, it changes everything. It has to.

When I weigh my reasons for remaining on Earth against destabilizing all of wanshiqi civilization, I know what I have to do. I have to live through my seventeenth birthday. Grandfather is offering me everything I've ever wanted if I do it. He'll protect my parents. He'll undo what Octavius did to them. But what about Bess? "Can you help a human live longer?"

"If you tell me where Octavius is, I might be willing to help."

That is the one thing I can't tell anyone. But Bess. How can I let her die? "Is there any way to stall Death?"

He tilts his head. "That's the first interesting question you've asked me. Like anyone, Death will trade up."

"Meaning?"

He leans forward. His eyes burn with intensity. "You must give him something he wants more. He is known to request whatever would cause you the deepest agony. I once traded 2000 years of accumulated power and wealth." He says it like he lost something precious. He sniffs. "He'd smell the desperation on you, my dear. You'd probably have to sacrifice someone you love deeply to help that human."

There's a reason I've never heard about deals with Death before. Only someone who is as dark and twisted as Xia could have made this kind of agreement with Death. Killing someone you love…I couldn't do it. Not even for Bess. Grams and Hunter respect Death. They never try to make deals with him. I think I understand why now.

The cost is too high.

As I struggle with that realization, Xia is the picture of patience with his hands folded in his lap.

He waits for my promise, my nuoyan. It's a binding agreement. The punishment for a broken nuoyan is 10,000 years of imprisonment. No reincarnation. No tonggan. Most go insane. I've never heard of any who have recovered from it. They go dormant. Inhabiting a grain of sand for eternity. Refusing to take conscious form again. It is a near extinction of our qi.

I whisper, "I'll live to my seventeenth birthday."

He stares at me as though he's calculating my authenticity. "A nuoyan for a nuoyan. Proper wording is required. Add an *I promise* and substitute *through* for *to*, my dear."

"I promise to live through my seventeenth birthday."

"Good girl." He pats my head. "In return, I promise to protect your family and your tonggan and have your parents' memories restored."

Turning seventeen means that I will go through qifa and trigger Han's return. "Why do you want Han back?" When I was in his memory, I'd swear he wanted Han gone.

"My enemy's enemy is my friend." He heads to the door.

"Wait, who is your enemy?"

He ignores my question. "I'll be back on your birthday to collect on our bargain." He shuts the door behind him.

I can't stop trembling. Humans fear the devil. I don't. I just made a deal with someone far worse.

CHAPTER THIRTY

IN THE MORNING, I wake slowly and roll over to Hunter's side of the bed, but it's still empty. I couldn't bring myself to go home last night. My house is too empty without Grams and Gramps.

In my mind, I play over what Xia said yesterday. Despite my misgivings and fears, I feel a glimmer of something else inside me. It's the first time I've had the possibility of having my parents back. Five minutes with who they were is worth 5000 years with who they are now.

I get up, shower, make breakfast. I'm about to leave when I get a text from Tav, and my tiny bubble of hope bursts. *Meet Mom and me at Scripps' Park above La Jolla Cove at 11.*

His mom was the person I planned to save with my last curse before I promised Xia that I would live. I don't want to let her die, but I can't sacrifice a loved one to save her. Unfortunately, there's no simple solution here like kill a criminal and save Bess.

Is Bess okay? I type back.

She wants to see you is all he writes.

It's one thing to weigh one human life against all of the wanshiqi realm and make the choice I made, but to look into her eyes and see the life slipping out of them and know I could have kept her alive—I don't know how I'm going to face her. It takes me a few minutes to summon the courage to get in my car.

All too soon, my car is in traffic, lurching past the shops and hotels crowding Prospect Street in downtown La Jolla. I take a steep right down Coast Boulevard toward the water and grab the last parking spot near Scripps' Park.

I lock the car and look across the grass, past the pockets of trees that grow horizontally, toward the walkway with the ocean view. Bess is on a bench bundled in a sweater coat, scarf and hat. It's 70 degrees out. My smile slips. I force it back into place and wave.

They don't see me.

Tav frowns and shakes his head. Bess takes his hand in hers. She's wearing gloves. Things are going cold inside her. I know what that means. She doesn't have much time left. I don't need to hear any words. I feel the cancer mocking us. Tav for having hope. Bess for trying to live. And me for not being able to save her.

To give them time to finish their talk, I meander along the cement path that hugs the edge of the cliffs and skirts the grass. In the cove below me, snorkelers lurk just beneath the surface, trying to identify the sea creatures that clutter the inlet. The water rushes to shore only to change its mind and drag sand and rocks back out to sea.

When I get to Tav and Bess, his voice trails off. I hug him. He holds himself still, enduring my sympathy. I let go, and he lowers his chin until his hair covers his eyes.

"I'll be down on the beach." His voice reminds me of driftwood abandoned along the shore. I watch him make his way down the rocks to the shore below.

Bess pats the wooden bench. "Come sit with me."

Sunlight glints on the waves of bright-blue water in front of us. "I could spend all day here."

"I wish I could." She wraps her sweater coat tightly around her, trying to ward off the chill that's already taken hold of her. "We played here for hours when Tav was a kid."

"Collecting seashells or building sandcastles?"

"A bit of both, actually." A ghost of a smile haunts her lips. "I made mosaics from them. I wish I had time to make him one more." She lifts her face to the breeze. Her eyelids slip shut. "I love the ocean."

Even in the sunshine, her face is devoid of color. She coughs a dry, barky cough.

She leans against me. "I need you to be there for Tav, Kali."

Nausea crashes into me like the ocean slamming into the rocks. Sweat springs up on my skin. The worst guilt robs me of words. I can't save her, and I can't be here for him. I hate this. It's not fair. If only there was a way for me to keep my nuoyan to Xia and still help Bess.

"You can't give up." My voice comes out pitchy and raspy, like a cat clawed my vocal cords.

"The doctor says the cancer is spreading rapidly." Her sigh is a mix of world-weary and acceptance. "I want to enjoy my last weeks with Tav."

"Don't you want the possibility of more?"

"Always. But cancer doesn't work that way." Her voice flatlines. "I need to prepare Tav." Veins of anguish nurture her voice. "Leaving my son behind—that's the worst pain."

Tears fill my eyes. She can't leave Tav. When you've had someone love you the way Bess loves him, it's impossible to go on without it. Maybe that's why I keep surviving. My parents have never loved me that much, even before Pompeii.

CHAPTER THIRTY-ONE

I DON'T LIKE IT, but tonight I have to think like Xia because he is a master of loopholes. Luckily, I've been inside his mind for a moment. I pace around Hunter's cavernous living room. My bare feet slap against the hardwood floors. How do I get what I want and ignore the collateral damage like Xia does?

I promised to live through my seventeenth birthday, but I never promised I wouldn't die after my birthday. Wait. Could I cast a curse to stall Bess's death? Xia said I did something no one thought possible when I trapped Octavius in Pompeii. Maybe I can get around dealing with Death. I just want to give her an extra ten or fifteen years with Tav before she dies. Do I have that kind of energy left?

I run to the bathroom to check my eyes in the mirror, but only a tiny dot of brown remains. I don't have nearly enough energy to fuel a curse to help Bess. If I had more brown, I might be able to do it. And there's my shiny loophole. One person can give me more brown: Hunter.

It's a risky plan, but it's the only one I've got. When Hunter returns, I have to convince him to tase me. I won't think about what that may do to me or him. The risks I'm taking. I will put it into the collateral damage box and ignore it like Xia does. Now that I have my loophole, my mind slows down. I sit on the couch and lean my head back and close my eyes. Exhaustion overtakes me. I'm out before I know it.

I awaken in Hunter's arms and snuggle into his warmth. "What are you doing?" Sleepiness slurs my words.

"Bringing you to bed." His voice is deep, reverberating in my ear.

I start to slip back into my dream until I remember what's at stake. I jerk awake.

His arms tighten, securing me against him. "Careful, I almost dropped you."

"I need your help."

He lays me on his bed, but I quickly sit up against the headboard.

He sits next to me. His eyes are bloodshot. "What's wrong?" He sounds like he hasn't slept in days.

I tell him about Bess's cancer. The hospital. My talk with her at the beach. My voice quakes with the realization. "She'll die if I don't help her, and I don't have enough energy to help her unless you tase me." If he gives me energy, I will be able to fuel a curse without dying. I hope.

"Why would I help Tav?" His eyes go Arctic Ocean cold. So does his voice.

For wanshiqi, humans are toys. We never put ourselves at risk for our toys. "Because I'm your tonggan and you always help me."

"Emotional blackmail." I can't tell from his tone if he's upset or intrigued.

Outside his window, it's still dark, but a dark that is giving way to the light.

"Why do you care so much about these humans?" He says it without much inflection, but I know it irks him.

"His mom is like me. She'd do anything to keep her family together." My voice curls inward like a long-forgotten love letter. "Tav is the center of her world. And he'd do anything for her. It's really beautiful."

Hunter looks at me with sudden tenderness. "It's everything you've ever wanted." He caresses my cheek.

A golf ball of longing lodges in my throat. "Yeah."

"When would you want to do this?" He hasn't agreed, but he hasn't said no. It gives me hope.

"As soon as possible."

"Can't we wait a day or two?" Dark circles rim his eyes.

"The sicker she gets, the more energy I'll need to help her." This large of a curse may activate the self-destruct gene in my DNA. I may get sick. Prelude-to-death sick. The kind of sick that Grams and Hunter can't reverse.

I'm the only wanshiqi that can heal Bess right now. Grams isn't around, but she can't heal someone who's started their death spiral. Hunter can send energy into Bess to make her stronger, but since her body has entered the death spiral, he can't do anything to stop her death.

If only I'd asked him weeks ago to help her. He could have made a difference then but not now. Now, I'm the only one who can help her. I can't stop death, but I can push it back. Yes, I'll weave a curse to delay her death. To give her more time with Tav here on Earth. I'll put the cancer in remission. It has to work.

He rubs his temple. "I get it. Let me sleep on it."

"Okay."

"It's dangerous." Hunter's voice is weighted with consequences. "Too little energy from me, and you die during the curse. Too much energy shot into you, and you end up brain dead with no ability to end your existence. You'll live through your seventeenth birthday whether you want to or not."

He has no idea what dying would mean for me. Wanshiqi imprisonment. I force lightness into my voice. "We've always played well with fire." Hunter's the one who burned down Bodie for me.

I wish I could fall back to sleep with Hunter, and I try. I lie there beside him for two hours before I give up. I start my day with the sunrise. I brush my teeth and pace across the bathroom's cement floor, passing the black soaking tub. On my third loop, I turn the rain shower on so the water warms up. The water dances over the pebbles that line the floor of the shower, creating a sound that usually soothes me.

I step in to the shower and put my face under the hot spray. My conversation with Hunter didn't go as well as I'd hoped. I dread telling him about my nuoyan to Xia to live through my birthday, but I have to. He needs to know why it's better to leave me brain dead than to let me die. I practice what I'll say, trying to find the words that make this sound less awful. By the time I turn the water off, I feel almost ready. I dry off and slip into my blue silk robe.

I pad down the hallway and into the kitchen. The gray granite tiles cool my feet. I waltz around the black appliances, preparing breakfast and setting the glass table in the corner for us.

The scent of brewing coffee pulls Hunter into the kitchen. He wraps his arms around me from behind. "Food can't fuel my wan-shiqi powers. I'm going to have to go borrow some energy." He kisses my cheek and heads toward the door.

He's gone for twenty minutes. Strolling around on each floor, siphoning energy from every human in the building. They'll be tired for a few days, but they'll survive.

When he returns, his skin glows with energy. The dark circles have disappeared. He's brimming with power.

"Do you still want breakfast?" I'm not sure I do. I have this overwhelming desire for him.

He gives me a wicked grin, leans in, and kisses me. It's a delicious kiss. A kiss that claims me completely. I melt against him, wanting to get as close as I possibly can.

He pulls back and sits down at the kitchen table. "Thought you might like a taste of what you're asking me to do."

I touch my lips. Energy vibrates inside me, humming in my ears from one kiss. It's never been this intense.

"Eat your breakfast." He says it in such a calm voice that I swear he's laughing at me.

My legs bend on their own, and I take my seat. I lift the fork to my mouth and swallow. Eat without tasting the food. Completing the task so we can get back to each other.

He devours his food. "Did you write up your curse?"

I tap the side of my head. "It's all in here." I composed it while I laid in bed beside him this morning. The words and images are scorched into my psyche. "I just want to get Bess through the next ten or so years."

"Good." He bites into his toast.

My voice dips and rolls over each word. "There's something I need to tell you."

"Is it about Xia's visit?" He smears more jam on the toast.

"You knew?"

He gives me his Kali-are-you-kidding-me face. "My chair reeked of licorice."

I tear tiny pieces from my napkin and ball them up. The words rush over my lips like barrels over Niagara Falls. "He wants me to live past my seventeenth birthday."

Hunter frowns and forks his eggs. "That makes me side with you about dying."

I explain the memory Xia shared with me and how the wuwang power struggles are linked to me. I even mention how the lishihui fear me.

He stares at the table with a lowered brow and a tense jaw, like he's doing a trigonometry problem.

I roll the tiny balls of napkin on the table. "Do you think I'm dangerous? I mean do you fear what I could do after qifa?"

"No." His expression softens. He reaches across the table and takes my hand in his.

"But the darkest curses always come easiest to me. Saving curses take so much from me. That has to mean something." My voice thins and almost rips.

"Whatever you are, I am, too. Do you think I'm bad?"

"I think you're wonderful."

"I think the same about you." His eyes glow in a way that warms my qi. I could spend eternity staring into them, but he shifts back to his thinking face again. "Zhangzhe don't just share memories. He did it to get something from you. What did you give him?"

I look down at the eggs. Hunter's not going to like the next part. "A nuoyan."

Hunter's coffee mug clatters on the glass tabletop. He leaps up. "What?"

"I promised to live through my seventeenth birthday."

"Without talking to me first?"

That's like asking me to check in on the status of the Earth revolving around the sun. "Hunter, you've always wanted me to turn seventeen."

"What about Grams and Gramps?"

"I can't ask them since they aren't around." Bitterness butters my voice.

Hunter towers over me. "What did Xia promise you?" Each word comes out slowly, dropping around my shoulders. When I don't answer, Hunter drags his chair close to mine and sits down. He rests his hand on the back of my chair. "It had to be something you prize more than being with your family."

I hate that Hunter knows me this well. I group the pieces of shredded napkin into piles of ten, trying to organize the chaos I've created. "He's going to protect you and my parents and restore their memories."

He slams his palm on the table. The dishes jump and rattle. "Xia will triple-cross you before you can contemplate breaking your nuoyan."

I rest my hand on his thigh. "I'm not stupid. I know he only wants to help himself, but it might benefit me, too."

Hunter shakes his head. "You don't get it. Everything, everything I've been doing is for you, and you go off and make this nuoyan. How can I protect you now?" His words come out fast and fly around the room. "What if there is more to the story than what Xia showed you? What if you living puts us at an even greater risk?"

"Then I'll break my nuoyan." I try to sound brave, but my qi shivers. Ten thousand years of imprisonment will break me.

"You can't break a nuoyan." Horror hollows out his words. "You won't survive."

Ice fills my veins, but I don't allow the fear to drip into my voice. "I won't let you or my parents or my grandparents suffer for me again."

CHAPTER THIRTY-TWO

Hunter and I remain deadlocked with me sitting on his couch and him standing by the window. Thick gray clouds blanket the sky. Thunder threatens.

I finger-comb my hair into a ponytail and rest the back of my head in my hands. "I promise to do everything I can to keep my nuoyan."

"Don't go making any more promises." He crosses his arms and lightning lashes the ocean. "How do you not see what you are doing to me? You'd be sentencing me to 10,000 years of my existence without my tonggan." The rumble in his voice rivals the thunder.

I release my hair and lean forward. "Don't you realize I'd only break my nuoyan if it meant saving you from something worse. I'd risk me for all of you because you're that important to me."

He takes a few steps toward me and stops. Sheets of rain slam into the window. Thunder and lightning collide. "I want you safe. It's all I ever wanted."

His truth strips away all my anger. "Pompeii would have been so different with you there." I rest my cheek on my hand and look up at him.

"I will never let anyone hurt you, Kali."

What I see in his eyes breaks my heart and shatters my voice. "That's exactly how I feel about you and my family."

"I can't spend 10,000 years without you. I won't." His voice is husky. Rich in emotion. Tangled in fear. I hear it all.

"I don't want to lose you either."

He sighs, rubs his forehead, and walks in three small circles. "Talking isn't getting us anywhere."

"So stop talking." I stretch my arms out to him and slide to the side. The bottom of my robe hikes up, exposing most of my thigh.

He moves toward me like a wave toward the shore. His arrival is inevitable.

I wrap my arms around him and pull him onto the couch beside me. The heat he exudes has nothing to do with his frustration. He's been holding in all that energy he gobbled up this morning. He needs this release as much as I do.

I nuzzle his neck. "Let me help Bess."

"I have every incentive to overload you with energy, so you keep your nuoyan no matter what Xia does."

I pull back and stare into his turquoise eyes. "I trust you." I say each word slowly and wait for it to register in his eyes.

"Do you?" There's a question deep within his eyes.

I rest my forehead against his. "I do." I say it with all the conviction I have.

He kisses me with such intensity. His lips trail down my neck. My skin tingles in their wake.

It's so hard to think when he touches me. He unties my robe and slides it off my shoulders. His lips continue kissing their way lower and lower. A moan gathers in the back of my throat. I tear his T-shirt over his head. My fingers fumble with the button on his jeans.

A chuckle echoes in his throat. "We have all afternoon."

My nerves and my desire for him overwhelm me. "I can't wait."

He cradles my face between his palms. "Everything is going to be all right."

My throat is too full of fears. No more words. I run my fingers through his hair and pull him closer to me. He presses his lips to mine and lets me take control of the kiss. I deepen it. Extract his energy, pulling it into me a little at a time.

Every touch imparts a flash of energy. I want to wrap my skin around him and absorb it all. It's instinctual—this desire for a tonggan. But Hunter and I, we've always had more. Some greater connection that I can't name.

His lips on my skin. My flesh to his flesh. It's an agony of desire. A hurricane of need building inside me. My world flattens to him.

The present becomes an eternity. Every inch of him laid bare for me.

His eyes burn mine. "I love you."

"I love you, too."

It's pleasure. It's pain. It's too much. It's not enough. I can't find the words to tell him. My body spasms. The energy consumes me. A wildfire engulfs my qi.

It's impossible to decipher what is actually happening and what is my brain short-circuiting from Hunter's energy overload.

I come to consciousness in a place of shadows and darkness screaming, "I'll kill you," and threatening Octavius with a knife. A sharp pain slashes through the back of my brain. Everything goes blue.

Then I'm back in Pompeii in Livia's bedroom. My wrists are bound and hung from that awful hook in the ceiling. I squeeze my eyes shut. Oh Goddess, not again. Please not again. When I open them, I'm still there.

"You have to suffer for what you've done, demon." Dad's expression is viciously happy.

One by one, pus-filled boils swell on my arms. He lets Octavius squeeze each one until it explodes. I scream and scream and scream until my voice becomes a silent whimper.

"This is what you deserve." Mom practically sings the words to me.

I open my mouth to beg for their help. To tell them this is wrong. All wrong. But my voice is gone.

"Silencing you is the first step." Octavius's smile slices through my qi. He leans close and whispers, "You never understood what was going on, did you?"

I can't bear to watch him dismember my body. I close my eyes.

Everything fades away. I'm in a fog. I don't know how long I'm there or if it's another nightmare. I don't care. I'm so grateful to be free of Octavius.

Suddenly, it's afternoon. Bright sun blinds me. I shield my eyes with my hand. Tombstones stretch across the grass like notches on rulers, marking time gone. Tav sits in front of a pink granite tombstone. His gray eyes are lifeless.

The name on the tombstone reads *Bess Ponte.*

Bess died. I didn't save her.

I failed.

Everything goes dark. Not evening dark. Wanshiqi prison dark. No light. No exit. The walls surround me, pressing in on my qi. Inescapable.

It's worse than I imagined. Ten thousand years of worse than I imagined. I can't survive this. I won't.

The darkness devours me.

I don't know how much time passes before my skin senses anything again. Something warm and comforting surrounds me. It reminds me of being inside my mother, sloshing around in the warm fluid. The only warmth she imparted to me in each lifetime.

I'd swear I'm floating in water. Panic swells in my lungs. My fingers clench, and water squirts out of my grasp.

"I've got you." Hunter's voice vibrates in my ear.

It's not just water surrounding me. It's Hunter. I nestle into his body. I open my eyes and realize we're in the big black tub in his bathroom. And everything's spinning and tilting like gravity doesn't quite apply in this room. I clutch his arm and wait for things to settle down.

"What happened?" My voice comes out hoarse, like I've been screaming for hours.

"You spiked a fever." He sounds calm, but his voice is frayed around the edges.

"How long was I out of it?"

"A day. How do you feel?"

The inside of my mouth is parched. Scorched. Torn up. "Like I ate a rollercoaster."

Hunter shifts, and the water sloshes against the side of the tub. "It felt that way."

I look down at his forearm resting on my stomach. A red welt slashes across his arm. "Did I do that?"

He traces tiny circles around my belly button. "Among other things."

My head is too heavy to hold up. I let it roll back against his shoulder. Hazy memories assault me. Nightmares. I brandished a knife at Octavius. Except Octavius is still buried in Pompeii. Confusion cripples me. "I...cut...you?"

"You didn't mean to."

"I'm sorry." I never mean to hurt Hunter, but intentions aren't enough.

He kisses the side of my head and presses his palm to my forehead. "It's okay."

It shouldn't be. "What else did I do?" My voice comes out breathy.

"You hallucinated and trashed the apartment. You had a couple seizures. Then the fever took you."

"I'm sorry." I touch the scar and feel an awful pain in my own heart.

"I was afraid I'd fried your brain. That you wouldn't wake up." His voice deepens, slipping into a fissure of fear.

Tremors rock my body. Nerves twinge and muscles jerk. "Something's wrong with me."

"It's too much energy for you to hold inside." He sweeps his knuckles along my jawline. "Are you ready for the curse?"

"Yeah." My stomach rumbles. It's not hunger. It's the energy inside me trying to find a way out.

I lace my fingers through Hunter's and wrap his arms around me like a comforter. I shut my eyes and imagine Bess. Bess with beautiful brown hair and nickel-gray eyes. Bess with pink cheeks. Bess at La Jolla Cove, smiling and laughing and hunting for seashells.

Bess strong and capable and alive.

I imagine her watching Tav in his burgundy-and-gold cap and gown, graduating high school. Helping him move boxes into his college dorm. At his college graduation, she whoops and claps. I see her helping him hunt for his first apartment.

I see Bess's life as it would be with years of remission. I can't remove the cancer, but I can stall its progression for a while.

The heat that burns inside my body radiates out of me beyond the bathwater to fuel the curse to defer Bess's death date. The fever flees. A chill creeps up my legs. When it reaches my head, my teeth chatter so hard I'm afraid they'll shatter. Shivers rack my body.

Hunter holds me as tightly as he can, trying to contain the coldness.

I should stop. I've gotten Bess to where I promised I would.

But it's not enough.

Inside my mind, I see Bess at Tav's wedding. Then she holds her first grandchild. Tiny lines radiate from Bess's eyes. Parentheses embrace her lips. I see Bess watching her grandchild grow. Gray streaks appear in Bess's hair. She wears reading glasses. Her clothes become more practical. Deep lines unfurl across her forehead. Her skin sags with age.

I want Bess to have a lifetime with her son. I want Tav and her to have the family I've always wanted. I want them to live the life I crave.

CHAPTER THIRTY-THREE

FROST BITES MY FINGERS and toes. An agonizing cold radiates from my bones. I will never be warm again.

But I hold on to the image of Bess in my mind, seeing her reach her 60s.

"Kali, stop this, you'll kill yourself." Hunter's voice goes primal as it calls to my human instincts to save me.

I listen to him and let Bess go in her 60s, but I can't feel my body. Not even my frozen fingers.

"Don't you die on me." Hunter sounds so very far away from me.

I can't see him. I can't feel him. I don't even know if we're still in the bathtub.

All I feel is numbness. Numbness is bad. It's what comes before death. Everyone thinks it's painful to die. It isn't. It's painful to start dying. The dying part, though, it's painless. Your body is tricked into death. Because it doesn't see it coming. Pain is a warning that something is wrong. Numbness is a state of calm. Right before everything ends.

People who fear death don't understand. It's the easiest thing you can do. Dying is letting go. Giving in to the numbness. Surrendering yourself.

Death is a reward.

"Stay with me." Hunter's sorrow stings my heart.

I don't want to leave him. Not like this. But I don't know how to stop my death.

A jolt to my heart shatters the numbness. Pain rushes in to fill the space. My lungs burn like they've been deprived of air for too long. A gasp rips through my throat.

The cold cement floor in Hunter's bathroom presses against my back. My eyes open. Hunter's face is inches above mine. Drops of water slip from his dark curls and wet my face.

"You almost died." His voice is gritty and raw like he came through a sandstorm and swallowed too much.

I try to explain, but I can't make my mouth work. I tell my hands to move, but they don't listen. My blood hurries through my veins, trying to outrun my fear. My eyes dart around, but I can't move.

He sits back on his heels with his chest heaving like he's fought a terrible battle and won. Gently, he touches my face. His fingers find the pulse point in my neck, lingering there until he's sure of my heart again. "Are you all right?"

I blink twice for no. Please let him understand.

He leans closer, staring into my eyes. "Your eyes have only amber left." His voice is threadbare, worn through by what it means.

When the brown disappears, I've activated my own death spiral.

This paralysis is my prelude to death.

I want to tell him I love him. That I was foolhardy to do so much for Bess. That he was right. He's always right. But the words, the damned words, won't form.

"Can you understand me? Blink once for yes, twice for no." Worry lines layer his forehead.

I blink once.

"Can you talk?" His voice is steady, but he can't keep the concern from filling his eyes.

I blink twice.

He picks me up and carries me to bed. "You need to rest."

It's the most comforting lie he can tell us. Rest can't fix what I've done.

The sunlight streaming through Hunter's windows tugs me out of my dreams. I roll toward warmth and curl into Hunter's strength. He strokes my hair.

"How do you feel?" Apprehension and worry and frustration flicker across his face.

My tongue rolls around my mouth. "Tired?"

His face relaxes. He pulls me across his chest. "You're okay."

"I'm okay." The paralysis from last night has passed. It wasn't a temporary glitch; it was a glimpse of my oncoming death. We both know it, even if we don't say it.

My lips are tight and dry. They feel like they are about to split open. "I'm thirsty." My stomach wails.

"Breakfast time?" I hear the smile in his voice.

I put on his boxers and T-shirt. He slides into yesterday's jeans. We make our way to the kitchen. While he makes breakfast, I sit at the table. I gulp down my orange juice, and he refills my glass. It stings the cracks in my lips, but it tastes so good.

I coat my toast in a layer of butter and another of pumpkin butter. I'm on my second slice before I ask, "What day is it?"

"Friday."

My arm jerks. My butter knife clangs against the glass table. "Friday?! I missed four days of school."

"You nearly died and that's your concern?" Before I can reply, he says, "I had your dad call the school for you." Hunter slides scrambled eggs onto my plate.

"How'd you manage that?"

"I talked to him about how Xia has been stirring things up and trying to see you." Hunter pours the rest of the eggs onto his plate and sits across from me.

"You did what?" My voice leapfrogs over the table toward him.

"It was the best way to secure his help." He says it with that confident calm that I find madly endearing.

I should be happy that he took care of it, but all I can think is that I lost four of the final days of my human life. I barely realize that my thoughts slip from my lips. "I traded four days for twenty years added to Bess's life."

"Twenty years?" Hunter's coffee sloshes over the side of his mug. He slams it on the table causing a clatter. "You said you were giving her ten more years."

I play with my eggs. "I just...I saw...I couldn't stop myself."

Hunter rubs his forehead. "I didn't give you enough energy for that. Hades, your heart stopped. I had to get it started again." His expression darkens like the sky before a hurricane. "You almost died."

"I didn't plan it. I just did it." In the moment it felt so right, but now my words sound so inadequate.

His chair screeches across the gray tile. He stands up. "When are you going to realize you can't just go rogue? You aren't only endangering your future. You're endangering my future!"

"I'm sorry. I just..." Tears burn my eyes. "I wanted her to have her family for longer than a few years. Is that so wrong?"

"No, it's wonderful and compassionate and why I love you. But consequences, Kali. Consequences." He says it like I never consider them.

I don't know what to say. He's right, and I hate that he's right. I grab my fork and take my first bite of the eggs. Inside my mouth, they are mush, flavorless mush. I spit them back onto the plate.

Hunter gives me his what-in-Hades face. "Now you hate my eggs?"

"They taste weird."

He scoops some up with his fork and tries them. "They taste just like mine. Delicious."

I grab the salt and shake it all over my plate. I scoop up another forkful. It's bland and boring. Tasteless. I sprinkle salt on my palm and lick it. I taste nothing.

"What is it?" Dread and confusion wage a battle across Hunter's face.

I've been trying to ignore it, but my right hand has a slight tremor. I try to control it and the shaking worsens. This has happened before. The tasteless food, the tremors. I can recognize the symptoms now. It's the prelude to how I will die.

I hate the knowing. The feeling of my body dying while I'm still in it. I hold my hand up to show him.

"What's happening?" Hunter doesn't want to see what's in front of him.

"It's Parkinson's," I whisper. I've suffered through the degenerative disorder of the central nervous system twice before.

"I didn't give you enough energy." He rubs his face, trying to remove the guilt.

"It's my fault. I went rogue and triggered my self-destruct." Each body has a self-destruct programmed in. Once it's activated, Hunter can't stop it. Grams can't undo it. One more curse would do me in. My death is an accelerated inevitable.

"Can you make it through your birthday?" I hear 10,000 years of fear building in his voice.

"As long as I don't curse." My voice is fragile, like what remains of my human body.

He goes to the fridge. The tremor in my hand worsens. I can barely hold on to the fork. I stab the cardboard eggs.

Hunter returns with a bottle of maple syrup and pours it over my eggs. "This might help."

The next bite is delicious. "I'm sorry."

Hunter's eyes sear mine. "So am I."

CHAPTER THIRTY-FOUR

HUNTER'S CAR IDLES IN my driveway. A quick shift, and we are out of here. All I have to do is ask. But I won't.

"Are you sure you want to do this?" Hunter already knows the answer, but he wants to give me one last out.

I stare down at the labradorite ring he gave me. My heart is too full of him today. "I have to face my parents." I just wish Grams and Gramps were here to help defuse the tension.

"I can come in with you." He turns his car off.

"Thanks, but I need to do this myself." I reach for the door release, but something inside me refuses to leave. "Hunter?" Somehow I manage to make his name sound like a question.

"Yeah?"

"I'm sorry for all the crap I've put you through. I'll be sorry until I die." My voice is swollen with remorse.

"Your human body or your qi?"

"Both." I lean in and kiss him. It's not a goodbye kiss, but a promise-to-be-better-for-him kiss. It's a few minutes before I manage to pull the door release and step out onto the pavement.

My parents sit across from me at the dining room table. No food. No water. Nothing of sustenance at the table. Grams would have made sure we had something to occupy our hands and soften the tension in our stomachs.

The chestnut-paneled walls feel stifling. The air is stale. Like the life has fled from this house. My parents stare at me. My contact lenses show them just enough brown in my eyes to put them at ease.

Dad plants his palms on the table, trying to bridge the distance between us. He molds his voice to sound compellingly casual. "What have you and Hunter been up to?"

I think about all the sex until heat creeps over my cheeks. "We hooked up."

"Let's start with Sunday. Walk me through everything you did on Sunday." Mom taps her blood-red nails on the table and cross-examines me.

"Sunday?" That's a week ago. "Why Sunday?" Before she can respond, I add, "Oh wait, that's the last time you saw me."

Dad's gaze slides to Mom. He almost looks surprised by her bad parenting.

I drop my voice to a confidential quiet. "Look, we just wanted to get some alone time before my birthday."

"Because you are going to be separated for a while?" Hope bleeds into Mom's words.

"For qifa?" Excitement burns in Dad's pale-blue eyes.

They want to hear that Kali is going to be a good girl and survive her seventeenth birthday. It's childish, but for all the centuries they didn't give me what I want, I refuse to give them what they want.

I lean back in my chair and kill the inflection in my voice. "If all goes well."

Dad's eyes ice over. "No cursing for three more days."

"This is the closest we've come to your seventeenth birthday." Mom sweeps her hand over her dark hair, making sure no strand threatens to go astray.

"I'm doing my best." I whine so much that my mother's brow tightens, and her eyes snap shut for a moment.

"Do better." The intensity of Dad's gaze reminds me of centuries ago when he led legions into battle.

"Fine." I shift in my chair. "I've got to get going."

"You're not leaving our sight for the next three days." Mom's smile seethes. "We are not letting you die this time."

"No." I stand up and step behind my chair.

"What did you say?" The corners of her eyes tighten, a feral focus, causing me to take a step back. A step toward who I never want to be again.

Panic bubbles inside me like lava inside Vesuvius. Pushing me to do something dire. If I lose control, I'll curse. I can't let Hunter down. I won't break my nuoyan. I bite my tongue until I taste blood. Then I give them what they want. "I promised Xia I'd reach my birthday. In three days, you'll get to return to your wanshiqi existence and be free of me. Win-win-win, right?" My sarcasm drips onto the floor.

"When did you see Xia?" Mom's face is at war with her emotions. Confusion, frustration, and annoyance battle it out.

"Same day you saw him."

For a split second, she looks almost uncertain. "Impossible."

"He pretended to be Dad a while back." I know it's spiteful to say, but I can't stop myself. "Fooled you good, too."

"Kali, you're not making any sense." My father gives me a warning look like he doesn't want Mom to find out about Xia.

Maybe Grams was right about Dad working with Xia. The air goes out of the room. I can't breathe around this possibility. My father betraying me by choice is the worst pain. It takes me a while to gather my next breath.

"Tell us everything." Mom stands up, trying to intimidate me back into my chair.

I grip the back of my chair. I'm done letting my parents push me around. "We don't have that kind of relationship. You made sure of that across every lifetime."

Mom sputters.

Dad lays a hand on hers. "Let it go. If she made a nuoyan to Xia, she has to keep it. There are no loopholes." My father's voice sinks under the weight of what a broken promise will mean for me. For a second, I almost think he cares about my imprisonment.

"You have to let us go home." What could be a plea sounds like an order from Mom.

That's all she's ever wanted. To be back amongst our kind and to take any form she wants. I've always been an afterthought.

I turn to leave.

"We aren't done here, Kali." Mom's voice is brutal in its indifference.

I walk toward the door. "But. I. Am."

"We didn't raise you to be so rude." Dad's tone chafes my ears.

My laugh comes out like burnt sugar, caramelizing over my pain. I spin around to face him. "You didn't raise me. Grams and Gramps did." A tremor weaves down my right arm. My fingers vibrate on their own.

Mom stalks toward me with a way-too-determined look in her eye. Her heels *damn-damn-damn* the herringbone floor.

Before she can reach me, I cross my arms and pin my right against my chest to conceal the tremor. "You can't wait to be rid of me. The only thing you look forward to is my qifa."

"Your birthday, actually."

My voice verges on a sob. "Did you ever love me? Like even for a second in any of our lifetimes? Ever?"

"I've done all I could after what you did in Pompeii." She's colder than an iceberg, and more dangerous.

I choke back a sob. "You did everything wrong in Pompeii."

"You're overwrought. Sit down, Kalifornia, and talk to us." Dad's tone is placating—everything a father should say to his crying daughter. But it sounds rehearsed, not real.

Microscopic bees sting my eyeballs, but I will not cry in front of them. "When you remember, you'll be sorry, and it'll be too late."

My father's forehead creases like a suit in Florida humidity. "We know everything that happened in Pompeii."

"No, you don't." Centuries of frustration flood my voice and crash into the wood-paneled wall.

"You can't rewrite history." The disgust in Mom's voice could bruise my skin.

"Others can." I hate how shrill I sound.

My parents exchange an uneasy glance. They think I've lost my mind again.

I won't tell them what really happened in Pompeii because I can't bear to watch them have seizures. I will not hurt them, even when they hurt me. But some part of me needs for them to consider the possibility that I wasn't wrong. "But what if you didn't know everything that happened in Pompeii?"

Dad's tone turns conciliatory. "If you want to tell us how you saw things, we will listen."

"She can't change what she did," Mom blurts out.

"Let her speak." His expression entreats Mom.

They don't understand. They won't hear my truth. They never could. "Forget it."

Tav answers his front door on the third knock. "Kali?" He steps out onto the porch barefoot and tugs the door shut behind him. "Where have you been all week?"

"I was sick," I lie.

He steps back, leery of risking Bess's compromised immune system. "Should you be here?"

"Just a bad migraine. Nothing contagious." The lie comes more easily than I'd like. "How's your mom?"

"She's resting." Exhaustion and fear have hollowed out his cheekbones. "She wanted to come home." He doesn't say the "to die" at the end of that sentence, but I sense it.

"Doctors don't know everything." They don't know about me or how my curse pushed back her death date.

"That's the weird part. She's been better this week." He crosses his arms and leans back against the railing. "The doctor said she might get better right before she…" His voice trails off.

"She isn't going to die."

"She is." The fear in his eyes threatens to spill over. I try to hug him, but he grabs me and kisses me. A rough and desperate kiss.

I shove him away. "I'm with Hunter. Nothing will change that."

"We're sixteen. Everything will change."

"Not Hunter and me." Steel beams reinforce the conviction in my words.

In the porch light, emotions tumble across his face and kick me in the gut. "What about the beach?"

"That was a mistake."

"I'm a mistake?" Hurt braids his words.

"You're wonderful."

He starts to come toward me, and I put my hand up to stop him. "You need someone who can be with you."

"Someone like Mandy?" He says her name with a softness that scratches at my heart.

"Yes." My throat tightens around that word. It's the biggest word I've ever tried to say.

Recognition flickers in his eyes. "You can't stand the idea of us together."

"That's not true."

He closes the space between us. "You like me."

If I were human, I would be tempted to reach out and touch him. But I'm not, so I grip the banister. "You're very likable."

His lips are several inches from mine. "You want me."

"No." It comes out too breathy to convince him.

He tries to kiss me again, but I stumble down the porch steps, putting a few feet between us. "I wanted to check on your mom and you. That's it."

"Why do you care so much about me and my mom?" He makes it sound like I did something awful.

"I'm trying to be your friend."

"My friend?" Disbelief douses his face.

I back up until I bump into my car door.

"I don't want your friendship," he yells before he goes back into his house and slams the door.

CHAPTER THIRTY-FIVE

I DON'T KNOW WHERE to go, so I drive. I probably shouldn't because my right hand is trembling something awful. But I can't stay still. I merge onto the Five in my VW Beetle, heading downtown to the heart of San Diego. I'm hoping a little distance and a lot of city light will distract me from the emptiness inside me. I get off the freeway, and green traffic lights send me past Juniper and Grape toward Broadway. It doesn't matter how many people are around me on the streets, emptiness still threatens to overwhelm me.

I can't let Hunter see that Tav upset me. I won't go back to Mom and Dad. All I can do is keep driving. I change course leaving behind the brightness of the city center and heading to the darkness of the summit. I speed north on the freeway and get off near La Jolla. I find my way to the winding road that takes me up Mount Soledad and into the darkness. I go as high as I can and park the car. The darkness wraps me in its embrace as I wander into the overgrown grass and shrubbery. There's a narrow, sandy trail that I follow. The breeze ruffles my hair and carries a hint of hope. The path ends at a bench. I sit alone above the city, the ocean, and my problems.

It's after 1 a.m. when I slip through the front door of my house and into the main room. The whole house is dark. Shadows creep up the walls. I fumble for the light switch, but the lamp on the side table bursts to life. My mother sits in an armchair in her black silk robe. Her dark hair shrouds her face. She stares into the empty fireplace.

The stairs are in sight. The sanctuary of my room is a flight away. I take a few deliberate steps toward them.

"What did you mean about Pompeii?" Her voice creaks like the worn-down floors of an old house.

My neck muscles tighten, and it's hard to get my next breath. She doesn't know the fear I felt when I watched her eyes glaze over and her body twitch. How scared I was that she wouldn't come out of it. The relief when her muscles finally stopped spasming, and her eyes focused and saw me. I can't go through it again. I won't. "Nothing."

"Your father and I did the best we could with you." She wants to send me on a guilt trip.

I should run away from the truth like my parents do. Instead, I pivot on my heels and face her.

"If you must tell me something about Pompeii, now is the time to do it." It sounds like a taunt, but there's a catch in her voice, a paperclip of uncertainty.

"Nope." I won't risk hurting her, even if this silence kills me.

She stands up. Her black silk bathrobe slithers down her legs. Without her heels, she's a few inches shorter than me. "Don't you want to go home?"

"When has what I wanted mattered?" My voice goes up and down like the rollercoaster of emotions her words unleash inside me.

She folds her arms. "I have lived in exile as a human for over 1900 years. For you."

"And you've reminded me of it daily."

"Because each day is an agony. You have no idea what you've done to your father and me." She grabs at my arm.

I step out of her reach. "In a few days, you will have everything you want." My self-control shimmies like a car about to go off the road.

She rests her cheek against her hand. Her expression is almost vulnerable. "I have always cared about you. Not like a human mother, but like a wanshiqi parent should."

"Never the way I needed you to." The ache in my chest comes from a hollowness nothing will ever fill.

The next morning, the house smells of Grams's gardenias. The air is fresh like all the windows were thrown open to the ocean breeze. And the house feels alive again. When I walk into the dining room, the table is covered in breakfast foods. Grams stirs her tea, and Gramps slathers apricot preserves on his toast like they didn't disappear for a week.

"When did you get back?" Relief warms the pit of my stomach.

Grams looks at Gramps and squints like she's trying to see a clock that's too far away. "About 4 a.m."

I slide into my seat and reach for the oatmeal. "Why didn't you wake me?"

"We wanted to talk to you after your mother left." Grams pours me a cup of coffee.

"Your mother asked me about Pompeii." He doesn't say it, but I feel a reprimand.

I ignore it because I've got bigger issues. I pour a bucket of honey into my oatmeal. It's the only way I can eat anything with Parkinson's. Drown it in sweetness and swallow it. "What did you say?"

"The same thing we've said for hundreds of years. That things aren't black and white." Gramps takes a bite of toast.

Grams tries to read the emotions on my face. "What did you want us to say?"

"I wish you could tell her the truth. I want her to look at me the way she did before Pompeii." But that's a fairytale ending. And I don't get those kinds of endings.

"I wish we could, dear." The genuine sadness in her tone clogs my throat with tears.

I fight to keep myself from crumbling. "She'll find out after my birthday."

Grams pats my hand. "I'll do my best to heal her, but remember there are no guarantees."

She doesn't know about my deal with Xia yet. "Thanks," I say weakly.

"You've never come so close to your birthday before." Gramps forks his ham and prods me along.

They need to know why. "Xia came to see me."

Gramps drops his toast jelly side up on the table.

Grams's spoon clangs against her porcelain teacup. "When?"

"While you were gone."

Gramps slams his fist on the table. Everything rattles and shakes, including me. "What did he want?"

I lock my ankles around my chair legs, needing to feel more stable. "A trade."

"What was he proposing?" Gramps's expression turns Zeus-like, threatening all of mankind.

"A nuoyan for a nuoyan." I fight to keep my voice level.

"You sent him away." Grams says it like it was my only option.

I can't bring myself to look at her.

Gramps knows me better. "What did you promise him?" His voice is harsher than a Siberian winter.

"I'll turn seventeen, he'll protect Mom, Dad, and Hunter, and he'll fix Mom and Dad's memories."

"Oh Kali." Her disappointment lengthens each word. "You shouldn't have."

"You should have told me Gramps was Zhou of the wuwang. How come Hunter and Xia told me more about you than you ever did?" My voice spirals.

"It's not that simple." Gramps looks ancient. "We were protecting you."

"And I'm still hurt. If I had known what was going on..."

"What could you have done, dear?" Her tone reminds me how powerless I've been.

"We'll never know because you didn't give me the chance." I toss my napkin on the table and dart out of the dining room.

CHAPTER THIRTY-SIX

I DON'T KNOW WHAT I'm doing at my father's beach house or why Mom's car is in his driveway, but I sneak in through his bedroom window to find out. His room is done in shades of gray with black highlights just like his qi. I tiptoe across the hardwood floor and peek out into the living room.

My parents sit on the couch with their backs to me. An impeccably dressed man that I don't recognize stands facing them. Sunlight pours through the sliding glass door behind him. He sees me. My pulse almost darts out of my wrist. He gives me the slightest nod, but doesn't let them know I'm there.

"How did you secure her nuoyan?" I hear a little awe in my father's voice, and now I know why. He's talking to Xia.

"The girl has a soft spot for her family." Xia picks a piece of lint off his suit and discards it the way he discarded me all those years ago.

"You threatened us?" Mom's voice rises. She's either shocked or annoyed by his tactics. But not surprised, no, definitely not surprised.

"I merely reminded her of the difficulties ahead without the proper alliances." Xia manages to minimize all his actions.

"This human hell will be over in a few days." Relief relaxes my father's shoulders.

Mom hesitates. "And my parents?"

"Should be fine." Xia's tone sets me on edge because his words dance with a delightful uncertainty that only he understands.

"Are you sure Kali can make it to her seventeenth birthday?" Dad still doesn't trust me.

"She's strong enough." Xia's eyes lock on mine. "Though the brown in her eyes is gone."

Dad shakes his head. "You're wrong. We just saw her last night."

"You only see what you want to see." Xia smirks. "Haven't you noticed the brown is there even as she begins her death spiral? She had special contacts made to hide her true eye color from you."

"We'd know." Doubt chips away at the confidence in Mom's tone.

"Because you're such good parents." Xia's truth sinks into them like venomous fangs.

Mom and Dad exchange a look.

"Enchanted contacts…" A gruff note of pride echoes in Dad's voice.

Xia's face is a mask of indifference. I cannot figure out why he told them about the contacts or why he's keeping my presence a secret from them.

I don't care that Xia revealed my secret. I'm done dying before my birthday. I don't need the contacts anymore. It's what my parents said to him that impacts me. My parents are colluding with Xia. They are working with him against me. I back away from their conversation and slip out the window. I stumble down the street. Tears blur my vision the way my parents blur the truth.

Something gnaws at my stomach and burns up my throat. Rage. Shadows demand to be allowed out of my qi. A curse sings from my heart. To die this close to seventeen would decimate them.

But I would suffer imprisonment. Imprisonment is not the way to get even with them. There is nothing I can ever do to equal how they've hurt me. Getting to even is impossible.

Trust is one of the most shatterable things. A crack can birth a thousand more. It can only be mended with time and truth.

I come home for truth. I stomp through the entryway of my house, and yell, "Grams, we need to talk."

She doesn't appear. I march into her sunshine room, but she's not there among her plants. I try her study. Empty. Gramps's study door is locked. I pound on it. The lock clicks and the door creaks open. Gramps fills the doorway with his billowing white hair.

"I need to talk." I try to step into his study, but he blocks the way.

"Let's go to Grams's study." He tugs the door shut behind him. The lock clicks into place again.

"Who's in your study?"

"An old friend," is all he says as he ushers me into Grams's study and shuts the door.

The room is ivory encased in gold. Elegant, warm, and so Grams.

I move like a bee, constantly changing direction and agitating the air around me. "Mom and Dad are helping Xia."

Gramps sits down in a Louis the XV chair. "He's got them on his side now." His voice settles around this news.

I take a breath, cling to it and then release, release, release it.

"Kali, sit down. I have to tell you something important." His tone is like a cast iron skillet—heavy and weighted with consequences.

I drop onto the couch. My knee bounces up and down.

"When Grams and I left, no one could know where we were going or what we were doing. It was too risky. We went to meet with Hunter's grandfather, Qin, in Atlantis."

"But you destroyed Atlantis."

"According to the history books." His smile reminds me that he's been playing power games for 100 times longer than I have. "All those centuries ago, I helped the demons submerge Atlantis to escape wanshiqi persecution."

My jaw drops and my thoughts free fall. "No, you couldn't." For millennia, Gramps was known as the destroyer of Atlantis and its demons. My parents tortured me in Pompeii because they thought I was a demon. It's like he carved the heart out of my voice with a wooden spoon. "You helped the demons?"

"Demons are the only ones strong enough to threaten the wan-shiqi. I never trusted Shang or Xia. I needed a place they couldn't find that was filled with my allies. Just because the five kingdoms united didn't mean we wouldn't fight for power again at some point." Gramps was playing the long, long game all along.

Right now, Xia's words echo in my head: *My enemy's enemy is my friend.* I no longer see Gramps in front of me. This is Zhou of the wuwang. I shudder and pull back into the couch.

Gramps leans forward. There's an undeniable fire in his eyes. Some part of him still enjoys the game. "Uncertainty over the next in line to rule has caused power bases to shift and alliances to alter throughout the realm."

"Because some want Han to remain gone and some want her to return." I tell him about the memory Xia shared with me of Han stepping down as ruler.

Gramps wipes his palm over his eyes, trailing it down to his lips, and cupping his chin. "Xia stopped before Han laid out the succession plan?"

I nod.

Gramps gets up and walks toward me with a determined look on his face. "I'll complete the memory for you. It will make everything clearer." He presses his pointer finger into my third eye.

I'm back in the wuwang meeting, picking up at the exact point that Xia's memory ended. This time, however, I'm seeing everything through Zhou's perspective.

"But if something happens..." Xia's voice is crème brulee smooth—completely untrustworthy.

"Such as?" Han sounds melodious and calming.

"Complications are common." Xia spreads his dark crow wings out.

"If I don't return, Zhou will succeed Shang and reign in my place for the next ten thousand years. Then Qin, then you, Xia." Han looks like a Chinese empress bestowing her gentle smile on everyone, but her eyes tighten with weariness. "Does that ease your mind?"

"It removes an element of instability," Xia says.

I hear Gramps's thoughts so clearly. When Xia knows the rules, he knows how to manipulate everyone to get what he wants.

Shang clears his throat. He is bathed in shadows in Zhou's memory. Darkness clings to him. I can't see his form. "And if anything happens to one of us?" There is too much surety in his tone. Something will happen to them.

"The next in line will rule," Han says.

"Just make sure you come back to us." Bile washes against the back of Gramps's throat, and I taste the sourness of Han's decision. Her stepping down will destabilize the realm. He tried to convince her to stay, but his words held no sway.

"Are you sure this is necessary?" Qin is a hawk perched on Gramps's shoulder. His claws nip at Gramps's shoulder, conveying his displeasure with Han's choice.

"One cannot rule forever." Han touches her third eye.

The other wuwang do the same, locking the memory away.

I blink, and I'm back in Grams's study.

"Why is Shang still ruling?" Qin was supposed to take over if Zhou couldn't rule next. At least according to the memory.

Gramps sighs. "When you were branded a traitor and punished, I chose to follow you here. Shang insisted he remain in power during such a *turbulent time*."

I snort. "The turbulence he created."

Gramps points at me. "Exactly."

My thoughts turn to the powers of the wuwang. Xia moves his qi in and out as he pleases. Qin can move others qi, but not his own. Gramps is a death dealer. He can kill or maim millions. I don't know what our enemy can do. "What is Shang's power?"

"He raises the dead."

"He's a healer like Grams?" That doesn't sound nearly as impressive as what Gramps can do.

Gramps shakes his head slowly. "He brings the dead back to do his bidding."

"Zombies?" I whisper.

"It's very hard to kill what's already dead." His voice is leaden, like he's reliving that battle in his mind.

"What about Han's power?"

"She is the most powerful of all of us. None can stand up to her. She was old when I was young." His tone tells me he won't say more about her.

Still I try to finagle for more information. "So could she bring the dead fully back to life?"

"Not that I know of." He gives me a secretive smile. "If she set her mind to it, she could accomplish anything."

I try to process everything he's told me. "According to the succession plan, if Shang takes out you and Qin, Xia would rule."

"Which makes Xia the final barrier to Shang's permanent rule of the wuwang."

My head spins at the betrayals and manipulations. All to be the ruler of the wanshiqi. My voice comes out tiny. "And I'm at the center of it all."

His expression tells me he'd have done anything to avoid what is happening to me. "Xia and Shang wanted you to violate falu in Pompeii, so they could delay your qifa and prevent Han's return." Gramps's voice is excavated, like explorers have tunneled through it and pillaged what they found.

"Shang wants me to die before my seventeenth birthday?"

"He and his faction will do whatever they can to get you to curse and kill your body."

"Why don't they just kill me?"

"It's not that simple. You must die from choosing to use your powers. That's what keeps your punishment ongoing and prevents you from reaching qifa. It also keeps me here with you and out of Shang's way." His world-weary sigh reminds me just how long he's been dealing with this endless power struggle.

My mouth can't catch up to my mind. The conspiracy Gramps was worried about includes everyone—the lishihui, the zhangzhe, and the wuwang. We could be facing a battle between the five kingdoms. Oh Hades. This is bad. Really bad. Wanshiqi war bad.

"We've got to do something."

"I am. But there are nuoyan that I must keep. And falu still applies to you."

"Forget about falu. Gramps, no one else is playing by the rules." Impatience blisters my voice.

"We are all playing around our rules." Millennia of experience reinforce his words. "Shang will come after you. I don't know when or where. I want you to stay here the next few days where I can protect you."

"He can't get to me here?"

"He can get to you anywhere. He's Shang. But I can help you here."

I know I should do what he says. It's the smart decision. But I know me. And I have to end my time here properly. "My friends deserve a goodbye."

"I figured you'd say that." There's a grim determination in his voice. Gramps walks to Grams's cabinet and pulls out an ornate silver bracelet with a large opal in the center. He puts it on my wrist. "If you need help, press the opal. It will send a message to our allies."

I nod.

"I need you to do one thing for me: keep your nuoyan and live through this birthday. Can you do that for me, Kali?"

"I can."

He doesn't look the least bit surprised. "Grams and I figured as much."

I used to worry that he'd caught me in this lifetime. But I think it was much earlier than I imagined. "How long have you and Grams known?"

"The first dozen or so lifetimes on Earth, we saw your surprise when your death came early. You were still figuring out what your powers did to your human body. After a while, that disappeared. It was like you wanted to die young."

"Why didn't you say something?" Misery nurses my words.

"Because we understood what you wanted—to keep your family together. To regain the parents you had before Pompeii. It was the safest option for all of us. So we let you do what you wanted to do."

"What about Mom and Dad?" The words claw their way out of my mouth, leaving a bloody mess behind.

"Your parents would never understand. They mistake your humanity for weakness. Your emotions have always been your strength." His voice flows like the eternal spring of his experience.

I chew the inside of my cheek. "I can barely summon any power from the lighter emotions. It's only the dark emotions that fuel my worst curses."

The intensity of his gaze makes me squirm. "Because you embraced the dark emotions after Pompeii."

"They saved me from Octavius." My voice goes pitchy.

"For centuries, you've dodged love and compassion. You refused to embrace those emotions. Is it any wonder they are so weak and hard to wield for cursing?" He gently leads me toward a realization.

Because of Octavius, I believed the lighter emotions caused my downfall. What if I had spent thousands of years living with the wrong lesson?

Gramps sits beside me on the couch. He wraps his arm around me. The realization reverberates through me. I tremble.

"I wanted to be a family. To help Mom and Dad. I love you all so much." My voice smashes like ancient pottery. I'm not sure I can salvage anything anymore.

"Grams and I tried to give you family."

I hear the slightest hesitation in his words and squeeze his hand. "You did in every reincarnation."

His smile warms my qi.

A loud crash from Gramps's study startles both of us.

He gets up. "I have to see to that."

"To what?" I ask.

"A demon that I've kept waiting far too long."

He's almost out of the room when I ask, "What can I do to help?"

"Whatever happens, keep your nuoyan. And I'll find a way to keep all of mine."

CHAPTER THIRTY-SEVEN

I UNBUCKLE MY SEAT belt, turn to Mandy in the driver's seat, and give her my best smile. I make sure to roll my words in sugar and cinnamon like her favorite apple cider donuts. "Just get Tav out of the house for an hour."

"I can't just ask him out." Mandy's fingers grip her steering wheel, and her voice tips toward panic.

"Tell him you need to talk to him." I have to see Bess one last time before my birthday. I press my palms together. "Please. I'd do it for you."

She slumps in the driver's seat. A defeated look crawls over her face. "Fine. One hour."

"Thanks." I hug her, slip out of her car, and crouch behind the hedges in Tav's yard. I pull a few branches aside, so I can watch Mandy park in his driveway and walk to the front door. Her hands fist and unfist. She knocks. While she waits, she walks in a tight circle. Anticipating a lie, she searches for the right place to drop it, like a hen with her egg.

When the door opens, she jumps. I can't hear what she's saying, but her arms flail about. Her eyes bulge. Tav's expression shifts from dumbstruck to complete confusion. He edges back inside. She hops around on the porch, looking more like an angry chimp than the captain of the cheer squad. She tugs on his arm. Tav gives in, shuts the door, and walks to her car.

Mandy makes her constipated face until I text her to smile. Her lips stretch like a hyena. Poor Tav.

Once her car disappears down the street, I make my way to Tav's front porch.

Bess answers the door with a turquoise-and-green silk scarf wrapped around her head like a turban. She's wearing a flowing peacock print caftan. Her toenails are painted bright blue. Surprise flitters across her face, but she smiles and hugs me. "Kali, it's good to see you again."

I follow her to the living room where she's got tea and lemon bars set out on the coffee table. "Tav and I were just sitting down for a snack, but he had to help Mandy. Perfect timing." Her voice tells me she suspects it's a little too perfect.

"I wanted to see you." I sit on the couch and Bess takes the chair. The opposite of the first time we met. The blinds are open and sunlight streams into the room, touching her crystal earrings and her cheeks. Both sparkle with life.

"You look gorgeous." Death has disappeared from her features.

Her cheeks flush cherub pink. "I feel like I got a shot of life in my veins." She pours the tea and offers me a lemon bar. "Last week, I had the strangest dream. You were in it. And you promised I'd see my first grandchild."

"Really?" I lift the teacup to my mouth, and my right hand trembles. Tea sloshes over the side and into my lap. "I'm so sorry." I dab at the spill, despising my failing body.

"Are you okay?" Worry lines race across her forehead.

"Just clumsy." I shift to hide the tremor in my right hand.

"In my dream, you healed me." She studies my face.

"That's pretty cool." I grab a lemon bar and bite into it, so I don't have to say anything else.

She takes my hand in hers. Her hands are so warm now. "Ever since that dream, I've felt healthy. I have an appointment with the doctor on Monday, but I think you know what he'll say." Her eyes pierce through me.

"You are going to beat the cancer and live to see Tav into adulthood."

Her voice slips under the carpet and crawls toward me. "You're not like me, are you?"

A thousand lies clutter my mind. A piece of the truth escapes. "You only have one chance. One ride on the merry-go-round of life."

"What about you?" She grips my hand. "Did you take on my sickness?" Guilt hunches her shoulders.

"I'm going to be fine." Centuries of practice make it easy to smile and pretend all is well. "But I have to leave California soon."

Her eyes go all shiny.

"You understand what it's like to leave behind the people you care about. The fear you have for them." I try to keep my voice steady, but it veers into sadness.

She nods.

"I need you to watch over Mandy for me."

"Tav and I will do that." She says it like a solemn vow.

I release the breath I've been holding too long.

"Do you really have to leave?" She nips at her lower lip. If she remembers the dream, she knows the answer.

"We still have half an hour before Tav returns."

She releases my hand and presses the sides of her fingers to her eyes, trying to keep the tears from falling. "Will you say goodbye to him?"

"After last night, I'm pretty sure he never wants to see me again." That admission triggers an ache deep inside my chest.

She presses her palm to my cheek. "If I know one thing, it's don't leave with regrets between you."

CHAPTER THIRTY-EIGHT

I KNOW SEEING TAV again will be awkward and difficult, but when he walks into the living room, and I look into his iron-clad eyes, I wish I hadn't listened to Bess.

"What are you doing here?" Tav asks as if I'm a cockroach infringing on his home.

"I came to see your mom." I shift uncomfortably on the couch.

"I asked her to stay and talk to you." Bess folds her arms and gives him a behave-yourself look.

"Why?" His voice is sharp enough to nick my heart.

I stand up. "This was a mistake."

"Kali, sit down." Bess rests her hand on my shoulder and eases me back onto the couch. "Tav, you've been slamming cabinets since she left last night. Talk. To. Her."

Tav tucks his neck into his shoulders, reminding me of a turtle protecting its head. "I don't have anything to say. To. Her." He starts backing out of his living room.

"Octavius, don't." Her voice is certitude forged in the fire of experience. "If there is anything the cancer has taught us, it's that time is precious. You never know what will be the last thing you say to someone."

He stops and stares at the tips of his sneakers. His neck is mottled with angry red blotches.

"Give Kali half an hour. And open up those ears and listen to her." Bess leaves us in the living room.

Tav stays because she made him, not because he wants to hear what I have to say.

"I don't want to leave things the way we did." I smooth the wrinkles out of my skirt. I wish I could smooth things out between us as easily.

"There's nothing left to say." The finality in his tone forces the truth from me.

"I messed up."

His eyes narrow and his lips thin—I'm not sure if it's disbelief or annoyance.

"I like you. A lot. But I shouldn't have kissed you."

"You didn't want to?" Something vulnerable creeps into his words.

I rub my forehead, trying to find the words between truth and false hope. "I wanted to kiss you, but I'm with Hunter. That made it wrong."

"So leave Hunter." His eyes are quicksilver.

"I won't do that." I get up and take a step toward him. "If things were different, if I were different, I'd have loved to have you as my boyfriend."

"Don't say things you don't mean." His voice is more fragile than meringue.

I won't damage him. "I never do."

His hair slides over his eyes.

I'm making a mess of things. Again. "I just wanted to say good-bye."

"We've still got a few weeks until summer break." He peeks at me through his hair.

"I have to leave California." My birthday ends my time here—if I survive I go to qifa; if I die, to wanshiqi imprisonment. Either way, I'm no longer here.

He slides his hands in his pockets and rocks on his heels. "So I guess I'll see you when you get back."

"I'm not coming back." I won't ever see him again. My eyes are hot. But I won't, won't, won't cry.

"This is goodbye?" Goodbye comes out clipped, like his teeth latched on to the end of the word and refused to let it go.

I nod, no longer trusting myself to speak. Everything wanshiqi in me tells me to walk out and not look back; everything human in me screams to touch him one last time. I fling my arms around his neck and kiss his cheek. He smells of limes and cedar like he always does. I close my eyes and sink into him for a second. If I were human, I could have fallen in love with him.

I don't bother knocking on Hunter's front door. I just use my key. I turn the doorknob, but the door opens without me pushing it. I stumble into the apartment, and Hunter catches me.

"You're here." I've never been so grateful to see him.

"It's your last weekend as a human being." His smile heals my heart.

I take a deep breath, inhaling his scent. Stars and oceans. Hunter. I burrow into the strength that is inherently him. I'm tired of talking. I need to be with Hunter for a while. He knows it, too. We melt into each other.

I can't help thinking about how this will all change soon. If everything goes as I plan, I'll turn seventeen and go through qifa and be completely different. I don't know how I will feel or who I will be when I emerge from qifa. My worst fear is that I become like my mother. Too many emotions attacking my too-human heart. I can't repress them anymore.

Fear claws its way up from the bottom of my belly to the back of my throat. My breath hitches in my chest. I feel that awful pressure of a sob building in my lungs. I tighten my arms around him and clutch at his shirt.

"Kali, your nails are digging into my skin."

A tidal wave of feelings rushes through my ears.

He picks me up and carries me to the couch. He sits down with me attached to him. "What is it?"

I try to speak over the roaring waves of emotion, but all those feelings choke me.

He holds me while I battle my emotions.

Finally, I gain enough control to whisper, "I need you. I have always needed you." I press my forehead to his so he can see the truth in my eyes.

"I need you, too." He cups my face. His eyes are like the waters off Lido, sweeping me under a sea of blues and greens and sucking me down until I don't want to breathe. "You've always been afraid to grow up. Afraid to change. But Kali, we are eternal, you and I. We get to grow together."

"I want to believe we will always be close. But deep down, I'm terrified qifa will change me. Us. We might become like my parents." My voice dips into despair. "I don't want *us* to change."

"You will always be my tonggan. Always."

My lips are so close to his, we share a breath. "You promise?"

"I promise." He uses his lips and hands to seal his nuoyan.

Hunter and I lie in his bed, legs entangled, sheets wrinkled, qi satiated.

I look up at the ceiling. "There's something that's been bothering me."

He rolls onto his side and looks down at me. "What's that?"

"Why did you let me keep dying if it put Qin in danger?" Every lifetime Hunter asked me to turn seventeen, but he always let me choose. And I chose to die every time. With Zhou stuck on Earth, the next threat to Shang's power was Hunter's grandfather Qin.

The tiny muscles in his jaw pulsate under his skin. "Tonggan comes first. It was what you wanted and needed."

I reach up and stroke his cheek. "And now?"

"Qin and your needs align." He leans down and kisses my neck.

It's a few minutes before I can think again. "Do you think Shang will let me turn seventeen?"

Hunter laces his fingers through mine and pulls me into his arms. "He has a plan and allies ready to help him achieve his goals. You are definitely in danger."

I listen to the reassuring beat of his heart. "Do you think we can beat him?"

"Zhou and Qin have their allies and their plan, too." He strokes my hair.

"Will it be enough?"

"It has to be." Hunter's voice is jagged like stones stolen from within the belly of a mountain.

CHAPTER THIRTY-NINE

Hunter's Porsche comes to a stop in front of Mandy's contemporary-style house. I fidget with my phone. This is my last and my hardest goodbye.

"You don't have to do this in person." He reaches over the console and tucks my hair behind my ear.

"I owe her a real goodbye." I reach up and capture his hand. I press a kiss to his knuckles to thank him for being here.

Hunter glances around the neighborhood. "What if Shang tries something?"

I lift my wrist and show him the opal bracelet. "Gramps says it's like a panic button. I'll be okay."

He pulls a book out of the back seat and reclines his seat. "I'll wait."

"It could be a while." I need to break my leaving to Mandy and pick up the pieces afterward.

"I'm very patient."

I can't tell him no. I take a deep breath and open my door. "See you soon."

I swear the night sky echoes the dark notes of Carmina Burana that are playing in my head. I walk past the tulips to the morning glories and the garden gnomes, by the fragrant roses beside the front steps. I reach the front door and knock. No one answers, but the lights are on inside. Someone has to be home.

Five knocks later, Mandy yanks the door open. Her face morphs from surprise to frustration. "What are you doing here?" she hisses at me.

Her tone makes me step back. "What's wrong?"

Her gaze darts inside her house like she doesn't want me to come inside. "Bad timing."

"I need to talk to you."

"Not now." She starts to shut the door in my face.

I push it back open. "It's really important."

She looks at Hunter's car and sighs. "You'd better send him home."

"Why?"

She steps close to me. Close enough that the roses don't mask her scent. Licorice. "Because he could get hurt if he stays."

"Grandfather?" My tongue trips over his name. "What did you do to Mandy?"

"Just get rid of him." Her voice is sharp and quiet like a razor slashing across my skin.

My heart triple beats in my chest, running a race it cannot win. I retrace my steps to Hunter's car. At the roses, I know I have to stay and save Mandy. As I pass the morning glories, I want to run to Hunter and escape. Near the tulips, I know what I have to do.

He rolls down the passenger window and looks up at me. "What's up?"

I lean inside and add a slight strain to my casual tone. "Mandy's having a fit over how much time I spend with you. She feels like a pit stop on my way to you."

"Isn't she?" His lips curve with confidence.

"Sort of." All humans are. "Can you wait for me at my house?" I grip the windowsill. I want to jump in that car and speed away from here, but I can't leave Mandy in Xia's clutches. "Mandy will give me a ride home." Sweat trickles down my spine.

He hesitates.

I jangle my bracelet. "You'll know if I'm in trouble."

He gives me a smile that melts everything inside me. "See you soon."

I watch his taillights fade into the night. Once they are gone, I turn back to Mandy's house and retrace my steps to Xia.

Xia in Mandy's body freaks me out because I don't know how this impacts her human soul. My evil grandfather also looks like my best friend. It's surreal to sit with him in Mandy's living room under the vaulted ceiling and exposed wood beams. I have sat on this brown leather couch watching hundreds of rom-com movies with Mandy.

Now, she sits across from me in a matching leather armchair with her legs folded under her like a teenager. I mean, she is a teenager. Well, her body is. It's just been commandeered by a wuwang.

"Is Mandy okay?" My voice clutches at *okay*.

"For the time being." The smile crawling across Mandy's face is pure Xia.

Creepy squared. "What are you doing back here?"

"You should have left like I said." He speaks so softly that I can barely make out his words. He gives me a look that I'd swear is pure regret.

The kitchen door swings open. An old man hunches over his cane. He drags himself into the room, looking weak and worn through by life. He comes closer and I smell fire. The kindling and burning of wood. I remember that smell from Xia's memory.

"Shang?" I whisper.

His eyes are completely black. No white, no iris, just darkness. They are utterly lifeless. "Last time I saw you, they called you Livia."

"That was a long time ago." My voice huddles around me, small and afraid.

"Two millennia is a long time?" The sound of Shang's voice sets me on edge. It's harsh. Mechanical. Inhuman.

Shang touches a strand of my hair. It's like a bat latched on to me. I shudder and pull away.

"We came to talk, not to torture." Xia grips the armrests.

"Quiet." With a single word, Shang reminds Xia who is in charge.

"We need the girl," Xia murmurs a reminder.

Shang's eyes sink deeper into his weather-beaten face. He lowers himself onto the couch next to me. Beneath the smell of smoke and fire, there's something else. Something awful. A whiff of decay hits my nose. Every cell in my body rebels against his nearness. I inch away from him.

"You have so many humans that you care for." Shang's words are a knife held to my throat.

I don't say anything. I don't move. I don't breathe.

"Did anyone ever tell you about my power?" He tilts his head like we're having a civil conversation.

"You raise the dead." My throat is so tight, my voice comes out an octave higher. "Is that what you are right now?"

"She's smarter than you said," Shang says to Xia, like it's a bad thing. His words send goose bumps cascading down my arms. "I'm using this dead human to talk to you. Consider it a proxy for me."

I reach for my bracelet to summon help when Shang says, "You know, for centuries, I sent my minions to live amongst you. They discovered something interesting. You always die young to keep your family together. Though sometimes you need a little encouragement." He turns to Xia. "Remember that time I dispatched you to Bodie to deal with your son?"

My hand freezes, and I don't touch the opal. "What are you talking about?" My gaze darts from Shang to Xia.

"What was that guy's name? The one you took over for one night." Shang uses his cane to tap Xia's foot.

"Farley." Xia's eyes are devoid of any emotion.

I feel like someone torpedoed my lungs, and they are sinking into my stomach. "You murdered my father?"

"I did what had to be done." Xia brushes it off without remorse.

I leap out of my chair. "You murdered my dad!" My voice bounces off the walls.

"I killed his human body. His qi was fine." Xia gives me a disdainful look, like my overreaction is embarrassing him. "Sit down." Xia's tone is powerful enough to get me to drop back onto the couch.

Shang gives me a look of pure malice. "You die tomorrow, or I will raise an army of the dead to kill all the humans you love. Then I will raise your loved ones and make them part of my dead army."

"Why would I risk my future for humans?" My voice squeaks on humans.

"No wanshiqi should." Shang studies me. "But you've never been like us, have you?"

"All this time as a human has given me insight into them." My voice warbles like a songbird fearing for its life.

Shang wraps his gnarled fingers around his cane. "The lishihui will be distraught to hear that." His delight bounds through the syllables.

"What about my family?" I don't want to know, but I need to know.

"I will imprison your parents and grandparents and your tong-gan." The authority in his voice is absolute. "You will speak of this to no one."

"You can't do this."

Before I can reach for my bracelet, Shang gives me a grim smile and grabs my wrist. "This is for Octavius."

My bones tighten and burn. My joints crackle. My muscles liquefy. I gasp. Pain floods my brain. My vision goes sparkly.

I try to touch my bracelet, but I can't move. Desperation drives me. Survival instincts kick in and scream for the shadows. Anger rises up. I'm on the verge of speaking a curse. Anything to escape from Shang. No. I can't let him win. I bite down on my lip until I taste my blood. The iron stings my tongue and sizzles down my throat.

My eyes slip shut.

I'm fading fast.

"If she dies by your hand, her punishment ends." Xia sounds worlds away from me.

The inferno in my bones subsides. My vision wavers and solidifies. Shang stands over me. "Tomorrow, Kali—you die or everyone you love suffers."

He blurs and disappears.

I pass out.

CHAPTER FORTY

I OPEN MY EYES TO a vaulted ceiling and exposed beams above me. Beneath me is something soft and warm. It takes me a moment to realize I'm lying on Mandy's couch. I sit up slowly, waiting for the room to stop tilt-a-whirling. My bones throb and my muscles ache. My mouth is raw. It's ten times worse than the flu. My head is so heavy I have to hold it in my hands.

I smell licorice right before Xia nudges me. He hands me a mug that smells of warm milk and honey. "Drink this." It's Mandy's voice, but Xia's words.

I hesitate to take it.

"It will help, I promise."

I gulp it down and relief slowly spreads through my body. I lean back into the couch feeling exhausted. "What did Shang do to me?"

"It was his zombie." Xia perches on the chair across from me. "The touch of the dead is usually fatal to the living. You're lucky you're a wanshiqi soul inside a human body, or you'd already be dead. Though a few more minutes of him touching you, and he'd have done you in, too." He shakes the keys to Mandy's car in front of me. "Let's get you home."

Everything Shang said rushes back to me. I stand up so quickly, I have to grab the couch to stabilize myself. "I'm not going anywhere with you. You killed my dad." My voice is shredded, torn apart by what he's done.

"Shang would have done far worse. My killing your father kept you here on Earth and out of Shang's reach. I am the lesser of the two evils."

He may be. But I can't be okay with what he's done. Even when I know what Shang could have done would be twelve times worse.

He tries to lead me toward the garage. But I don't budge. "I want to say goodbye to Mandy."

He shakes his head. "That's impossible."

"Can you leave her body for a little bit?" I hate asking, but I need to talk to her one last time.

His eyes drift closed like dealing with me is a monumental task. "Shang has assigned me to stay here until you die." His tone tells me there is no way for me to see Mandy. "I won't leave this body until then."

I hate that I can't give her a proper goodbye. It's not fair. And my body feels like it can't stay upright for much longer. "I want to go home." My voice shakes with the aftershocks of what I've learned.

"Let's go."

I follow him out to Mandy's Mini Cooper and fasten my seat belt with shaking hands. "Where is Mandy? What does she think is happening to her?"

"She's still here. I just nudged her soul over and put her in a dream state. She'll awaken when I leave." He pulls out of her driveway and heads toward my house.

The palm trees are black silhouettes against a dark sky. "What will she think happened?"

"She'll remember bits and pieces. Just enough to think she was here." He stares at the road ahead. His face is a mask of indifference.

"Why did you make me promise to live?"

The skin around his eyes tightens. "I thought it was the best option."

"For you."

"And you."

"But it isn't. You have to release me from the nuoyan now." My tone is pleading; I'm afraid of the outcome.

"No."

A single word decides my entire future. I need to understand what the outcome is for everyone. "If I die, everyone is safe and I suffer imprisonment?"

"That's how things look." His voice deepens and rolls over me.

"Is that how they are?" I hate how he speaks in riddles.

He arches Mandy's perfectly shaped brow. "Do you trust Shang?"

"No."

"Do you trust me?"

"No."

"Think about the rules, Kali. Then play the game like your very existence depends on it. Because it does." He says each word slowly, dropping them into my lap like a puzzle I have to assemble.

When I get home, Grams and Gramps and Hunter are waiting for me. My grandparents sit on the couch in the main room, and Hunter stands beside the fireplace. As soon as they see me, their conversation sputters out.

Hunter strides across the room and hugs me. He whispers in my ear, "Are you okay?"

"Fine." My voice comes out weaker than I want. I kiss his cheek and pull away. "What's going on?"

"You only have one more day to get through." Gramps's voice is iron bars protecting me. "I don't want you leaving the house tomorrow."

"Shang will try to force you to curse and die." Concern is baked into each of Grams's words.

I rub my forehead. "I'm wiped out. Let's talk tomorrow." I head toward the stairwell.

"She smells of licorice." Hunter's voice waffles between desperate and disappointed.

Hades. My throat tightens. Swallowing doesn't help.

"Did Xia threaten you?" Gramps asks.

"No." I turn back toward them. The three wanshiqi I trust and would face imprisonment to protect.

"Did he threaten someone you love?" Grams peers up at me like she can read a lie on my face.

I stick to one-word answers. "No."

"Did you see Shang?" Gramps asks.

They know me too well. I'm afraid of what Shang will do if I tell them what he said. My tongue bonds to the roof of my mouth like it's caught in a peanut butter trap. I try to find a way to answer Gramps. I have to lie if I want everyone to be safe. But that's what Shang is counting on—my fear making decisions and forcing me to follow his rules.

He wants to isolate me. Force me to play the game on his terms. Just like Octavius did.

But I won't.

I walk up to Gramps and press my pointer finger into his third eye and pour the memory of Shang into him.

Gramps, Grams, Hunter, and I sequester ourselves in Grams's study, trying to come up with a plan to deal with Shang and Xia. Hunter drapes his arm around me on the couch while Grams sits calmly in her chair.

Gramps moves around the room with his brow clenched in concentration. "I was preparing for a battle, but we need stealth. We need to expose the loopholes and string them together to form a plan. It's our only chance to keep Kali safe and bring Han back."

Hunter holds my hand in his. "Kali has to survive her birthday to avoid imprisonment. She has to honor her nuoyan to Xia."

My voice rises and falls with fear. "But Shang says I have to die on my birthday to protect my family and friends from him."

"Kali, you can't." Hunter's expression is horrified heartache.

Gramps stops moving around. "She has to live and die." He says it almost to himself, like he's formulating a way for both to happen.

Grams rubs her lips together. "Zhou, she can't do both."

"Can't she?" A slow smile sweeps across Gramps's face. "She only has to appear to die on her birthday."

"If her qi leaves her body, it will be lifeless." Grams's voice warms to this idea.

Hunter grips my hand tightly. "Qin could move her qi somewhere else. I could bring her body to Xia and Shang and show them she's gone."

"But what will happen to me?" I ask in a small voice. I'd do anything to save my loved ones. I just want to know what anything entails.

Hunter's eyes promise I'll be okay. "Your qi will be protected. Shang will be satisfied and everyone will be safe."

"But my body will be dead."

Gramps shakes his head. "Not necessarily." His gaze focuses on Hunter. "Can you pull enough energy out of her body to slow everything inside her down and make her look dead?"

Hunter chews on his lip, considering Gramps's request. "It's possible. Then I'll bring her body back to my place and give it just enough energy to keep it in a deep coma all day."

"Can you do that?" I don't mean to be skeptical, but I know what it takes for him to roll me back a curse or two. "This is beyond what we've done before."

"I can do anything for you." He sounds confident, but I catch a tiny note of hesitation in his tone.

Grams's expression turns thoughtful. "How will we get her qi back in her body? Qin can only move qi once in a moon cycle."

Gramps rubs his lips. Hunter recedes into silence.

My voice is hesitant. "What if I curse myself back into my body?"

Gramps looks into my eyes. "There's only amber left. Your powers are too weak to switch forms. You might be able to curse yourself free of the water. But you'd still have to find a way back into your body."

"I'm willing to take that risk if it saves everyone else," I say.

"Kali..." Hunter's voice begs me to rethink things.

I turn to him. "How else are we going to get me through my birthday? Do you have a better idea? A way to protect everyone I love and save me, too?"

"No." He grips my hand tightly, as if he's afraid to let me go. "But if this works and we get you to seventeen, what happens then? Shang's still coming for you and all of us."

Gramps's smile is ferocious. "Atlantis. He can't go there. I'll have the demons bring Kali's human friends and all of us there. It will give us time to prepare for what comes next."

"Humans? In Atlantis?" Hunter's voice rises so high it makes the hairs on my arm stand on end.

"Are you questioning my decisions?" Gramps's eyes are a meteor shower aimed at Hunter.

"What's the problem?" I glance from Hunter to Gramps to Grams. What am I missing here?

Hunter tightens his arm around me. "Demons feed on humans. They could devour your human friends."

"No, no. Absolutely not. We have to do something else." My eyes meet Gramps's, and I see the truth: There is no other way. I hold my head in my hands. I don't want to make this decision. It could end awfully.

Gramps's voice is much closer when he says, "It's the only way to keep them safe."

Grams gives me a patient smile. "I'll put them in a nice healing sleep for the trip there."

"Grams, you can't just knock out my human friends."

"Do you want to have them endure the physical pain of traveling to Atlantis?" Her brow rises with her concern.

"Physical pain?" My head tilts with confusion.

"It's 10,000 leagues under the sea," Gramps explains. "Human bodies travel there better when unaware of it."

"Is this really our only option?" I ask.

"We could let you turn seventeen, go back to the wanshiqi realm, and go through qifa. But do you really think that's safer?" Gramps's tone tells me it isn't.

"I get it." My shoulders slump. "We'll go with your plan." Even if it puts the people I love at risk. It's less risky than letting Shang and his zombies near them. Gramps and Grams can protect my friends from the demons. I will keep repeating that until I believe it.

Moonlight trickles through my bedroom window. Hunter cradles me in his arms. There are so many things I should be doing and saying, but being here with him feels right.

"I'm glad you showed us what's going on." His voice is warmer than the noon sun in the low desert.

Shang forbid me from telling them, not from showing them. "I'm through being the pawn of the wuwang."

"Are you prepared for what we have to do tomorrow?"

I roll onto my stomach, rest my chin on his chest, and look up into his turquoise eyes. I want to be confident for him, but the warmth in his eyes lets me be vulnerable. "I think so. I hope my parents don't mess things up." Even after all these lifetimes of living down to my lowest expectations, my parents can still hurt me.

He brushes the hair off my forehead. "One day, your parents will realize what you've done for them."

I force a smile. "You and Grams and Gramps know. That's enough for now."

"Is it?" His voice is softer than a stingray's skin and just as velvety. It does things to me.

I slide up the length of him, pressing every inch of my body against his.

"It has to be," I whisper right before I claim his lips.

CHAPTER FORTY-ONE

TODAY, five WANSHIQI ARE going to do the impossible. Grams and Gramps are going to save my friends, while Hunter and Qin and I save me. Gramps plans to put my parents into what he terms a "deep sleep," which is code for coma. We can't have them messing with our plans or leave them to be used against us by our enemies. Grams is confident she can reverse the comas when the time comes. I pray she is right.

Everything is riding on my last day as a human being.

I wish Mom and Dad could be part of the equation. I feel like I'll never get over the absence of my parents' love. It's something I still long for. No matter how impossible it becomes. No matter how often trust is broken. No matter how stupid it is. The only way to end this hurt is to go through qifa. To stop being the Kali I am and become the Kali I am meant to be. I know that. But deep inside, I still ache for the family we might have been if Octavius hadn't damaged them. He stole so much from me in Pompeii. I can't let him take any more.

Breakfast is a restrained affair in the dining room. The wood-paneled walls amplify the sounds of butter knives scraping across toast, forks clinking against plates, and spoons tinkling inside coffee mugs. Mom and Dad are seated across from Hunter and me. Their relentless gazes chafe my skin. Grams sips her tea, and Gramps drowns his waffles in syrup like it's an ordinary day.

"There's only amber left in your eyes." Mom spears a piece of melon. I'm pretty sure she's pretending it's me. "Surely you can go one day without cursing."

"One would think." I stare down at my toast, refusing to be baited.

"Kali does as she pleases. Regardless of how it impacts the rest of us." Dad's so quick to think the worst of me.

The hurt must show on my face because Hunter slams his fist on the table. "It would serve you right if she did die today."

In Dad's eyes, a threat builds. If he uses his powers to influence Hunter's logic, I'm in serious trouble.

"If you hurt Hunter, I swear I will curse myself dead right now." My voice slides across the table like a list of demands in a kidnapping negotiation.

"Kalifornia, I wouldn't hurt your tonggan." Nothing in Dad's tone sounds genuine.

Gramps snorts.

Hunter flashes a wolfish grin. "I haven't eaten wanshiqi energy in a while." He could pull enough energy out of Dad to kill his human body. His wanshiqi soul would reincarnate.

"Hunter..." I rest my hand on his arm, a silent request that he stand down.

Dad tosses his napkin on the table. "I have work to do." His gaze locks on mine. "Don't die today." He doesn't realize those may be his last words to me in this life. But I do and it stings.

"Did you have to start something with your father?" Disappointment unfurls across Mom's face, like a flag claiming new territory.

"Me?" I can't keep my voice from flying around the room like a panicked pigeon.

Hunter reaches for my hand under the table and squeezes. "We should get going. We've planned a couple's afternoon."

That's our cover story for my parents.

"I'll be by Kali's side today." The determination in Mom's voice solidifies in her eyes. "I'm not letting her die today."

If it actually had anything to do with me, it would be sweet, but I don't delude myself. It's all about saving her.

Hunter gives her a slow smile. The kind that does things to me. "I never knew you liked to watch, Mrs. Brewster."

"I can't trust her to turn seventeen." Mom's voice could chill icicles.

And I can't have her sabotaging our plans. My gaze goes to Gramps, silently pleading for his intervention.

"She's going to turn seventeen. Let them have some time together before she does. Qifa is a long time to be apart for tonggan." His tone makes Mom sound ridiculous for crowding me today.

Mom's eyes narrow on me. Why am I always her target?

"Hunter will make sure she lives." Grams reaches for my mother's hand, but Mom jerks it away.

"You always let her do what she wants." Anger heats her voice and her cheeks. "She's not your daughter."

"If you were any sort of mother to her, we wouldn't have to intercede across all these lifetimes." Gramps's words are a terrible truth. The kind you don't tell unless you have no other choice.

Mom makes this awful gurgling noise in her throat. Her chair screeches back across the hardwood floor. "You get her through today then." Her voice is more animal than human.

Despite the overcast June Gloom sky, Hunter and I go to Torrey Pines Beach because Qin has chosen the ocean for my qi's temporary home. It's diffuse enough that no wuwang can sense or smell my qi. It should be enough to fool my parents and Xia.

Waves charge the shore and recede, revealing islands of sandbars. The scent of the ocean reminds me of Hunter. The warm sand shifts beneath my feet, and I work to keep my balance. Hunter leads me away from the small smattering of people building sandcastles and frolicking in the water. We keep walking until we find an isolated spot.

We lay our towels on the sand and strip down to our swimsuits like any other beach goers. The wind whips my dark hair around my face and chills my skin. Hunter laces his fingers through mine and squeezes my hand. I think it's meant to be reassuring, but there are doubts hiding within his grip.

I try to shake them off. Our plan is risky, but it's the only way to save my human friends and my wanshiqi family. We head toward the *whoosh* of the water.

My feet slap against the wet sand. Water rushes between my toes. It's freezing. Hunter tugs me after him. I don't have time to adjust to the cold. Each place the water hits me is a shock—my ankles, my knees, my thighs. Goose pimples gather in constellations across my skin. We keep going deeper, swimming when our feet no longer touch the bottom. My skin tingles and tightens. My teeth chatter. I don't stop. I can't.

When we are far from the shore, Hunter cups my face and stares deeply into my eyes like he'll see the truth there. "Are you sure?"

I press his hands to my cheeks. "It's the best option." That is what I keep telling myself.

"Let Shang come for all of us. We can fight him."

"I felt what he can do, and I won't let him do it to the humans or the wanshiqi I love." I still remember the screams from Pompeii. The lives snuffed out because of my curse. I destroyed an entire city. I won't let anyone else die because of me.

Hunter wraps his arms around my waist and kisses me like I'm breakable. I twine my limbs around him, needing more contact. More of him. An inferno of desire ignites at my core.

This time, Hunter doesn't fan the flames. He sucks them out of me. Through every pore of my skin, I feel my energy escaping. It's an awful sensation. My legs go limp. My arms sink into the water. The only reason my head stays above water is because Hunter holds me up.

We float farther from shore. I stare up at the blanket of clouds above me, but my treacherous eyes slip shut.

A heaviness comes over me, like a thousand pounds of satin heaped onto my body. I can feel the ending of me. Finally, I understand why humans fear death so much. It means the end of them. And if things don't go right, it might mean the end of me. Fear makes me scramble. I kick out, trying to escape death. Hunter holds me closer.

"I love you." His breath is the last bit of warmth I feel against my cheek before coldness overtakes everything.

Then I hear something. It's so faint. But then it grows louder.

The waves call to me. A beguiling chant I've never heard before. More seductive than a Siren's song. I can't escape it. I don't want to.

Everything goes black. Not nighttime black, but end-of-life black.

Except I don't go into dengzhong. I don't go anywhere. Qin summons my qi from my body and puts it into the ocean. Hunter's energy-sucking abilities have slowed everything inside my body to a visible standstill. I don't seem to breathe. There is no heartbeat.

My body appears to be dead.

I can't help freaking out as I watch my body float back to shore without me. I rush after him.

"Kali, you can't." Hunter's words are a warning I must obey.

It's not my body right now. It's the dead shell that he needs to show Xia. It takes a few moments for me to understand. It's still hard to float away from Hunter, but I force myself to let go. When I do, I feel free for the first time in a few millennia. My new body is now the ocean. I don't just ride the ocean waves, I am the ocean waves. I don't feel that empty, awful place my parents carved out of my heart because I don't have a heart.

I am so much more than I was. I feel full of life. The crabs scampering along the seabed stop to wave at me. The jellyfish undulate hello. I delight in the sheer connection I feel with everything in the ocean.

This is my first taste of what life will be like after qifa, and I want more.

My exhilaration falters when I remember that I still have to find a way back into my body. None of us know how that will work. Or if it will work.

Time slips away from me. Maybe it's an hour; maybe it's three. Xia stands on the shore still occupying Mandy's body. Her long, blonde hair is pulled back in a French braid. She stopped styling it like that in sixth grade. My parents stand beside him. Mom's fingers ball into fists. Dad's lips compress to invisibility.

Xia crouches beside my body. His fingers check each of my pulse points. He pinches my nostrils and holds his hand over my mouth to make sure I am not breathing. He even presses my pointer finger to his third eye. My qi isn't inside my body, so there is no memory to retrieve.

"She's dead." Xia squints at the horizon, and for a second, I fear he senses me. Then he looks down at my body again. Something flickers across his face. Could be disappointment, could be triumph. It's hard to tell with Xia.

Mom drops down beside my body and sweeps my tangled, wet hair back from my face. "You can't be dead," she whispers.

For a split second, I swear there's actual regret in her voice.

Dad touches my pointer finger to his third eye. Nothing happens. His sigh is centuries of failure. "She wasn't supposed to die."

"My parents were supposed to keep her safe." Mom's voice capsizes like a dinghy in a hurricane. "Her nuoyan..."

Dad rises slowly to face Xia. His expression is almost murderous. "You double-crossed us. You annihilated your own granddaughter."

I haven't seen Dad this emotional over me in centuries.

"I tried to help her." Xia words are edged with truth. "She didn't know how to play the game."

Hunter grabs Xia's shirt and holds him up in the air. "Don't talk to me about your stupid games. She's your granddaughter, and you forced her to die and break her nuoyan. You have taken my tonggan from me."

The sky rumbles and lightning flashes from cloud to cloud. Hunter is terribly convincing as the bereaved tonggan.

"Careful, you don't want to hurt her best friend." Xia smirks in a way Mandy never would.

Dad pushes them apart. "You promised we would all return to the wanshiqi realm."

Xia steps back and adjusts his shirt. "Kali breaking my nuoyan trumps her punishment from the fayuan. She will not reincarnate as human again. She will be imprisoned in our realm. You and your tonggan will transition back to full wanshiqi. In time, you can have another offspring. Hopefully, one that is less troublesome."

Xia kept his word to my parents about returning them to the wanshiqi realm. He kept his vow to Shang—I will not be able to undergo qifa and threaten Shang's rule. He even kept his word to me about protecting my parents, grandparents, and Hunter. Xia truly is the master manipulator.

Mom strokes my forehead, like she can revive me with her touch. "We never wanted this for you." I swear I hear genuine remorse. For the first time since Pompeii, she almost remembers what it means to be a mother, to be my mother.

"You have your existence back." Xia says it like she should be celebrating my death.

My father punches him. "You have no idea what family means."

Shock passes over Xia's face. It's quickly replaced with smugness. "I've been a father longer than you've existed. You have no idea what it means to be a father."

Now, Hunter has to hold my father back. "Get out of here," Hunter shouts to Xia.

"With pleasure." An orb of light streaks out of Mandy's chest, and she collapses onto the sand. Xia's qi has left her body.

Dad leans over and whispers in Mom's ear, "Kali is gone."

Mom grips my hand. "She's my daughter."

"Why did you betray her?" Hunter crouches near her, like a panther stalking its prey.

"We did everything we could for her." Dad's voice is a drought-destroyed well crumbling in on itself.

I think he really believes that, too. Sadness overwhelms me. He will never be the father I need. I wasted hundreds of lifetimes trying to get back something that was destroyed in Pompeii. Maybe in time Xia can restore their memories, but it will be too late. After qifa, it won't matter anymore to me.

It's better this way. I'll move on without them. It is the only thing I can do. I will keep telling myself this until I believe in it more than I ever believed in them.

Mom's eyes glisten; a few tears escape.

Dad pulls Mom away from my body. She collapses against him. He picks her up. "Take care of Kalifornia for us, Hunter." His voice thickens as he uses my nickname one last time.

I linger offshore, watching everything. After Grams appears to take care of Mandy, Hunter wraps my body in a blanket and takes it to his apartment. I stay nearby because I need to know Mandy is safe.

Mandy lies unconscious on a towel. Grams stands over her, whispering an ancient incantation to make sure Mandy doesn't suffer any damage from Xia's possession.

When Mandy wakes up, she's confused enough to believe Grams's story that Hunter twisted his ankle and I took him to the hospital. Grams takes her to the demons to be hidden in Atlantis.

Once Grams and Mandy are gone, I tiptoe up the coast. I can't find a current running north to ride on. I'm not sure how to generate one on my own, so I drift farther from shore and hitch a ride behind a dolphin. Traveling over water in a boat used to feel so fast, but traveling as water is indescribably faster. I've always loved the way water caresses my body when I'm swimming. Now, I am the ocean. I feel everything. It's beyond the scope of a human's senses.

I forgot how exciting it is to change form. Almost two millennia as a human, and I forgot what it was to be me. What I was meant to be. But I remember now. I am wanshiqi.

I will no longer run and hide from my future. I will face it.

Hunter leaves his bedroom window open, blaring *Patience* by The Pierces for me. It's the best way to tell where my stop is. I let go of the dolphin and merge with the waves heading toward shore. The rocks and sand tickle me as I rush back out to sea. I have to stay close to my body, but still off land until midnight.

Once I've lived through my birthday, I just have to find a way back into my body. Then I will reach out to our allies, the demons, to bring us to Atlantis.

The clouds above me split open. A bird-of-paradise sunset sprouts across the sky. The last rays hit my surface, warming me like Hunter's kisses.

Soon, night cloaks the sky. Tiny crystals wink down at me. The stars seem so much brighter now.

The wind rushes over me, chilling my surface. I don't mind. I'm a hundred feet deep. The crabs skitter around in their underwater dance. I gurgle with laughter, but it comes out as foam on a cresting wave.

I wish this didn't have to end. I wish I was already past qifa. That this form was mine to keep, but it's borrowed. A glimpse of my future that will be snatched away come midnight.

Für Elise starts to play from Hunter's apartment, signaling that it's midnight. I glide toward the shore. Light flashes in Hunter's bedroom. He's sending energy into my body. I've spent hours summoning my light emotions—love for Hunter, for Grams and Gramps, and for my friends. I use it now. A curse dances across my tongue. It swirls around my qi, separating it from its temporary home. The wind wails. No, it's me. Crying out as I shoot out of the air toward Hunter's window.

I see my body on his bed. I float around as an orb of pure energy. Qi.

Hunter looks up and sees me. "Come on, Kali, you can do this." There's a desperation in his voice that I've never heard before.

I circle my body twice, looking for an entry point. I'm not sure how I exited since Qin pulled my qi from my body, so I don't know how to get my qi back in.

Perspiration breaks out across Hunter's forehead. "Try the crown of your head." His voice is strained from sending constant energy into my body to keep it a breath away from death.

He can't keep this up forever. I dive toward the top of my head and bounce off like a tennis ball slamming into a racket.

I try my feet next. I can't push through them. It's like something is stopping me from entering my own body.

I'm energy. Pure energy. It shouldn't be this hard to break through human skin. I sneak up on my fingers and try to slip through the webs between them. But I'm propelled backward, like my body is rejecting my qi.

I circle and circle and circle. I need to get back inside my body, or it will die. My energy weakens. I bob around my body and drop onto the bed beside it. If I don't get in my body, it's over. I'm dead and my nuoyan is broken.

Imprisonment will end me.

Hunter reaches out and touches me. His fingers are warm and welcoming. I feel so much love and acceptance. I slip right through his flesh. I hesitate. Unsure what this will do to me.

To him.

To us.

"Do it." Sweat rolls down his face.

His body can't hold two qi for long. It will devour mine. That's what his power does. He knows it, too. But I have to trust him. I slip through all the layers of flesh and into him. My qi feels balanced. Invigorated. Alive. Recharged.

We lean over my body and touch my third eye.

There's a spark, and I'm sucked out of Hunter's body and into blackness.

My eyes open and all I see is Hunter.

"Happy seventeenth birthday, Kali." He leans in and kisses me.

Glossary and Pronunciation Guide

All the wanshiqi terms in the book are actually based on Mandarin Chinese pinyin romanization. That will be explained in future books.

For anyone unfamiliar with Mandarin Chinese, I created a sound guide for how to pronounce these terms based on the English language, which is found in the parentheses below.

wanshiqi (wan "with wan from wand" + sure + chee): An immortal being.

qi (chee): Immortal soul/spirit/essence of the wanshiqi.

qifa (chee + fa): Enlightenment; coming of age. It's a major turning point in the wanshiqi existence. Knowledge that was forbidden is now known. It is the closest a wanshiqi comes to death, and it changes everything about them.

falu (fa + lew "with lew from lewd"): The code of the wanshiqi, the laws of their civilization. Forbids post-qifa wanshiqi from using powers on pre-qifa wanshiqi without their consent.

lishihui (lee + sure + hway): The council of the wanshiqi.

fayuan (fa + you + on): The special tribunal of the lishihui composed of eleven members. The fayuan pass judgment on all wanshiqi who violate the laws of the land (falu).

tonggan (tong "with tong from tongue" + gon "with on from on"): The basis of wanshiqi relationships; eternal soulmate.

dengzhong (dung + jong "with ong from song"): Limbo; the place Kali goes between reincarnations.

daoqian: (dow + chee + en "with en from end"): wanshiqi apology.

wanwu (won "with on from on" + woo): everything.

nuoyan (noy "with noy from annoy" + yon "with on from on"): A wanshiqi promise. These are unbreakable; the penalty is 10,000 years of imprisonment of your qi.

zhangzhe (jong "with on from on" + ju "with ju from just"): An ancient wanshiqi—over 100,000 years old.

zhiyu (jur "with jur from jury" + you): Healing curse.

kuai (cu "with cu from cut" + why): Speed curse.

wuwang (woo + wong "with on from on"): the five kings/heads of the original five kingdoms of the wanshiqi realm.

Zhou, Xia, Shang, Han, and Qin are the wuwang. They are the five most powerful zhangzhe. The head of the wuwang rules all the wanshiqi.

Zhou (Joe): Kali's maternal grandfather (Gramps) and one of the wuwang. His ability is to spread death.

Yuan (you + on): Kali's maternal grandmother (Grams) and a zhangzhe. Her ability is healing.

Xia (she + ah): Kali's paternal grandfather (Grandfather) and one of the wuwang. His ability is to take any form and push the original qi or soul aside.

Shang (sh + ong "with on from on"): The zhangzhe that currently rules the wanshiqi realm. His ability is to raise the dead. Necromancer. One of the wuwang. His son is in charge of the lishihui, and his grandson is Octavius.

Qin (chin): A zhangzhe who can extract qi from any form and move it into another form. One of the wuwang. A friend of Zhou. Hunter's grandfather.

Han: (hon "with on from on"): The oldest zhangzhe. The pinnacle of power in the wanshiqi realm. A wuwang. The only one who can balance the four other most powerful zhangzhe (Qin, Shang, Xia, and Zhou).

Author's Note

Thank you so much for reading my novel!

I'd love to hear what you thought of it.

No matter how short or long, readers' reviews make a huge difference. I read all reviews and take your feedback to heart and improve my stories.

Hopefully, more readers will take a chance on my book when they see that others already have.

Thanks!

XOXO,

Kika Emers

Sneak Peek at Book 2: Forget Atlantis

For a sneak peek at Book 2 in this trilogy, turn the page…

INTRODUCTION

It's the perfect homecoming after a dangerous odyssey. Hunter's lips are soft and warm and welcoming. He tastes like cherries and joy. I lose myself in kissing him. It's a few minutes before I let him pull back. His face is so close to mine. I can see every speck of color in his beautiful turquoise eyes. They remind me of the clear water off Kata Noi.

Lying on his bed, it hits me. I made it back into my body. I lived through my seventeenth birthday. Relief and exhaustion and excitement roll through me. Hunter said we'd figure it out, but in the crevasses of my soul I had doubts. I wasn't sure I could get back to my body. But I did it.

No, *we* did it.

"Thank you, thank you, thank you." I kiss his cheek, his nose, his other cheek. There aren't enough kisses or words in the world to show my gratitude. He did something I thought was impossible. He shared his body, tempered his instinct to devour my qi, and helped me get back into my body. "I wouldn't be here without you."

"You're okay," he whispers. "You made it back to me." He sounds like he's struggling to believe this is real.

I reach out to touch his cheek. "You saved me again." The love I have for him deepens by hundreds of fathoms.

His smile sends warmth to my toes. "Always."

I can't help kissing him again. Half a day without lips, and I forgot how sensitive they are. Maybe mine are ultrasensitive because my body just came back from the brink of death. All I know is I want to kiss him forever.

Inside my qi, something tender and fragile unfurls. Hope. This is the beginning of a new era for us. From now on, I will trust Hunter with my life. I won't ever go back to how I doubted him.

He holds me in his arms, and for a few moments, I know peace and safety. This is the true tonggan bond. I can't believe I spent centuries running from it. From him.

There's so much I want to tell him. But it feels harder than usual to assemble the words. Something is off. My body feels strange. The more I try to move, the more I realize things aren't working right. I struggle to sit up.

"Are you okay?" Hunter helps me go from reclining to upright.

"I'm not sure. I feel off." When I try to stand, my legs are numb. Disconnected. They feel like someone else's legs. They don't listen to me and won't do what I want. I sway and fall back on the bed.

Hunter catches me. "Take it easy."

It's a few minutes before I can stand with Hunter's help. I look around his bedroom. Something shifts in the corner. Are my eyes not working, too? I glance back to be sure. I want it to be my imagination, but it isn't. In the shadow of the bookcase, there's movement. Something is standing there, shifting in the shadows. We're in trouble. I lean against Hunter and whisper, "We aren't alone."

He wraps his arm around my shoulders and whispers in my hair, "Everything will be fine. Trust me."

I nod, clinging to the calm in his voice. But I can't escape the fear inside me. It grips my heart. I want to trust him. I really do. But something feels so wrong here. Before I can find the words to tell him what I'm feeling, someone steps forward into the light. He's got a strong nose, dark-blue eyes, and sharp features that remind me of a feral lion. He looks human, but that doesn't mean he is.

He moves toward us slowly like time has no meaning for him. Like he knows we can't escape. That frightens me more. I catch a whiff of his qi. Butterscotch. He's one of the lishihui's minions.

I flinch at the memory.

He was Octavius's right hand, Ignatius, many lifetimes ago. He came to Pompeii often when I was Livia. The memories rise up in me, but I stomp them down. I can't fall apart right now. And the memories of what Ignatius did will break me. My pulse pounds against my temple.

Ignatius is a nightmare weaver. He can put you to sleep for days and torture you with horrors you never will forget. His nightmares feel more real than any day in your life. His power made Octavius's torture seem like a tea party. I should know. He used them on me.

He even testified against me before the lishihui. He sealed my fate as tightly as I sealed Octavius in Pompeii.

My hatred for him is only eclipsed by his for me.

Ignatius's smile fills me with fear. "It's time to come home, Kali." His tone promises I won't make it if I go with him.

A tremor starts in my hands and travels up my arms. My entire body trembles at what he will do to me. "That's Ignatius." I grip Hunter's arm and stare into his eyes. "What's going on? Why is he here?" My voice shakes with terror.

Hunter strokes my cheek and gazes at me. "You made it through you seventeenth birthday. You can finally go through qifa. Ignatius is here to escort you back." He makes it sound like he expected this to happen.

But I didn't.

We're supposed to go to Atlantis to meet Gramps. I can't go back to our realm where Shang rules. My mind screams, *This can't be happening*. My thoughts are so chaotic and jumbled. I can't make sense of any of this. "We had a plan." Why is he changing it? I want to ask, but I can't in front of Ignatius. I shake my head, trying to nullify what is happening.

Hunter cradles my chin in his hand. "It will be okay. This is what we wanted."

I won't go with Ignatius. I open my mouth to tell Hunter, but he presses his pointer finger to my lips. "I wasn't expecting the lishihui to send someone so quickly. I thought we'd have some time together before your qifa, too." He taps my lips twice.

That has to mean something. Please, let it mean something.

I glance down at my opal bracelet. Should I use it to call for help? I look back up at Hunter, and he gives me a tiny shake of his head.

He doesn't want me summoning help. Can I trust that? I promised myself I would believe in him and in us. But right now, the hardest thing to do is trust him.

I fall silent, praying I'm not wrong.

Hunter slowly leads me over to Ignatius. With each step, doubts assault me. Was Hunter working with the lishihui? Is he on Octavius's side? Did Gramps and I get it all wrong? No. No. No. I can't doubt him now. He did everything to save me for centuries. There's got to be a reason for how he's acting. What am I missing? The more I try to think, the slower my mind works.

I swallow. The dryness in my mouth is a salt lake of loneliness. Hunter wouldn't hand me over to Ignatius. He couldn't.

As Ignatius reaches for me, Hunter pushes me aside and grabs Ignatius's throat. I stumble and fall back on to the floor. Hunter's eyes glow in a way I've never seen before. They are darker than the deepest ocean. Ignatius struggles for a few seconds, then he collapses.

"Are you alright?" Hunter reaches for me and pulls me to my feet.

"I'm okay." I clutch at his arms, needing answers. "What was he doing here?"

"He arrived a little before you woke up. Somehow, he knew you weren't really dead. Kali, that means the lishihui know, and Shang knows."

My shoulders collapse. Thank Persephone Hunter didn't betray me. I can't believe I had a second of doubt. Old habits won't be broken as easily as I thought. But I will berate myself later. Now, we have to deal with the looming threat.

None of us foresaw that the lishihui would know about me living so quickly. That means Shang's plot goes deeper and wider than we expected. Gramps thought we'd have time to escape after I came back to my body. But we almost didn't.

I glance at Ignatius. He's so still. "Is he dead?"

"I devoured a lot of his qi. His human body may not survive it."

All I feel is relief.

"But more wanshiqi will be coming for you."

"This is bad. Really bad." I can't stop shaking. It's probably the trauma of coming back to life and almost being given to my enemy to be tortured. Even though the second part didn't happen. The possibility of what he would have done to me will haunt me for years.

Hunter puts his arm around me. I don't deserve the comfort he provides. But I take it anyway. He kisses my forehead and says, "Shang's people are the best at what they do. They must have created some sort of alarm for if you lived beyond seventeen." He rubs my arm gently. "I didn't think Ignatius was going to take you back to our realm, but I had to play along until I could get close enough to take him out."

There is so much concern in his eyes. I look away in shame.

"You know that I would never let him hurt you?" His voice holds more uncertainty than it should.

"I do." I give him the best smile I can, but my lips tremble.

Hunter looks around like he's expecting more arrivals at any moment. "We need to get to Atlantis, fast."

I press the opal on my bracelet to signal Gramps and his allies that we need help.

In front of us, the air pulsates. It's like the air itself is peeling apart layer by layer.

Hundreds of shades of blue and green whirl out of the layers like living creatures. It makes the aurora borealis seem plain. I smell coconut and vanilla. It's the most beautiful thing I've ever seen. Something I never thought I'd witness: a demon portal opening up in front of me.

These kinds of portals were thought to be lost forever with the demons and Atlantis. I have to thank Gramps again for not destroying them.

A demon steps out of the portal. I recognize him from the illustrations in our history books. He's eight feet tall with horns that spiral upward to piercing points, and sharp tusks that protrude from his mouth. He has two extra arms, and instead of legs, he has a merman tail. His skin is covered in red scales. His eyes are golden and glow with a ferocity we need to get us safely out of here.

"We have to go now to Atlantis." The demon says the words inside my mind.

"He's taking us to Atlantis," I tell Hunter and slide my fingers through his. I won't let go of him.

Hunter squeezes my hand and a bit of energy jumps from him to me. It helps me stand a little better.

The demon steps aside. Hunter and I step through the portal. Whatever comes next in Atlantis, we will face it together.

ACKNOWLEDGEMENTS

To Emerson Langley, my shih-tzu warrior lapdog. You were beside me every day for 16.5 years. You sat in my lap for so many revisions to this story. It's our last work together and I think it's our best. I couldn't have made it through all the years without you. Thank you for being my first baby boy. And for staying with me as long as you could. And for checking in on me when you can.

To my parents who stick with me and cheer me on for each and every book and read each newsletter. Thank you for giving me a home and for believing in me and the books.

To Akira Star, my reckless mayhem, for talking to me and making me take breaks to play with you. To Bentley, my quiet little gentleman, for letting me work and loving me as much as any dog can. You both bring so much joy back into my life and you make each day brighter.

To Grace Bradley for helping me make this the best book it could be. Working with you as my editor didn't feel like work at all! Your insightful comments and attention to detail are a gift. Thank you for sharing them with me. Also, I'm super grateful for your insights on the cover design.

To My Brother's Editor, for terrific copyediting and proofreading in the final stretch. To Gaelle Vaudaine, for maintaining my website and doing all the heavy lifting with updates. You are a gem!

To Rob Eagar, for teaching me everything I know about Bookbub and Amazon ads. To Mal Cooper, for being a Facebook ads guru. To Anna and Kat, for being beta readers and helping me make this book better.

To Moorbooks Design, for giving me the cover I dreamed of!

To Kelly, for loving my books and being an early reviewer! To Audra, for always asking about the next book and being a supporter of each one of them!

To Ant, for all the years of supporting my writing and reading each ARC. It means a lot that you make the time for me. To Dr. Pam and Gurusha, for being ARC readers and newsletter members—your support means so much!

To Jackie T. and Debb—for joining my ARC Team and taking the time to check the book for me! To Suyog and Carol—for reading the ARC and being early reviewers!

To all my ARC readers on NetGalley—you are the best! Thank you for supporting my books and posting reviews when the book first comes out. You help me keep writing! To my newsletter subscribers—thank you for all your support—I love your replies!

And to my readers, thank you for trying a new trilogy with me. I appreciate you sharing your precious free time with me and my characters. You're wonderful!

About the Author

Kika Emers makes her home in the hills of Connecticut with two quirky shih tzus, Akira Star and Bentley. Akira brings the mayhem and Bentley, the calm. Kika enjoys instapot cooking, reading monster romance, sipping loose-leaf tea, and bellydancing. Not all at the same time, though.

When she has spare time, she can be found doing Chinese Watercolor Painting, playing the harp, brushing up on her Chinese language skills, or napping with her shih tzus.

Kika Emers is a pen name created from her nicknames for her first and her third shih tzus, Emers and Kika.

Kika Emers also writes PG-13 YA time travel mysteries as K.C. Tansley, and paranormal suspense for adults as Kourtney Heintz. Kourtney Heintz minored in Chinese at Georgetown University and received a Master in Pacific International Affairs with a regional focus on China from UCSD.

You can find out more about her on her website: <u>https://kourt neyheintz.com</u>

Bonus Scenes from Remember Pompeii

There's always a few scenes that get cut from the book. I really liked these scenes, so I'm sharing them as bonus content. You can download them from here:

https://dl.bookfunnel.com/sraqzzu275

Also By

I have two other series you may want to check out.

K.C. Tansley writes YA time travel murder mysteries and **Kourtney Heintz** writes paranormal suspense for adults.

THE GIRL WHO IGNORED GHOSTS
BY K.C. TANSLEY

"Intriguing" (Publishers Weekly): While working on a school project, Kat and Evan are sucked into a portal and sent back in time to 1886—to the night a pair of newlyweds were murdered. Can they solve the case and return to the present before their souls slip away forever?

Read *The Girl Who Ignored Ghosts* ebook for free on Kindle Unlimited or 99 cents on Kindle:

https://www.amazon.com/Girl-Ignored-Ghosts-Unbelievables
-Book-ebook/dp/B00WZOJ028/

THE SIX TRAIN TO WISCONSIN

BY KOURTNEY HEINTZ

When his wife's telepathy spirals out of control, Oliver brings her to the hometown her abandoned where the secrets of his past threaten their future.

Read The Six Train to Wisconsin ebook for Free on KU or $4.99 on Kindle:
https://www.amazon.com/Six-Train-Wisconsin-Book-ebook/dp/B00CJIXKG2/

WANT INSIDE SCOOPS?

Sign up for author updates on my website: **https://kourtney heintz.com** and I'll immediately send you my unpublished short story, **And Then There Were Three**, and the **Bonus Prologue to The Girl Who Ignored Ghosts.** I'll also give you the inside scoop on my books—new releases, sales days, free book deals, giveaways, and behind the scenes info you can't find anywhere else!

I won't share your email address and you can unsubscribe anytime. You'll hear from me once a month and a little more often around a book release.